DEAD STRAIGHT

He was taking off over the Pflantzgarten jump at the Nür-burgring in the C3, but this time the nose kept going up and up. Blue sky filled the windscreen. Everything had gone deathly quiet. Then the front of the car dipped down and he could see a hillside and the track again. The sports car crashed down onto it, exploding in a storm of sparks, tearing metal and shredding fibreglass as it did so. It shot towards the Armco barriers like a berserk missile. Frantic-ally Jonty swung the steering wheel over, but it was no longer connected to anything. The next impact was like nothing he'd experienced before, as though he'd been hit in the back by a lorry and punched in the stomach by a sledgehammer. His eyes and teeth felt as though they were coming out of his skull.

Also by Andrew Neilson

Braking Point

DEAD STRAIGHT

Andrew Neilson

A STAR BOOK
published by
the Paperback Division of
W. H. Allen & Co. PLC

A Star Book

Published in 1985
by the Paperback Division of
W. H. Allen & Co. PLC
44 Hill Street, London W1X 8LB

First published in Great Britain by
W. H. Allen & Co. PLC, 1984

Copyright © Andrew Neilson, 1984

Printed and bound in Great Britain by
Cox & Wyman Ltd, Reading

ISBN 0 352 31497 4

*The characters and situations in this book are
entirely imaginary and bear no relation to any real
person or actual happening.*

To Sally

One

ANGELICA FLICKED the big sports car through the S-bend and accelerated hard onto Snetterton circuit's pit straight. Behind her the V6 engine roared and rammed her through the 150 miles-an-hour mark without the slightest sign of peaking. Its twin turbochargers glowed cherry red and whistled like kettles about to blow their tinny spouts off.

As Angelica shot past the pits she glanced right to find her pit signal. One of the men pressed against the double Armco barrier was leaning further over it than the rest, holding out a white fibreglass board with the red letters and numbers slotted onto it

P I

+ 35

L 2

First place, thirty-five seconds ahead of the next car, two laps to go.

And just beyond the signaller, amongst all the blurred faces turning to follow her progress, Angelica clearly saw Michael Church. For a moment the bright brown eyes in his boyish face met hers, and she felt an inner glow. Then she looked away and concentrated on the race again.

'It's just a round of our national sports car championship,' Michael had explained when he'd collected her from Heathrow Airport the previous day. 'About an hour-and-a-half's racing with one compulsory driver change. We'll use it to shake the car down.'

Well Michael's had his shakedown, and I've had my holiday cruise, Angelica thought, and now I'm going to find out what this baby can really do.

She ground herself down into the C4's racing seat. It had runners under it, so she had been able to slide it forward when she'd taken over from Michael halfway through the race. The six-belt safety harness wasn't so easy to adjust. Its metal buckle was bruising her belly, and the crutch straps were abrading the inside of her thighs. And the cockpit ventilation was bad – non-existent was a better description. When they'd arrived at the Norfolk Circuit that mid-April Sunday morning, the wind had been so bitingly cold that Angelica had put on a thick pullover and her old Austrian Olympic Ski Team anorak. Now, after forty minutes in the cockpit in just her race-suit, she was soaked in sweat. It was like sitting in an oven in which tyre rubber and brake pads were being roasted as well.

To Angelica these were just irritations to be noted and corrected before the next race. A more serious problem was her aching neck muscles. As Austria's leading lady racing driver she had mostly driven single seaters, and looked down on sports cars as big and slow in comparison. To her surprise and delight, this one generated enough cornering force to drive her helmet down onto her shoulders. She would have to devise an exercise programme to cope with that in world endurance championship 1,000-kilometre events, let alone the 24-hour race at Le Mans.

Angelica looked over the top of the small black leather steering wheel and through the sharply curved and raked windscreen at the track. All she could see of her own car were the crests of the wheel arches and the streamlined wing-mirrors mounted on top of them. Vibrating images of the cars behind her danced in them. She overtook two open sports racers, saw that the rest of the straight was clear, and lined up on its right hand side. Then she glanced down at the eight gauges set into the black metal dashboard. Her piercing green eyes read seven of them quickly, then settled on the eighth –

the turbo boost gauge. Its yellow needle hovered at one-point-two. Angelica's left hand dropped from the steering wheel to an aluminium knob under the dashboard. She twisted it to the right, glancing at the boost gauge until its needle had climbed to one-point-five.

When Angelica looked back at the straight she was doing just over 200 miles-an-hour and had reached her braking point at the end of it. She squeezed the brake pedal, changed down into fourth gear with her right hand, then into third, steered left, snatched second gear, came off the brakes, and accelerated round the tight right-hander. As she built up speed the whistling sound of turbochargers joined the engines's muzzled snarl, and there was a distinct shove in her back as they cut in again. She thundered under Snetterton's bridge and moved the C4 to the very left of the track, then dived into the trickily cambered right-hander with her foot hard down on the accelerator.

She had never taken it flat out before, but something about Michael's car gave her the confidence to do so now. Its nose gave a twitch of protest and tried to understeer towards the outside of the bend. Angelica gave the wheel a decisive flick that pointed it back on line, and like a wilful thoroughbred that had tested its jockey and recognised a master, the C4 tracked through the difficult bend in a neat arc. As a result its speed continued to build up exhilaratingly quickly. It slid to the outside of the track where there was a back-marker in her way. Without lifting off the accelerator Angelica worked the sports car back to miss it, and then turned into the long right-hander called Coram Curve.

She was going in on a tighter line than usual. This time the cornering force felt like a giant trying to shove her out of her seat. The safety harness cut into her body but held her firmly in place, but there was nothing to restrain her red-and-white striped helmet. It was being bent relentlessly down towards her left shoulder, compressing one set of neck muscles and stretching the other to tearing point. With her head so far over, Angelica was finding it hard to see where she was going.

Gritting her teeth she jerked her head upwards.

Pain ripped through her neck and she screamed out in agony. For a moment Angelica lost vision in her left eye, and instinctively backed off the accelerator. She had rounded Coram Curve now, and as the track straightened out her head lolled upright. Sickening waves of pain pulsed through her body, but adrenalin suddenly exploded into her bloodstream and she was shouting angrily at herself.

'That's right, you stupid bitch! Lift off and spoil the whole lap!'

Angelica stamped her foot hard down again and her helmet banged against the headrest. Downhill and ahead of her she could see the S-bend before the pit straight.

'Flat, you bitch!'

She was fighting the C4 across to the right of the track to get back onto the ideal line, and then suddenly she was at the turn-in point with her right foot hard down. Angelica felt a hollow moment of panic as she wondered if she had talked herself over the limit. Then her eyes widened in astonishment as the car tracked cleanly left and right and slid neatly out onto the pit straight. What the hell had happened? The C4 had taken the complex as though they'd been doing fifty miles-an-hour, not 150, as though the giant who had tried to tear her head off had decided to push the car down onto the track instead.

Some car, Angelica thought, glancing right to spot her pit signal again.

Last lap.

Beyond the signaller she saw Michael again, but this time he was staring down at his stopwatch.

Some designer!

Michael Church was a strongly built twenty-eight-year-old of medium height with a distinctly boyish face. Unruly brown hair curled over his forehead and ears. Large brown eyes sparkled with fun, and his full lips were almost permanently parted in a lopsided grin.

He was still wearing the cream race suit in which he had driven the first half of the race, but now he had a maroon team anorak over it to keep out the chill Norfolk wind. In his hand he held a stopwatch, and as Angelica flashed past him he pressed down its red stop button with his thumb.

'Christ!' Michael said, jerking his head back in surprise. 'Am I reading this right?'

'Fifty-four-point-two!' the lanky mechanic on Michael's right said, staring down at his own stopwatch. 'That's two seconds inside the outright lap record!'

'What was my best time, Ian?'

'Fifty-six-point something, Guv'nor. If you don't buck up we'll have to drop you this season!'

Michael was telling his chief mechanic where to go when the commentator's excited voice boomed out of the loud-speakers.

'And we've just had word of an incredible lap by Angelica Hofer, Austria's top lady racing driver, over here to co-drive Michael Church's C4 today – fifty-four-point-three seconds! I repeat, fifty-four-point-three seconds. That's way inside the outright lap record set by a Formula One car in . . .'

The rest of his sentence was drowned as a line of assorted sports cars blared noisily past the pits.

Now Michael and his mechanics were standing on tiptoe trying to spot their car as it came into sight on its last lap. Suddenly they could see it approaching Coram Curve, a screaming maroon blob that rapidly enlarged into a recognisable shape. Wedge-like bodywork rose sharply to cover the front wheels, then dipped gently on either side of the cockpit before rising again to clear the rear wheels. The cockpit and engine cover was like a teardrop squashed down the centre line, with the sharply curved windscreen just behind the front wheels, and the pointed end at the back of the car. An upside-down wing spanned the rear bodywork, supported on each side by shark-like fins.

Ian glanced down at his stopwatch. 'She'll be quicker still this time,' he said in an awed voice.

The C4 raced round the long right-hander, its 650 horse-power Glaser engine shrieking a war cry. It was visibly quicker than before, the back end twitching alarmingly out of line as Angelica kept the accelerator hard down. As it shot towards them the engine note kept on rising. Then Angelica's red-and-white helmet was clearly visible, leaning left as she turned into the S-bend flat out. The front of the car bucked as she changed direction. For a moment there was clear air under its front right wheel. The C4 was centrifuged out to the edge of the track. Its left wheels rode up the kerbing, then over it so that they were racing along the grass, but the sports car kept going at un-diminished speed. Gradually Angelica eased it back onto the track.

Michael started to breathe again. Beside him Ian was staring at his stopwatch and babbling disbelief.

'What time, you idiot?' Michael asked. 'I forget to stop mine.'

'Fifty-three-point-one! Can you believe it?'

Michael's mouth fell open, and then his full lips stretched into a huge grin.

At the end of the pits, a sports-jacketed man had stepped out onto the track with the chequered flag. As Angelica flashed past him he swirled it down and round to signal the end of the race.

Gradually she backed off the accelerator and let the growl-ing and whistling behind her subside into a drone. As she did so the adrenalin disappeared, and waves of pain replaced it. Her heavy helmet sagged forward. Inside it, Angelica bit her lower lip and forced back the tears that were welling up in her eyes. She took one hand off the steering wheel and began to massage her aching neck. The safety harness was intolerable now, and she grappled with its buckle with her other hand, letting the C4 find its own way for a while. The buckle sprang open and spat out the metal end pieces of the straps. Angelica sagged down in the seat. It took an enormous effort to concentrate on the track now, and she nearly ran into a back-marker. Slowly she com-pleted the lap.

When she reached the pit straight again, marshals were standing on the track and waving her on to the finish line. As she drove slowly past the pit, Michael and his maroon-overalled mechanics were climbing over the Armco barriers. A flicker of a smile played on her lips as she saw him. Angelica stretched out her hand to turn off the ignition switch, but she had already stalled the engine. The big maroon sportscar rolled uphill, under its own momentum, the swishing of its hot and sticky tyres now the loudest sound. She braked it to a halt amongst the rapidly growing crowd on the finish line, and put it into gear. Then she opened her right-side door and pushed it up and forwards. Slowly, painfully, she levered herself out of the cockpit.

As Angelica stepped out of the C4, Michael was jogging up the track towards her. He noticed that her movements were unusually awkward. Normally they had the grace and strength of a lithe athlete. Now she stood unsteadily beside the car and pulled off her helmet and balaclava.

Sun-streaked hair tumbled down over her shoulders. She was twenty-eight years old, the same age as himself. Her long, deeply tanned face was too strong-featured to be pretty, but it was unforgettable. Dark green eyes flashed a disconcerting fire. Her mouth was large but well-formed, set above an equally aggressive chin. Standing there in her red race-suit, he thought she looked like a space age Amazon. She had a kind of fierce beauty that moved him deeply.

As Michael neared her he held up his arms in triumph. 'Fantastic! Unbelievable! You've smashed the lap record!'

How it happened he wasn't quite sure, but Angelica stepped towards him and suddenly they were pressed against each other. Michael felt her hold onto him, and instinctively he put his arms around her. She was about three inches shorter than him, and as she bent her head back to look into his face her smile turned into a grimace of pain.

'You okay?' Michael asked.

'Sure. Hurt my neck a little, that's all.'

An official was standing beside them now, explaining that they wanted them on the victory rostrum. Michael opened his arms, but for a few moments Angelica didn't let go of him. Finally she stepped back, and they followed the official towards the tower at the top of the pit lane. They climbed the stairs to a balcony overlooking the track where the commentator was waiting for them, microphone in hand. He started gushing as soon as she reached him.

'Well Angelica, we didn't expect the outright lap record to go today, and we certainly didn't expect a beautiful lady to shatter it! Just how did that last lap feel?'

Michael stood beside her, listening to her being interviewed for the first time. Now he understood why Glaser, the Swiss car maker who had loaned him their endurance racing engine for the season, had made her inclusion in his team part of the deal. In her slightly throaty voice and charming Austrian accent she was answering the banal questions with relaxed and amusing answers, praising the car and especially the engine again and again. She was one very experienced interviewee, Michael realised. Then it was his turn.

'How do you feel about your co-driver now Michael?'

'She's made me think about retiring!'

Angelica's startled eyes met his, and he smiled back reassuringly. As the commentator babbled on they continued to gaze at each other, and a new emotion began to sparkle in their eyes.

'Was this a one-off arrangement, or will you two be co-driving again?'

'I hope we'll be together all season,' Michael said, looking straight at Angelica.

Her lips parted in a slight, secret smile.

Finally the question and answer session was over, and they were presented with a large silver trophy and a bottle of champagne. Angelica shook it up, and then showered the crowd under the balcony to squeals and shouts of encouragement.

Watching this, Michael forgot the pain he had read on her

face when she'd climbed out of the car, but as they started back down the stairs she stumbled and gritted her teeth. He grabbed her arm to steady her.

'What's wrong Angelica?'

'I think I've pulled a neck muscle. Would you take this,' she said, handing him the half empty champagne bottle. As soon as she was free of it she put both hands up to her neck and tried to squeeze away the pain.

'You go back to the motor-home. I'll try and find something for that,' Michael said.

He left her and hurried round the back of the pits to the first aid centre. There, a St John's ambulance man pointed out that Snetterton wasn't a flipping football stadium, but managed to find a tube of anaesthetic embrocation for him. Then Michael crossed the grassy paddock to the team's maroon-painted motor-home and knocked on the door. There was no reply.

'Angelica?' he called out, opening it and stepping inside.

There was no-one in sight. To his left, a concertina door partitioned off the motor-home's sleeping accommodation.

'In here,' her muffled voice came from behind it.

Michael stepped towards the partition and slid it back. On either side of a narrow corridor were bunk beds, then a shower cubicle and toilet, and finally three couches arranged in a U-shape. Angelica was sitting on one of these with her neck cradled in her hands. Her race-suit was unzipped and rolled down to her waist, revealing the long-sleeved fire protective vest underneath it.

'I . . . I found this,' Michael said awkwardly, holding out the tube.

'Thank you, Michael. Come in,' Angelica said.

He stepped past the partition, shut it behind him, and began to walk towards her, holding out the tube.

'Maybe you can help me,' Angelica said, bunching up the vest and easing it over her head.

Michael caught his breath as he saw her deeply tanned skin and surprisingly girlish breasts.

15

'It hurts worst here,' Angelica grimaced, turning her back towards him and lifting her hair away from her neck.

Michael sat down beside her. His hands were trembling slightly as he twisted the cap off the tube, and it slipped out of his fingers and rolled across the floor. Angelica sat quite still. He felt his heart pounding as he squeezed cream onto his fingertips. He reached out to her, hesitated, then gently touched her neck. Angelica shivered. Then Michael began to rub the cream into her skin with a circular motion.

'You drove beautifully,' he said.

Angelica tried to laugh, but it came out as a grunt of pain. 'Thanks. Some car you've built. I couldn't resist finding out what it could do.'

'Think we can take on the Porsches with it?'

'I think we can take on anything, Michael.'

She winced as he pressed on a knot of torn muscle, and Michael lifted his hand. Then her own was covering his and pressing it down onto her neck again.

'Go on Michael; that's so good.'

For a few moments neither of them moved. Then he began to circle his hand again with hers resting on top of it.

'Would you like me to take you home after this?' he asked quietly.

'Your home?'

'Yes.'

'I'd like that very much,' Angelica said.

The maroon-overalled mechanic walked into Snetterton's Clubhouse and joined the noisy three-deep queue at the bar. Dennis Morrell was a stocky twenty-year-old. Thick lips and pudgy face topped by curly fair hair gave him a slightly moronic look. He sucked his tongue and tutted irritably as he waited.

The man who positioned himself on Dennis's left was also stocky but older, thirty perhaps. But there was nothing even vaguely thick about his freckled face and red hair -- foxy was more like it.

16

'Didn't your lot do well then!' the stranger said.

'What? Yeah, fantastic last lap eh,' Dennis said in a slow voice with a Cockney accent.

'Fantastic. They've got a lot to thank you for though.'

Someone pushed between them clutching two pints, and they squeezed into the gap so that they were facing each other.

'Me?' Dennis said.

'Yeah. I saw you sort out that misfire in practice. The car wasn't doing anything special till then.'

'Oh that,' Dennis said dismissively. 'Just the black box overheating. Moved it six inches to the right, and that fixed it.'

'Is that what it was! We'll have to watch out for that on ours. Look out! That cheeky sod behind you's trying to butt in.'

Dennis edged backwards, blocking the overtaking manoeuvre. 'Ours?'

'Sorry. Should've introduced myself. Ralph Cambell, chief mechanic for the Lomax Team. We're running a Glaser engine too this season.'

'Oh yeah, I've heard about you. Why weren't you racing your car today.'

'It's not finished yet. We've got so much on at the factory we don't know where to turn. Stick your arm out and one of us might get served . . . what's your name?'

'Dennis. Dennis Morrell.'

Ralph Cambell put out a hand to shake Dennis's, and waved a five pound note over the bar in the other one. 'Pleased to meet you, Dennis. As a matter of fact, we're so short staffed we're looking for more mechanics.'

Dennis had just started to say something when Ralph Cambell caught the barman's eye and started to yell his order above the background din. 'Whisky and ginger. What's yours Dennis?'

'Four pints of bitter and two of shandy for the lads, but you can't pay for that lot.'

'I'll order them anyway. You can pay me back later.'

'Thanks. As I was saying, I'm just an amateur; I mean an amateur race mechy. I'm a sparks by trade, you know, an electrician. I just help the Church team at weekends.'

'You didn't look amateurish to me this morning,' Cambell said, passing an overfilled glass to Dennis. 'You'll need a tray for this lot.'

'Yeah, thanks,' Dennis said, taking a battered metal tray from him and starting to balance glasses on it as Cambell passed them to him.

'You could make motor racing pay you know.'

'Maybe, but I'm happy where I am.'

Cambell placed the last of the pints on Dennis's overloaded and warping tray, and then cleared a path for him with his right arm. 'Well, think about it anyway. We'll be ready for Silverstone, so I'll see you there.'

'Right, thanks,' Dennis said, concentrating on balancing the tray as he edged out of the Clubhouse.

It was only when he was halfway across the paddock that he remembered he hadn't paid Cambell for the drinks. It wasn't even his own money – the lads had given him the price of the round. A slow grin parted Dennis's thick lips. Ralph Cambell had been right – motor racing was starting to pay him already.

Two

MICHAEL TURNED his Vauxhall estate car off the main road into Reading, and drove down a side street. Lines of ochre brick terraced houses bordered it on both sides, and in the half moonlight they all looked virtually identical. He parked halfway down the road and turned towards Angelica in the passenger seat. Now she was wearing navy blue cords and a bright red ski pullover with a white hoop round it.

'Here at last. How's your neck?'

Angelica moved her head cautiously from side to side. 'Much better.'

Michael climbed out of the car, lifted its tailgate, and pulled their helmet bags past a Hewland gearbox. A low brick wall fronted the pavement. He pushed the wooden gate in it open with his back, and then led the way up the short path to his house.

'No time for the garden I'm afraid,' he said, nodding down at the tiny patch of uncut lawn and the weed infested border around it. His neighbour's looked like an exhibit at a flower show.

'I didn't have you figured as a gardening type,' Angelica laughed behind him.

Michael opened the black-painted front door, and switched on some lights. A narrow corridor ahead of them led to the kitchen. Stairs to their left went up to the top floor. Both were covered in the same plain contract carpeting, and the walls were whitewashed, giving the house an almost office-like feel. He closed the front door behind Angelica and started to climb the stairs, but she stopped at the foot of them and looked at the framed photographs on the opposite wall.

'Who are they?' she asked.

'That's my dad, Peter,' Michael said, stepping down to join her beside the portrait nearest the front door.

Peter Church must have been in his early thirties when it was taken. He bore a distinct resemblance to Michael, although his face was squarer, and protected by fifties goggles and a white pudding basin helmet. Michael's father was hurling a Lister-Jaguar sportscar round a right-hander in a full-blooded drift, and the photograph had captured the exhilaration of the moment on his face.

'So that's where you get it from,' Angelica said.

'Yes. Dad was a bomber pilot in the war. All he wanted to do afterwards was race cars, so he started a garage business. That paid for his sport, and got Conrad and me started.'

'Conrad?'

'My eldest brother. That's him in a Chevron B8 at the Nürburgring,' Michael said, moving down the hallway to a colour photograph. A rear-engined sports car was riding high round the Karussel Curve. Its driver was still wearing an open-faced helmet, but his mouth was hidden by a fire-protective bandana. The car was painted maroon.

'Does he still race?'

'No. Dad died from a heart attack in '76. Conrad had to pack it in to run the car distributorships. Nearly broke his heart as well.'

Angelica moved past the door leading into the living room, and studied the third photograph. In it an open sports-racing car was flashing past the chequered flag, but the driver's head was covered by an all-enveloping helmet. Only his brown eyes were visible glaring out through its narrow eyeslit.

'My baby brother, Jonty,' Michael said. 'He's the real ace of the family. Well, was anyway. He had a hell of a shunt last year, and reckons he's packed it in.'

'A real motor racing family! I'd like to hear more about them.'

'After I've had a bath. Sorry, I was forgetting my manners – I'll run one for you first.'

'Thanks,' Angelica said, turning to face him, 'but you better take yours before me.'

'You're the guest.'

'But I take a long time.'

'Me too.'

Angelica laughed. 'You don't know *how* long I take, otherwise you'd get in there while you could.'

'Well it's a big enough tub. If we can't decide who's first we can take it together.'

Suddenly the light-hearted atmosphere had disappeared. In its place was a pulsing electric tension. Angelica lifted her head so that her brilliant green eyes were looking straight into Michael's.

'I'd like that,' she said throatily.

Michael's mouth opened, but no sound came out. He stood quite still, feeling his heart beginning to pound against his rib cage. Then he stepped towards Angelica and put his hand up to her face. He caressed her cheek with his fingertips, then slid them under her wild brown hair and cupped the back of her head.

'I've felt this way about you since we met in Zürich last month,' he said.

And then they were in each other's arms, hungrily kissing each other and pressing their bodies together.

'And I've wanted you since you touched me in the motor-home,' Angelica said. 'The bath can wait.'

Dennis Morrell crossed the Thames by Chelsea Bridge, praying that the police wouldn't stop him now that he was so near home. The headlights of his nine-year-old Ford Escort flickered weakly into life, then died again. To his left, the monstrous funnels of Battersea power station were silhouetted by the half moon.

'Shit!' Dennis swore, hunting the roadside for bald-tyre bandits. He knew he should have fixed the lights before leaving Snetterton, but after a day's work on a *real* car he just hadn't felt like it. His banger wasn't taxed or insured either. If they pulled him now he was for it.

Dennis turned into Battersea Park Road and drove along it until block after block of high-rise flats towered up to the south. He steered towards them and found a parking space at the foot of one. With a great sigh of relief and fatigue he switched off the Escort's clattering engine and peered at his watch – 10.45 pm. He pulled a floppy yellow kitbag off the back seat and trudged towards the entrance to the flats.

Inside, the light fittings had been smashed and there was a horrible smell of stale urine. Dennis pressed the lift button and waited, but as usual it didn't come. Swearing horribly, he began to climb the stairs that wound round the lift shaft. He stopped at the eighth floor gasping for breath, then went up to the faded orange door in front of him and jabbed the bell. Nothing happened. Impatiently Dennis stabbed it again.

'Who is it?' a muffled voice asked from inside the flat.

'Who d'you think it is, Sharon? Open the door.'

'What time d'you call this, then?'

'Just open the bleeding door will you!'

The girl who did so was nineteen years old. She had long curly blonde hair, big blue eyes, and a five-month pregnancy stretching her faded pullover and jeans.

Sharon was one of those doll-like little girls whose looks had stayed with her after puberty. Then she had become the target for every hot-blooded boy in the neighbourhood, and a major worry to her father. He was a Battersea publican who didn't think any of them were fit to kiss his only beloved daughter's feet. That hadn't stopped Dennis, the local electrician's son, from taking her out. Nor had it stopped him from getting her into the back of his Escort, with surprisingly little resistance. Two months previously they'd had to get married.

Without saying a word, Sharon turned round and walked down the corridor to the tiny living room. A curtainless window at one end overlooked the concrete wasteland far below. Someone had once papered and painted the flat in coordinated oranges and yellows, but the brightness had long vanished from the scheme. In its place was a depressing grubbiness and a smell of old cooking fat. The television was on, and Sharon lowered herself into the battered brown arm-chair facing it.

'How're you? All right then?' Dennis asked from the doorway to the living room.

'Yes.'

'I'm starving.'

'There's some pork pie in the fridge.'

'Great,' Dennis muttered ironically, dropping his bag on the floor and shuffling towards the kitchenette.

The almost empty fridge finished any idea of alternatives, and Dennis extracted the lonely half pork pie. It was already on a plate. He opened a can of Tesco beans and tipped half the contents around it. Then he walked back into the living room and slumped down on the sofa to beside Sharon. She continued to stare past him at the drama on the screen. Two delicately beautiful girls were throwing a man out of a helicopter.

'We won today,' Dennis said forking pie into his mouth.

'Oh yes.'

'Broke the bloody lap record too. The *outright* lap record Shar, you know, set by a Formula One . . .'

'Shush Dennis! I'm watching the film.'

He slammed his plate down on the low table in front of him. 'For Christ's sake Sharon! I've been away all day, and when I come home you don't even say hallo or ask how it's been!'

'Yes! And I've been cooped up in this stinking flat all day doing nothing!'

'Well that's not my fault is it. I mean, I can't help it if your parents don't want to know you any more. I mean, you don't seem to be interested in anything. You're not interested in what I do, are you. What the hell are you interested in?'

Sharon's mouth began to pucker. 'Look Dennis, I don't feel too good you know. You may not have noticed it, but I *am* pregnant.'

23

'Oh I've noticed that all right!' Dennis yelled. 'A quick grope in the back of the Escort with Miss Shirley goody-two-shoes Temple, and my life's down the fucking pan!'

'Your life! Your life! It takes two to make a baby Dennis!'

'It takes one not to take the Pill or . . . or *something*.'

'God!' Sharon said, shaking her head despairingly and throwing herself back in the arm chair.

'You're meant to be a cook aren't you. How about making me something decent to eat, if you're so bored?'

Sharon shot upright again. 'What with, Dennis? What with, for Christ's sake? You don't earn enough money as an electrician to feed us properly, and still you take time off to work for that team you want me to be so proud of, that's so bloody marvellous they don't even pay you.'

'That's not fair Shar,' Dennis said, suddenly on the defensive. 'I mean, I'm learning the game. You can't expect them to pay me until I'm worth it. When I am they'll see me right.'

'Oh grow up!' Sharon shot back. 'You're just another mug who'll work for them for nothing. And I'll tell you something else Dennis Morrell – I'm not putting up with it much longer!'

Michael leaned back in the bath, then swore and sat up quickly as the hot tap burnt his back. A wave of water surged to the other end and splashed over Angelica's breasts.

'All right?' she asked, wriggling backwards to give him more room.

'Sure. You're worth getting burnt for any day.'

Angelica smiled almost shyly and looked down at the bubblebath foam floating on the water.

'What's the matter?' he asked, putting his hand under her pointed chin and gently lifting her head up again.

'Nothing . . . Well . . .'

'Tell me, Angelica.'

'Well . . . it's just that . . . I don't want you to think I made love with you to keep the drive.'

Michael stared at her in astonishment. Then he started to laugh, but stopped when he saw the hurt in her eyes. 'What

24

the hell are you talking about? You've already got the drive – it's part of my engine deal with Glaser, and you've just proved you're faster than me into the bargain.'

'You're a kind man Michael but you must know . . . everyone in the sport knows my reputation.'

Michael caressed her cheek again. 'Listen Angelica, I don't care what anybody else says or thinks about us. It's what you and I feel that's important, and I'm . . . I'm falling in love with you.'

Between them the foam was beginning to disappear so that Angelica's fit, tanned body was visible. She lifted her hands out of the water and began to sweep in more bubbles from the sides of the bath to cover herself.

'Don't do that,' Michael said, grabbing her wrists.

She shook her head miserably. 'I know I'm not beautiful. I know . . .'

'Are you fishing for compliments or really serious?'

'My thighs are too big, too much ski racing, and my tits are . . .'

But Michael had bent forward and clamped a hand over her mouth. 'You're crazy. All I know is you're incredibly beautiful to me. All I know is I want you.' He took his hand away from her lips and stroked it down her neck, over her firm breasts, hard belly, and then on down her body under the water.

'Michael, Michael!' Angelica gasped.

She bent forward to kiss him, and as she did so ran her fingertips along the insides of his thighs until she found him. Now it was his turn to shudder with pleasure.

Suddenly Angelica let go and wriggled round in the bath, starting a tidal wave. She knelt down with her foam-covered backside towards him. For a few moments Michael just stared at her magnificent body, deeply tanned and glistening wet. Her full-muscled thighs looked immensely strong, but above them her buttocks were small and tight. Then the rebounding wave of water splashed back against them, washing away the foam and exposing her. Michael fought for breath, feeling all

25

his blood and strength rushing to his loins.

'Go on,' Angelica whispered hoarsely, looking at him over her shoulder.

Bracing himself against the end of the bath Michael clamped his hands around her waist and pulled her onto him.

As he impaled her Angelica threw back her head and gave a long, high-pitched cry of animal ecstasy.

Three

THE TWO remote-controlled racing cars shot down the straight side by side, banged into each other and slithered apart again as they turned onto the banking at the end of it. One was a twelfth-scale replica of Porsche's Le Mans-winning 956, and it had pulled out a slight lead by the time they swooped off the banking onto the return straight. The second car was a home-built special with a balsawood wing fixed high above its un-painted tin bodywork. But suddenly the prototype was gaining on the Porsche and overtaking it.

'Aha! Aha!' the man working its radio control box went triumphantly. Rico Glaser looked more like a typical Swiss mountain guide than an industrialist. He was a squat man with a big leathery face and a bulbous nose. Silvery hair swept back from a wrinkled forehead and shrewd grey eyes.

The fourteen-year-old boy standing next to him was nearly as tall as his father, but Willi Glaser looked bored as he worked the controls of the blue-and-white Porsche.

Father was beating son as the cars reached the banking just in front of them, but then the prototype shot up and over the edge of it as though it was a launch pad.

'*Scheisse!*' Rico snapped.

The Porsche carried on round the banking and then slowed to a halt.

'Must be breakfast time, papa,' Willi said.

'No no, let's get it working properly,' Rico replied, already

27

examining his car for damage and then putting it back on the track.

Willi sighed, then made the Porsche start along the straight again. His father had built the miniature track in their garden after he had sold his company the previous year. It was meant to be a very special present for Willi, the Glaser family's afterthought, but Rico had certainly had his fair share of its use. Beads of sweat formed on his forehead now as he worked the prototype back into contention. It caught the Porsche on the return straight, only to go into orbit over the banking again. Rico's muttered oaths were lost in the shout from behind them.

'Breakfast!'

Frau Glaser stood in the kitchen doorway of their modern house just outside Bülach, twenty kilometres north of Zürich. She was in her mid-fifties, about the same age and height as her husband, but she had put on considerably more weight in the last ten years. A delicious aroma of hot sweet dough drifted past her into the garden. Willi spun away from the track and hurried towards the kitchen.

'You go on,' Rico said unnecessarily, staring down at the broken car in his hands. 'I'll fix this, don't worry.'

Five minutes later Willi was starting on his fourth waffle covered with golden syrup, and his father still hadn't appeared. Frau Glaser walked to the back door and opened it once more.

'Rico! The boy will be late for school!'

'I think I've found the problem. I just need . . .'

'Come and have breakfast *now!*' Eva Glaser ordered, holding the door open and waiting until her husband came in.

He sat down at the breakfast bar and distractedly pulled the plate of waffles towards him.

'Old fool,' Frau Glaser scolded. 'Every Monday morning the same thing – something you have been playing with at the weekend, and the poor boy is late. Coffee?'

But Rico wasn't listening. He had picked up two of the waffles and rested one on top of the other to form a T. 'Lever action!' he announced, as though he had seen the second coming.

'What?'

'We think we know so much, but time and time again we find we know nothing.'

'All I need to know right now is whether you want coffee?'

Rico nodded impatiently. 'I put the rear wing as high as possible to find clean air. It found it all right, but the support arms are so long that they lever the nose up and make it understeer. And all these years . . .'

'Rico! *Please* stop talking and eat!'

He grunted, broke up one of the cold waffles and stuffed a piece into his mouth. 'Must remember to tell Michael Church about this.'

The nineteen-year-old girl blinked her long-lashed eyes as she gradually woke up. A pale blade of light cut between the curtains of her bedroom window and fell across the pink-satin-trimmed bedclothes. She blew a strand of jet black hair away from her lips. There was a Swiss sullenness about them, but her sloe eyes were distinctly oriental.

The sound of running water came from the bathroom, and she rolled onto her side so that she could see its partly open door. Beyond it, her lover was shaving in front of the pink basin.

Curtis Stockwell was a thirty-six-year-old New Yorker. He had a lean aggressive face and a severe haircut that suited him and somehow didn't make him look old-fashioned. He made some final careful strokes with the razor, dabbed his face with a towel, and then splashed on aftershave. It smelt musky and expensive. Turning sideways to examine himself in the mirror, Stockwell breathed in and ran a hand over his taut stomach muscles.

He might be twice as old as her, the girl thought, watching him, but he was in good shape – three tennis matches a week made sure of that. And she had nothing to complain about in their affair either. For a start there was this little love nest less than a kilometre from the centre of Zürich. From the bedroom window she could look at the River Limmat drifting lazily through the best parts of town to the Zürichsee. Then there were the expensive clubs and restaurants they frequented. No, she had nothing to complain about the arrangement, but she wondered what Mrs Stockwell would think if she found out about it, or whether she knew already. Screw Frau Stockwell, she thought. If she wasn't capable of keeping her man interested that was her problem.

Curtis Stockwell finished combing his short brown hair, bent towards the mirror and plucked out a greying strand. Then he walked back into the bedroom and crossed it to the built-in cupboard in the far wall. He selected a pale blue shirt and began to put it on.

The girl was playing at being asleep, but now a smile formed on her pouty lips. Time for his morning treat, something to remember *her* by during his busy day. Rolling onto her back, she slid the pink satin sheet down over her young body revealing a triangle of tiny black public curls.

'Morning darling,' she said softly. 'Don't put that on yet.'

Stockwell turned towards her but continued to button up the shirt.

'Save it,' he said, hardly managing a smile. 'I've got to break somebody else's balls this morning.'

Rico Glaser drove the metallic-red sportscar past Kloten Airport and on down the autobahn towards Zürich. The 822 was the larger of the two models they built, but like its baby brother it was front-engined, with a long aggressive bonnet, two doors, and a sloping roofline just high enough to make them two-plus-twos. But this one was special. Ever since Rico had designed and built his twin-turbocharged racing engine he had been pressing for a turbocharged road car. The 822 he was driving was the experimental version. Now there seemed to be even less enthusiasm for it, Rico thought regretfully, playing with the exhilarating kick in the back the turbocharger produced when it cut in.

Just over a year earlier a Swiss-American holding company had made him an outstanding offer for his firm. There was more hard cash than Rico knew what to do with, and as he would still be the company president Rico couldn't see why he should refuse. But since the takeover, Glaser SA had changed dramatically, not so much physically as in spirit and attitude. The holding company had insisted on putting their own man on the board as vice-president. Fair enough, except that they had imposed Curtis Stockwell on him, a Harvard Business School graduate of Swiss-American parentage. Curtis Stockwell didn't seem to have any more love for cars than for packs of cigarettes, and openly said he thought they should be sold in much the same way.

Love? Rico thought to himself. Wasn't that expecting a bit too much of any modern manager? No damn it! he decided: not where automobiles or anything to do with them was concerned.

Ahead of him the autobahn curved right and then narrowed into a two-lane dual carriageway. Rico hung back for one last blast. For a few moments he relived the thrill of his racing days, when he'd been Swiss hillclimb champion three times, and an outstanding sports car driver. Then Rico had to stand hard on the brakes to make the turn-off to his left.

The Glaser factory was in a modern industrial estate just off the Kloten-Zürich autobahn. Rico drove down the access road and turned into the car park at the front of a large rectangular building. It was clad in navy-blue metal panels, with rows of round office windows set into the front. Whatever the architect had intended, the building looked remarkably like a cruise ship. Over the central front entrance was Glaser's stylised logo, a gold G leaning forward, with its cross bar streaking back through it. Rico parked his 822 next to Curtis Stockwell's metallic-silver version, and walked into the reception area. On either side of it corridors led to offices, and ahead of him was a flight of cantilevered stairs leading up to the first floor. He climbed them and turned left at the top, then opened the first door on his right and walked into his room.

A full width window overlooked the shopfloor. Rico went

up to it, leant his hands on the sill, and sighed contentedly. Below him were three production lines: two for the 422, of which they produced about twenty a week; and one for the special-order 822 model.

'Herr Glaser!' a worried woman's voice suddenly said behind him.

Rico turned to see his middle-aged secretary standing in the doorway that joined their offices. Normally Frau Rabensteiner was immaculately dressed and quite unflappable, but now her pinched face looked distinctly flustered.

'Have you forgotten Monday's special board meeting? You're fifteen minutes late, and I think they've started without you.'

'*Special* board meeting?' Rico snorted. 'There's one every day now. That doesn't make them special anymore.'

Frau Rabensteiner didn't waste time arguing. She opened the door by the corridor, making it quite clear by her schoolmarm expression that she expected him to hurry through it. She followed him out of the office, briefing him as she did so. 'Today it's marketing and promotions. Here's the file on last year's marketing expenditure; this one is current expenditure predictions; this one is the racing project.'

Rico stopped walking. 'The racing project? We're not discussing that today.'

'Herr Stockwell's secretary seemed to think you might be,' Frau Rabensteiner said, lowering her voice to a conspiratorial murmur. She opened a door halfway down the corridor, waited until he had walked through it, and then closed it behind him.

The board room had no windows, but had lights set into its white suspended ceiling. In the centre, a round beech wood conference table floated above a powder-blue carpet. Five men sat round it in beech-framed chairs with matching blue upholstery. In one of them, Curtis Stockwell was talking in his precise Swiss-German with only a trace of an American accent. He broke off in mid sentence as the company's president came into the room.

'Morning Rico. We were just having an informal discussion until you arrived.'

'Sorry I'm late; traffic,' Rico said, moving to the vacant chair alongside the American and sitting down in it. 'What was it about.'

'Dream cars.'

'*Dream* cars?'

'Yes. Francis has drawn some fascinating sketches,' Stockwell said, nodding at the young design director he had recently appointed. Francis Jaggi's fair hair was combed down over his forehead. That and his Andy Warhol glasses made him look more like the director of an art gallery.

Rico turned the drawings towards him and began to study them. He had to stifle an urge to burst out laughing. They looked like vehicles for a space fantasy film, the most outlandish creation having four front and four rear wheels.

'Eight wheel drive?' Rico asked the designer.

'They're static display concepts actually.'

'Meaning that they don't actually go?'

'If you want to put it that way.'

'I see,' Rico said, feeling anger pumping into his head. 'And who are these . . . static display concepts intended to impress?'

'That brings us right into the first item on today's agenda,' Curtis Stockwell said smoothly, 'product image creation. What I feel . . . what *we* feel is needed is a sophisticated marketing approach to increasing the desirability of owning our products. A series of outstanding dream cars displayed at the major motor shows would generate an enormous amount of publicity for us.'

Rico Glaser bit his lower lip, and waited for somebody else to speak. He looked round the table. On his right sat Norbert Dürr, the finance director and an old ally. Beside him were Kurt Fontana, the production director, and Hanspeter Brack, the personnel director, also long-standing friends. Francis Jaggi and Curtis Stockwell completed the circle.

'It's a new approach, but an interesting one,' Norbert Dürr said.

'It's crazy idea,' Rico said, looking reproachfully at the finance director. 'Since when have we been in the business of making cars that look good but don't work? That's going to change our image all right, into one of those Italian design studios always trying to create a sensation with weirder and weirder ideas.'

'I knew it!' Francis Jaggi said petulantly. 'Just because it's new concept you won't even listen.'

'I'll listen to sense, but this is nonsense. The fundamental way to improve our image is to make well-designed, well-built cars that are fast and reliable. To that we add the prestige of our racing involvement. These dream cars would cost god knows what, and are none of these things. They're mere fantasies, and as you say in your country Herr Stockwell, you can't fool all of the people all of the time.'

'That depends how good your advertising agency is,' Stockwell said evenly. 'As to cost, Francis and Norbert have done a preliminary evaluation, and it's certainly fundable from the existing marketing and promotions budget.'

An alarm bell sounded inside Rico's head, and he flipped open the beige folder marked RACING PROJECT that Frau Rabensteiner had given him. A sentence underlined in red biro leapt out at him – 'Expenditure on motor sport will now be included within the overall marketing and promotions budget.'

'By sacrificing what?' Rico asked. 'At the finance meeting last week we agreed that budgets couldn't be increased this year.'

For the first time Curtis Stockwell looked uncomfortable. 'We thought we should look at the racing engine again, Rico.'

'Now listen to me!' Rico started, but there was a knock on the door.

All eyes turned towards it as a young secretary entered with a tray of coffee. She put it down on the table in the tense silence, and nervously rattled a cup onto a saucer.

'Coffee, Herr Glaser?'

'What? Yes. Now listen . . .'

'Milk?'

'Yes. No. What I'm . . .'

'Sugar?'

'Good God!' Rico exploded. 'If anyone else tries to make me drink coffee this morning I'm going to pour it over their heads! I'm sorry my dear, just leave it and we'll serve ourselves.'

As the confused girl left the board room, Norbert Dürr eased his embarrassment by pouring coffee, and Rico took deep breaths to calm himself down. Curtis Stockwell broke the silence.

'Isn't the real issue that motor racing is becoming more and more irrelevant in the eighties?'

'You can't be aware of the International Automobile Federation's changes,' Rico countered. 'Take endurance racing sports cars. They have to be built to Group C regulations now. A road car manufacturer can still build any petrol engine he cares to, and put it in anybody's Group C chassis. But now the cars are only allowed a strictly limited amount of fuel for each race. That makes the technology highly relevant to us – a performance car manufacturer in a resource-conscious era.'

Stockwell pursed his lips: 'But the risk-reward ratio is too high, whatever they do to the rules. There's just no way you can guarantee results, is there.'

'Look, we've built a highly efficient racing engine. We've lent it to two outstanding British chassis constructors, Michael Church and Derek Lomax. Whichever of them performs better at the start of the season wins our full support for Le Mans. That's a highly competitive formula for success – *and* we've put a German-speaking driver in each car to ensure publicity.'

Stockwell smiled condescendingly. 'As a marketing tool, motor racing's hopelessly unsophisticated.'

'Enough!' Rico snapped, banging his fist down onto the conference table, so that everyone stared at him wide-eyed. 'Every meeting turns into an attempt to kill this racing project, and I've had enough of it! We vote once and for all to continue it this year, before we go any further.'

'But Rico . . .'

'Those in favour?' Rico demanded, glaring round the table.

Kurt Fontana and Hanspeter Brack raised their hands immediately. Norbert Dürr glanced at them and then followed suit.

Suddenly Stockwell held up both his hands in a conciliatory gesture. 'Then let's make it unanimous. You mustn't take this so personally Rico. It's my duty to put all the possibilities to the board. But now that we've definitely decided to go ahead with the racing promotion I do feel we need to appoint a man to control it.'

'But *I've* always done that,' Rico said.

Norbert Dürr laughed and clapped his hands together. 'Now, now, Rico. You can't go on doing *everything* yourself, and you can't win *every* battle. It has to be right that this considerable investment is properly managed.'

'Well . . . as long as it's someone who understands motor racing.'

'But of course,' Stockwell said.

Four days later Curtis Stockwell stood in one of the arrival halls at Zürich's Kloten Airport waiting for Thursday morning's flight from London. A Harvard Business School contempory of his ran a ruthless and highly successful headhunting agency over there. Although Curtis's requirement was too low grade to be worth their while normally, he had done it as a favour to an old friend.

The electronically controlled doors from the customs hall swished open, and pink-and-white faced English businessmen began to walk through. Stockwell mentally ran through the description his friend had supplied him with, and spotted Alexander Fitch without any difficulty.

He was in his late thirties, only slightly older than Stockwell, but his tall frame had literally gone to pot. Alex Fitch was born into merchant banking money, and he'd gone through his share of it in double quick time. A chubby, soft-faced child with curly fair hair and weak blue eyes, he had shown little sign of any intellectual or sporting ability. A good private school hadn't been able to do much about that, but it had reinforced his conviction that Britain owed people of his birthright and family wealth a living. In his twenties, still chubby and at rather a loss for something to do, Alex had discovered international sports car racing. Minimal talent and a lot of money had made him a midfield runner. More importantly, it seemed to give him immense prestige and status amongst his friends. Greatly encouraged by this, Alex ran through his seemingly inexhaustible wealth in five seasons and was faced with a horribly urgent need to find something to do.

The public relations industry saved him. A cigarette company was running a motor racing promotion, and a friend of Alex's got him into it as a link man with inside knowledge of the sport.

Sponsors came and went with alarming frequency, and Alex drifted along with them, adding an urbane if not dynamic veneer to their campaigns. The latest of these had just folded because of the recession when Stockwell's friend had contacted him. Now Alex Fitch walked into Kloten's arrival hall wearing a slightly shiny blazer, his old school tie, and a hopeful expression on his bloated face.

The American moved to intercept him. 'Alex Fitch?'

'You must be Mr Stockwell,' he said in a plummy voice. 'Very kind of you to meet me.'

'No problem.'

Stockwell led the way to the underground car park. There he loaded Fitch's battered leather suitcase into the back of his Glaser 822, and then climbed into the driving seat beside him.

'Pleased you could make it at such short notice,' Stockwell said, manoeuvring out of the dark car park. 'From what I've been told you could be just the man we need.'

'Jolly good,' Fitch said, confidence beginning to show on his face.

'You used to race yourself, didn't you?'

'Rather. Very keen on it. Packed it in to concentrate on the public relations side of things, but it's always in your blood.'

Stockwell accelerated the car along the autobahn access road. 'Personally, I feel motor racing's rather a questionable marketing tool. I think one should at least consider the other promotional possibilities available to the industry. What do you think?'

Alex Fitch glanced uncertainly at the American, then recovered and looked back at the road. 'Absolutely Mr Stockwell. I mean, one should certainly investigate all the errr . . . marketing tools available before choosing any particular one.'

'Good, good. But when you meet our president Rico Glaser I think you should play up your mutual motor racing interest rather strongly. There's a file on the seat behind you detailing his sporting achievements. You've got about five minutes to learn them.'

Alex Fitch twisted round and picked up the folder. 'I really do appreciate this advice Mr Stockwell.'

The hard American turned his head long enough to look straight into the Englishman's soft blue eyes. 'And *I* will really appreciate and reward your personal loyalty. Do you understand what I'm saying?'

'Oh *absolutely,* Mr Stockwell,' Alex Fitch said.

Four

WOLFGANG SCHNERING strolled up the Circuit Paul Ricard pit lane smoking a cigarette and wondering why he wasn't full of the joys of spring. The thirty-four-year-old German was of medium height, but had the gaunt figure of a jockey. There was something of a jockey's look, too, in his bony face, with its haunted grey eyes above prominent cheekbones. The late April sun was warming Provence, and a heat haze was already beginning to soften the vivid blue sky. Wolfgang was dressed in co-ordinated Lacoste shirt and shorts to make the most of it. So what was wrong?

Maybe it's this place, he thought, blowing out bluey-white tobacco smoke.

The Circuit Paul Ricard should have been one of the world's classic motor racing tracks. It was built in the late sixties, on a plateau in the hills between Marseilles and St Tropez. From its southern edge, one could look down past two-thousand-year-old hilltop villages and vineyards to the Mediterranean, shimmering like sealskin far below. But somehow the circuit, shaped roughly like the outline of an automatic pistol, was bland and soulless. A series of flat, accurately radiused corners led to an interminable runway-like straight. And the three-storey smoked-glass and white-concrete pits building looked like a minor airport terminal.

Bring back the Nürburgring, Wolfgang thought ruefully, picturing the great old circuit that snaked through the Eifel mountains. He had raced there for fifteen years in everything from saloon cars to single-seaters, and knew the fastest line through every one of its seventy-odd corners. Above all other tracks, the 'Ring had made him the professional he was now – not the fastest driver in the world, but one with enough experience and judgement to survive in top level sports car racing. But now the 'Ring was disused, an anachronism replaced by 'safe' circuits like Paul Ricard.

Maybe I'm an anachronism too, Wolfgang thought with sudden bitterness. Every year brought more pretty boys onto the scene, who could lap these identikit tracks faster than he could. Even girls. One bitch in particular!

He had reached the end of the pit lane and turned round to walk back. Ahead of him, Wolfgang could see the Glaser-Lomax sports car he had come to test. Something about it made him uneasy. The plain white Group C car had a conventional shovel-like nose, but its back end looked like a catamaran. The two protruding booms were linked by small biplane wings, a design meant to give it an aerodynamic advantage. But unusual bodywork was horribly often like the decor in a chichi restaurant – easy to make, and a cover for basic faults. Wolfgang couldn't help wishing he was driving the Porsche 956 further up the pit lane, a four-square brutally efficient looking machine.

Derek Lomax, the white car's tall and studious looking designer-constructor, was supervising final preparation of the car as Wolfgang reached it.

'We'll be ready for you in a few minutes,' Lomax said to his works driver.

Wolfgang nodded and stepped into one of the pit lane garages to change.

Five minutes later, he stepped back out onto the pit lane, kitted up in his black-and-gold helmet and cream race-suit. The one-piece rear end of the Glaser-Lomax was off. Ralph Cambell, the foxy-faced chief mechanic, was bent over the engine revving it in a series of dog-like snarls to warm it up. Wolfgang eased himself legs first through the car's right-side door, and settled down into the racing seat. He fastened the

40

safety harness, and took over the rhythmic blipping of the engine with his right foot. Behind him its note was suddenly muffled as the mechanics replaced the back end.

'Ready when you are,' Derek Lomax said, and shut the driver's door.

The mechanics pushed the car forward to help Wolfgang select first gear, and he accelerated away from them along the pit lane and down onto the pit straight on his left. It was enormously wide and hemmed in by double Armco barriers on either side. Every few hundred metres, a giant Marlboro cigarette pack stuck up beside it. From the tops of these, metal arms stretched over the track with signal lights on the end of them. Wolfgang navigated a series of turns that contrived to point him back in the general direction of the pits. On cold tyres he took them cautiously, with the engine burbling contentedly behind him. Then he was taking the last left-hander before the Mistral Straight, disappearing ahead of him into the distance. Wolfgang drove down it checking his instruments. He went past the back of the pits and paddock, under a pedestrian bridge, and eventually came to the famous Courbe de Signes right-hander at the end of the straight. At this speed it was no problem. Wolfgang arced neatly through it and the following series of predictable corners that led him back to the pit straight.

Now he checked his instruments once more, wiggled the steering wheel from side to side to scrub a bit more heat into the tyres, and then speeded up. Behind him the turbochargers started whistling and the engine note rose to a menacing roar. Through the tight corners the Glaser-Lomax slid about a bit at first, but then gripped the tarmac reassuringly as the smooth slick tyres reached working temperature. Wolfgang accelerated hard onto the Mistral Straight, taking the Glaser engine to its rev limit all the way up to fifth gear. This time the black bridge whipped over his head, and as the Courbe de Signes rushed closer it didn't look so easy anymore. Just before it, he lifted off slightly, then squeezed down on the accelerator again and turned into it at over 200 miles-an-hour.

For a few moments the car tracked neatly through the right-hander. Then its back end flicked violently out. Instantly Wolfgang fed on opposite lock, but kept his right foot absolutely still. The Glaser-Lomax had slewed diagonal to the track and more than halfway across it. Suddenly it snapped back into line, but now it was pointing off the circuit. With incredible self-control Wolfgang backed gently off the throttle, feeling for grip and delicately coaxing the white car round. He sucked in breath as the left-hand wheels drifted over the edge of the tarmac. Rows of catch fencing flashed past in an opaque blur as he gradually slowed down and eased back onto the track.

'*Wunderbahr!*' Wolfgang snapped sarcastically.

The next bend was a much slower 180-degree right-hander. Keeping tight to the inside, Wolfgang deliberately loaded up the car until the back end broke violently away again. This time he had left himself plenty of room to deal with it. He completed the lap at reduced speed, and pulled off into the pit lane on his right. Derek Lomax opened his door when he stopped beside him.

'How was it?'

'The engine is good. The handling is shit.'

'Shall we fit softer springs?'

'How about a chassis that doesn't flex?'

Derek Lomax's head rocked back as though he'd been punched in the mouth. 'Oh Christ,' he murmured. 'That bad?'

Out on the circuit, a forty-five-year-old Californian was thoroughly enjoying his first drive in a Porsche 956. Harvey Trip drove the dark-blue-and-yellow Group C sports car cautiously onto the Mistral Straight and began to accelerate down it. Inside the helmet, his big round face formed into a wide grin.

'Mo-ther!' he shouted out loud.

Harvey Trip had made his fortune by building up fast-food chains and selling them cannily ahead of changes in taste. He had found the current Mexican food craze a literal pain in the arse, so the big man from Los Angeles had finally decided to indulge himself in his childhood ambition – race driving.

International sports car racing catered for the Harvey Trips of the world. At the top it had its highly skilled professionals, with the specialised experience and self-discipline to do consistently well. But a large number of drivers' basic qualification was that they could pay for the ride. Endurance sports car events had prestige and glamour, didn't required ten-tenths driving, and many of the cars were made as easy to drive as possible. Which explained why Harvey Trip was tooling around the Circuit Paul Ricard in a £200,000 Porsche 956, ten seconds off the pace.

Back in the pits, the private German team who owned the blue-and-yellow car were praying that he was having fun – enough to make him hand over $300,000 dollars to have some more fun in the ten rounds of the world endurance championship.

After nine more laps, the Californian drove the Porsche back into the pits and was helped out of the cockpit by the team owner. Standing on the pit lane, he lifted off his electric-blue helmet with HARVEY signwritten on both sides in silver letters. His fleshy face was flushed and excited, and sweat plastered his thinning hair to his head.

'Jesus!' he said happily, 'don't it just motor down that straightaway!'

'And the handling?' the team owner asked.

'Aaah . . . fine, that was just fine.'

For a few minutes Harvey effused excitement about the Porsche. Then the son of a wealthy Italian jeweller took his place in the car, and he left them to it. Harvey never did things by halves, and he had arranged a second test drive that day. He walked down the pit lane until he reached Derek Lomax.

'Ready for me to try your machine now?' the Californian asked.

'We certainly are, Mr Trip,' Lomax said with a good attempt at a confident smile.

He helped squeeze him into the white car whilst Wolfgang looked on impassively.

'Not much room in this baby, is there,' Harvey complained.

'We can move the seat back a little,' Lomax said, kneeling on the door sill and struggling to make his potential customer comfortable. When he had done the best he could he went over the instruments and controls, showed him how to start the car, and then backed out and shut the door.

Harvey Trip accelerated cautiously out onto the circuit. Driven slightly below their limit the handling of most racing cars feels impressive, and there was no way he was going to lap as fast as Wolfgang had done. Even so he didn't like the Glaser-Lomax as much as the Porsche. It rocketed down the Mistral straight just as fast, and the brakes felt fine at the end of it, but there was a different feel about it. Harvey found it hard to put into words, but the Glaser-Lomax wasn't as *together* as the Porsche somehow. After half a dozen laps he brought it back into the pits.

'How did you like it?' Derek Lomax asked.

'Aaah . . . fine, just fine,' Harvey said.

But Lomax had seen his reaction when he'd climbed out of the rival Porsche. He knew he was going to have some hard selling to do that evening.

The Hotel de l'Ile Rousse was a favourite with racing drivers and the beautiful people who hung around them. For that reason Derek Lomax had offered to book Harvey in there, when he'd phoned from California about a test drive.

Twenty minutes south-west of the circuit, it was a rather ugly five-storey concrete box built on an exclusive promontory in Bandol. One side overlooked the forest of yacht masts in the Mediterranean harbour below. On the other side was a private sandy beach beside a bay. In the mouth of this was the tiny island from which the hotel took its name.

The hotel restaurant's interior had been decorated in old-France style – dark wooden ceiling beams, a large stone fireplace, and Louis Quatorze reproduction furniture. Now it was the off-season and nearly empty. Derek Lomax and Wolfgang Schnering sat at a table next to the panoramic windows overlooking the bay. They leant towards each other deep in conversation, with smoke from the German's cigarette drifting up between them.

Lomax was forty years old, with a long, intelligent face and slightly curly black hair. 'It's early days yet,' he said in a conciliatory tone. 'There's lots of things we haven't tried yet.'

'We've changed everything we can on the suspension and its still undriveable,' the gaunt-faced German said. 'That means the chassis just isn't stiff enough.'

'All right then, we'll stiffen it.'

'And then there's the tail. I'm not convinced that the downforce balance . . .'

'Look!' Lomax suddenly snapped. 'We'll do whatever's necessary, but I suggest you keep your doubts to yourself for the moment. I've gambled everything on this car. My company's not making any other models this season, and if it doesn't sell we go under. Finished! Kaput! Bust! I stress the *we*, Wolfgang, because at this stage of the game I wouldn't rate your chances of another works drive too highly.'

Wolfgang stared at him impassively, then nodded once. 'Don't worry, I'll be a good boy.'

Just then Harvey Trip appeared in the restaurant's entrance wearing a pearl-buttoned shirt and burgundy trousers.

'Glad you could join us,' Lomax said, standing up and pulling out a chair for the Californian.

The head waiter arrived and for some time they struggled to translate the menu.

'How did the cars compare then?' Lomax asked when they had finished ordering.

Harvey Trip's eyes narrowed. 'Frankly Derek, I took quite a liking to that Porsche I drove today.'

'Oh sure,' Wolfgang said, 'the customer 956s are made nice and easy to drive – a real rentadriver's car. You must have felt that when you drove it didn't you?'

'Aaah . . . yeah, that's right,' Harvey said with just a hint of hurt pride.

Lomax picked up the line of attack. 'Of course, if it's a rentadeal you're after we'll understand, but we wanted to involve you in the team rather more than that.'

'Just how did you figure on doing that, Derek?'

'Well, you'd buy a chassis and meet part of the running costs so that you'd actually own an asset at the end of the day. But as part of our works team you'd have free Glaser engines.'

Harvey's grey eyes enlarged, and Lomax could read the jackpot signs in them as clearly as if he'd pulled the winning combination on a one-armed bandit.

'Part of the works team?'

'One of our official works drivers.'

'That does sound good . . . a good deal I mean,' Harvey said almost to himself. 'Hell, I'm none too keen on Porsches anyway. They're rather like herpes – every prick seems to have them nowadays!'

Lomax roared with laughter. 'It'll be great to have you in the team, won't it Wolfgang?'

The German was staring at Harvey Trip in blank incomprehension. 'Wonderful,' he said with as much enthusiasm as he could manage. He didn't feel hungry anymore. As Lomax and Trip began to talk money, Wolfgang pulled another cigarette out of his pack and lit it.

Before I just had a shit car, he thought. Now I'm going to have a shit co-driver as well.

He might be able to talk Lomax into hiring a decent third driver, but Trip would still be in the car some of the time. That would kill any chance of them being really competitive, even if they managed to sort the car out. Yet another season seemed to be going down the drain, and with it his chances of being world endurance champion. And the really infuriating thing was that the Glaser engine was so damned good, a real alternative to Porsche power.

Wolfgang inhaled deeply and felt the smoke tickling his

throat. Then another bitter thought took away even that pleasure. Somebody else had the use of the Glaser engine, somebody he knew very well. The last thing he'd read was that she'd broken some lap record or other in England. Suddenly he could picture Angelica quite clearly – wild brown hair, that aggressive, beautiful face . . .

God, if that bitch beats me in the world championship! Wolfgang thought savagely.

Five

THE FIERCE midday sun blazed down on the Alps of the Austrian Vorarlberg, setting millions of ice crystals afire and turning the snowfields into an infinite jewel box. It was late April and what was left of the snow was already wilting under the onslaught.

On a slope high above the ski resort of Zürs, two girls and a man had set their skis face down in the snow to form makeshift sunbeds. Angelica turned over onto her back on hers. She was wearing a tiny white bikini that accentuated her deep tan, and her hair was even more streaked by a week back in the mountain sun. Flicking it away from her face, she put on her sunglasses and looked at her best friend lying beside her.

Ingrid was twenty-six, two years younger than her, but they had been in the Austrian ski team together for three seasons. Stockier and shorter than Angelica, she had been a slalom specialist. Ingrid had a cute heart-shaped face and short blonde hair, but powerful thighs stretched the frayed bottoms of her cutoff jeans, and magnificent breasts swelled her turquoise bikini top.

Beyond her, Angelica's father was showing off horribly for her benefit. Sigi Hofer had insisted on stripping off as well. He was prancing about in his ski boots and a tiny pair of red underpants, building up to his usual gymnastic display. Sigi was over fifty now, and his long hair was almost white. A beer belly flopped over the top of his briefs. But there was no way he could resist trying to get into Ingrid's pants.

Incredible! Angelica thought as she watched the performance. But then she really shouldn't be surprised – her father had laid half the available women who'd been to the resort, including her mother.

Josey 'Sigi' Hofer was born in 1932 in the nearby village of Stuben. His father was a farmer who had avoided war service by hiding out in the caves above Zürs. That had made his family local heroes. As if that wasn't enough of an advantage with girls, his youngest son Sigi had the muscular physique and swarthy good looks of a fifties film star. Sigi helped on the farm during the summer, and taught skiing to the ever increasing visitors to Zürs in the winter.

Not least of its attractions for a surprising number of women was the ski instructor with the handsome face, and bulging muscles under tight ski clothes. From November to April Sigi lived in an amoral sexual paradise that he had never imagined even in his adolescent dreams. Slipping from bedroom to bedroom in the best hotels, he served a clientele who rewarded him with gold watches, silk ties and leather belts. Even more extraordinary to him was that the staunchly Catholic villagers seemed to find his behaviour highly amusing.

'You can't blame Sigismund for being so beautiful,
It's not his fault everybody loves him,'
they laughingly quoted from the famous *White Horse Inn* operetta.

But Angelica's German mother was a different matter altogether. She was *'Die reiche Hur,'* the rich whore.

Carola first came to Zürs when she was seventeen, the languidly beautiful daughter of a Munich clothing manufacturer who had made a postwar fortune. Her parents considered skiing a healthy reward for their hard work. They were not so sure when Carola fell head over heels in love with her ski instructor, Sigi. When he got her pregnant during their next visit they knew they had made a ghastly mistake.

Carola's father forced a marriage on Sigi, bought them a house in Zürs, and then virtually disowned them. Four months later their only child, Angelica, was born.

For a short time Sigi managed to play the faithful father, but then another skiing season started and he was back in the corridors of pleasure for good. Carola hid herself away in their home, an outcast living in a cocoon of bitterness.

She would be there now, Angelica realised, waiting for her to get back. And on her mother's lips would be that knowing smile that always made her feel so guilty – 'you prefer to be with your father: no wonder you've turned out how you have.' Angelica was brought back to earth by her father's shout.

'So you don't think I can do a somersault eh?' Sigi was demanding of Ingrid.

'Go on then, let me see you do it,' she laughed, sitting up on her skis.

Turning to face her, Sigi set his boots apart, put his hands on his hips, and revolved his torso in a grotesque sexual parody. 'Just . . . warming . . . up,' Sigi panted.

Angelica studied Ingrid's face as she clapped and egged her father on. An unmistakable spark of arousal glinted in her bright blue eyes. Sigi climbed a few paces up the slope and began to make circus acrobat noises.

'Alleeeeeeez-*oop!*'

He jumped up into a tuck, somersaulted round, and splashed down beside Ingrid. Somehow he overbalanced so that he sprawled on top of her, coating her with snow as he did so. Ingrid screamed and squealed with delight as Sigi brushed it off her body.

Watching all this, Angelica couldn't decide whether she was amused or disgusted by her father, whether she loved or hated him. Who am I to judge him anyway, she thought with a sudden rush of guilt. After all, she had learnt to perform her own kind of tricks to get where she was. Maybe her mother was right – like father, like daughter!

Angelica stood up and started to pull on her skin-tight red ski-suit. 'Come on,' she said sharply. 'We'd better get down before the snow goes off.' Turning her skis over, she brushed snow away from the bindings and stepped into them. She wished she were in England with Michael now – anywhere but here. It had been her idea to spend some time at home before the motor racing season really got under way, but as usual it was turning sour on her. Angelica felt the familiar pain and anger welling up inside her. Grabbing her ski sticks she threw herself down the slope as though she were starting a race, feeling instant relief as she did so.

'Come on, you two!' she yelled over her shoulder. 'I'll be down before you've started!'

Then her father and Ingrid were coming after her yelling mock insults. Angelica made sweeping S-turns to let them catch up with her.

'So you think you can still ski better than me?' Sigi shouted once he was alongside. 'Sat on your arse in a racing car nowadays – what muscles does that exercise?'

Suddenly, Angelica slalomed towards and away from him in an incredibly fast series of turns. Every second one shot a wave of slushy snow up at him.

'Get away from me, you little cow!' Sigi yelled.

She kept it up until he tried to swerve away and crashed over and over in an explosion of the treacherous snow. Angelica gave a whoop of laughter, but then Ingrid came past tucked into the egg position. Instantly she forgot about her father and went down into a similar crouch. Downhill racing had been *her* speciality, the fastest and most dangerous of the alpine events.

As they reached the bottom of the slope they were already doing fifty miles-an-hour. Ahead of them was what was left of a piste at the end of April, mud-streaked waves of snow battered into shape by the now departed army of holiday skiers. Ingrid checked in a flurry of muddy snow to slow herself down but Angelica shot straight on.

'Oh no you don't!' Ingrid shouted, charging after her.

Now they were flying from crest to crest, whirling their sticks to find balance, crashing to earth and being launched into space again. Angelica had a savage grin on her face as she expertly chose a line, pre-jumping some bumps and using

51

others to launch herself over unskiable ones.

Suddenly Ingrid gave a panicky yell behind her as she lost balance and fell heavily. She slithered downhill in the filthy snow until she smacked into a huge bump and lay groaning at the base of it. It took Angelica several seconds to stop, and by then she couldn't see her friend. Her father hadn't appeared either.

'Are you all right?' she called out in a concerned voice.

But inside Angelica's head a devil's voice shouted triumphantly even as she was saying it.

You beat them! You can still beat both of them!

That same afternoon, Michael Church parked his estate car on the forecourt of his brother's garage in Reading. Turning up the collar of his maroon team anorak, he climbed out and hurried across the soaking wet tarmac.

The box-like showroom ahead of him was fronted by tinted glass. In bright sunshine it shone like silver, but today it was a lifeless rain-streaked grey. Pushing open one of its central doors, Michael stepped inside. The rectangular showroom was filled with family cars from a French manufacturer's range, except for the central display ahead of him. A wedge-shaped stand had been covered in royal-blue carpet tiles. On them stood a black Glaser sports car, with wooden chocks under its front wheels to stop it rolling down the slope and crashing through the plate glass window in front of it.

'Michael!' someone called out.

He turned to see his eldest brother coming out of his office at the end of the showroom. Conrad was thirty-three but looked nearer forty. He was shorter and heavier than his younger brothers, with darker hair and a fuller face. Usually there was a suggestion of disapproval on it, but now he was smiling warmly. In contrast to Michael's anorak and black cords he was wearing a charcoal suit over a blue shirt and tie.

'How are you?' Conrad asked as he reached his brother. He put a hand on his shoulder and began to steer him towards his office.

'Fine. How's business?'

'I keep hearing the recession's over, but nobody seems to have told my customers.'

Michael chuckled and pointed to the Glaser 822 on the wedge-shaped stand. 'Are those selling?'

'The image isn't quite right yet. People know the Swiss make great watches but they're not sure about Swiss cars. They'll buy a Rolex, but they'd rather play safe and get a Porsche.'

'We're hoping to do something about that this season.'

'That's why I persuaded Rico Glaser to lend you his engine,' Conrad said, pushing back the door of his office and waiting for Michael to go in first.

Apart from a large rosewood desk and the black leather chair behind it, the room looked like a miniature motoring museum. Behind the desk, glass shelves on the wall supported Conrad's collection of motor racing trophies and model racing cars. There were scratched fifties Dinkys, cheap plastic kit cars with their transfers peeling off, and expensive replicas of the sports cars Conrad had raced, painted in his maroon colours. On one side of the office, a rosewood bookshelf was stacked with motoring books and magazines. Michael glanced at the opposite wall. The large black-and-white photograph of their father still hung there. So did the picture of himself in one of his Lolas. But between them a rectangle of the pale blue wallpaper was slightly less faded than the rest. A tiny steering wheel from a racing car only partly covered it. Jonty's portrait used to hang there.

'You did me a big favour putting me onto the Glaser deal,' Michael said. 'The fuel consumption at Snetterton was over two kilometres per litre. That should mean we can run flat out for the whole of a 1,000-kilometre race on the 510 litre fuel allowance.'

Conrad tilted his chair back. 'Yes, the *car* was all right.'

'Meaning?'

'Frankly, the team was a shambles when you were driving – no-one leading them, part-timers bumping into each other trying to work out who should be doing what.'

Michael sighed and sat down on the edge of Conrad's desk. 'What we really need is a team manager and six professional race mechanics, but the budget just won't stand that.'

'Maybe I could . . .'

'Don't think I'm after you for more money. I know business isn't exactly brilliant, and you've done enough already.'

Conrad shook his head. 'That's not what I was thinking. One of my men helped build up the racing engine last time he was at the Glaser Factory on a training course. His name's Steve Driscoll, and he's not only a good mechanic, he's a bloody good organiser. He used to be team manager for some racing team or other before he got married. Why don't I lend him to you for the races?'

'Hmmm,' Michael went. 'We do need someone to take charge, and my lot would respect him if he knows his stuff.'

'Done, then, and I'll lose it in our accounts so that he won't drain your budget either. Now what about drivers?'

Michael started to colour. 'Well, Angelica certainly seems up to the job.'

'I'd noticed how well you two were getting on,' Conrad chuckled. 'What I meant was who's going to be your third driver in the 24-hour races?'

'I've renewed Jonty's licence, and entered him for Le Mans anyway. D'you think he'll drive for us again?'

The teasing smile disappeared off Conrad's heavy face, and a disapproving frown took its place. 'No way. And *you're* as much to blame as he is.'

'*Me?*'

'Well, you paid for his racing since he was seventeen, instead of letting him work for it like the rest of us.'

'Come on, Conrad – you know he was far more talented than either of us. I knew that the first time I let him try my Lola.'

'He was a spoilt brat! You put motor racing on a plate for him, so the first time it got difficult he just chucked it in.'

'He had a hell of a shunt.'

Conrad drove himself out of his chair with a disgusted

snort, and stalked away from the desk. 'We've all had prangs and got over them. Not everyone gets the chance to go on racing though. If you don't mind I'd rather you didn't mention the little sod.'

Quickly Michael suggested another driver, wishing he'd kept his mouth shut. It wasn't just that Conrad had been forced to give up racing when their father died. There was bad blood between him and Jonty for a reason that was a taboo subject. Michael had thought Conrad might have forgiven and forgotten by now. Glancing at the unfaded patch of wallpaper under the steering wheel again, he realised just how wrong he'd been.

It was nearly 2am and the dance floor of the Kensington basement club was nearly empty. Behind a smoked glass screen overlooking it, the disc jockey had run out of patter and was letting smoochy records do the work for him. In the middle of the floor a young couple clung to each other as though the corny words had been written especially for them.

Jonty Church looked startlingly like his elder brother. His face was almost identical to Michael's – the same mischievous brown eyes and slightly lopsided grin, same untidy brown hair tickling his ears. Only his unlined skin showed that he was six years younger.

The blonde girl had a fresh-faced just-out-of-school look that had brought her instant success as a model. A feline quality in her eyes suggested that she'd had more than luck on her side.

'Want me to take you home?' Jonty murmured.

Lindsey looked up at him, her little-girl lips suddenly inviting. 'I want you to take me to bed.'

Holding hands, they walked off the dance floor, threaded between tables and chairs in disarray, and came to a foyer that smelt of cigarette smoke. A strongman in a white dinner jacket opened the front door, and cool night air flooded over them. They stepped out into a dark well just large enough for the stairs leading up to street level. Lindsey shivered and snuggled up to Jonty.

'Come on,' he said, holding her against him and starting up the steps.

They turned towards the Old Brompton Road and jogged along the pavement, still holding tight, until they came to Jonty's white Lotus Esprit. He unlocked the door of the wedge-like two seater, jumped in, then leant across to open up for Lindsey who slid in beside him.

'Brrr! Turn the heater on.'

'It'll just blow cold air until we've been going for a bit,' Jonty said, starting the engine and pulling away from the pavement.

He drove surprisingly slowly, waiting for the traffic lights to turn all the way from amber to green before even starting to cross them. Jonty turned right onto Fulham Road. It was almost deserted and well lit by undisturbed pools of yellow light. Wanting to get the heater going, he changed down a gear and speeded up a little. The Lotus was doing forty-five miles-an-hour as it approached the next crossroad.

'Everyone's in bed,' Lindsey said.

Then it happened.

The Fulham Road traffic lights were green, but just as they reached them a red Cortina came shooting across in front of them. Jonty had an impression of laughing faces as he stamped on the brake pedal. He felt the tyres lock up and smelt burning rubber as they shrieked across the tarmac. Beside him Lindsey was screaming as well. The Cortina kept coming as though they weren't there. Jonty flung the steering wheel left but nothing happened. Instinctively he lifted his right foot enough to let the tyres find grip. As they did so the Lotus swung violently left, just missing the boot of the Cortina. Now they were heading straight for the traffic lights on the far side of the crossroad. Jonty aimed straight for them, balanced the car, and only then swung the steering wheel over. He hit the brakes again and brought the Lotus to a stop at the side of the road.

'How did we miss it? How did we miss it?' Lindsey whispered in a shocked voice.

Jonty said nothing. He was sitting back in his seat with his arms stretched out to the black leather steering wheel and his white-knuckled hands locked round its rim. He hadn't heard Lindsey's question, and he wasn't seeing the Fulham Road either.

He was taking off over the Pflantzgarten jump at the Nürburgring in the C3, but this time the nose kept going up and up. Blue sky filled the windscreen. Everything had gone deathly quiet. Then the front of the car dipped down and he could see a hillside and the track again. The sports car crashed down onto it, exploding in a storm of sparks, tearing metal and shredding fibreglass as it did so. It shot towards the Armco barriers like a berserk missile. Frantically Jonty swung the steering wheel over, but it was no longer connected to anything. The next impact was like nothing he'd experienced before, as though he'd been hit in the back by a lorry and punched in the stomach by a sledgehammer. His eyes and teeth felt as though they were coming out of his skull.

'Are you all right?'

Jonty shook his head and turned to see who was speaking, his face deathly white.

'Jonty, are you all right?' Lindsey repeated.

He nodded, unable to control his shaking limbs.

'God, how did you miss that maniac?'

'I don't know,' Jonty said quietly.

He started the Lotus again, every movement a conscious effort now, and glanced at Lindsey as they drove along in silence. In a few minutes they would be back in his flat, and she would console him with her sweet young body. This time he was in one piece and could take what was offered.

For a moment a picture of the wrecked Group C car filled his mind again.

There's no way I'll ever drive one of those fucking things again, Jonty swore to himself with absolute certainty.

Six

ANGELICA PURRED contentedly in her sleep and tried to turn onto her side. Something was stopping her doing so. Michael? He had met her at Heathrow Airport the previous evening, and since then they had been making love as though they'd just invented it. She reached out to touch him, but her hand flopped down onto her own body.

Blinking her eyes open, she realised that she was curled up in the seat of his estate car with the seat belt stretched tight across her. Michael glanced at her from the driver's seat and smiled broadly.

'With us again? What's made you so sleepy?'

'You should know,' Angelica yawned, stretching like a cat. 'Want me to drive for a bit?'

'No thanks. We're nearly at Silverstone.'

She looked at her watch – nine o'clock on Saturday morning – then out of the car windows at the landscape. They were driving fast along an undulating country lane. On either side were hedges, trees and fields in a spectrum of greens from vivid lime to matt ivy. Even inside the car she could smell their rich damp odour. Above them, lead-bellied clouds drifted across a gunmetal sky, but the rain was holding off. Early May in Northamptonshire.

Then Silverstone Circuit was on their right, and Michael slowed down to turn into the competitors' entrance. A roadway led to the *Daily Express* Bridge. As they drove up onto it Angelica could see the track. It followed the perimeter of a wartime airfield, but despite that unpromising heritage Silverstone was full of atmosphere and character. Across the track to their right, a group of houses and farm buildings formed a tiny village. Beyond that grassy fields and crumbling concrete runways dipped towards the southern corners of the circuit.

The Vauxhall clattered across the bridge and then dipped down onto the road to the pits and paddock complex. This was made up of parallel tarmac strips, with the pit straight forming the northern boundary. A wide breeze block wall topped by guardrails separated it from the pitlane. Opposite this was a long line of garages, broken only where the pedestrian bridge crossed the track two-thirds of the way down the pit straight. Behind the garages was the paddock.

Michael slowed to a crawl as he reached it. Mechanics were rolling freshly-fitted tyres across to their garages, and struggling to get them past the line of vehicles outside them. The works Porsche team had three identically painted trans-porters and a luxury motor-home, but further along, the privateers had a multi-coloured assortment of less pristine equipment. Beyond the pedestrian bridge, the works Lancia team raised the image stakes again, and just beyond them he spotted his own maroon transporter, a converted removal lorry.

'Here we are,' Michael said, parking beside Conrad's black Glaser 822.

But Angelica wasn't listening. She was staring at the beige transporter next door. Large chocolate brown letters down its side read: GLASER-LOMAX WORLD ENDURANCE CHAMPIONSHIP TEAM – Drivers Wolfgang Schnering, Harvey Trip.

'What's the matter?' Michael asked.

'Nothing,' she said, quickly climbing out of the car so that he wouldn't see the expression on her face.

The up-and-over door of their garage was open so that as they walked round the back of their transporter they could see the sports car inside it. Maroon-overalled mechanics were working around it, but they hardly looked up as Michael and Angelica walked in.

'Morning all,' Michael said.

There were a few grunts in response. Angelica stared at the mechanics in surprise. What had happened to the amusing atmosphere she had so enjoyed at Snetterton? Even Dennis Morrell hardly managed to return her smile. He was the young, slightly stupid-looking electrician who had saved the day at Snetterton by tracing an electrical misfire. Angelica had made a friend by praising him for it in front of the others. At least she thought she had.

A bearded figure in a maroon team anorak and matching slacks walked across the garage towards them.

'Hallo Michael,' he said, shaking hands with him, and then turning to Angelica. 'We haven't met. I'm Steve Driscoll.'

'Oh yes, the new chief mechanic. Michael told me about you.'

As she shook hands, Angelica studied him. He was in his early or mid-thirties, quite tall and thinly built. She sensed weakness behind his full beard of wiry black curls, but maybe it was just that she had a prejudice about men who wore them – Wolfgang had grown one once, and she'd made him shave it off. Angelica was standing sideways on to the mechanics, and in the corner of her eye she caught their hostile glances at Driscoll. Now at least she knew *who* the problem was.

'How's the car?' Michael asked.

'Just needs fuelling up,' Driscoll said. 'I was waiting for you to tell me how much you wanted in.'

'Hour-and-a-half practice sessions, aren't they? Quarter full then – twenty-five litres. We'll go for a quick time first, and then set it up on full tanks for the race.'

'Fine,' Driscoll said, and started to give orders to the mechanics.

Michael put his hand on Angelica's back and steered her towards the pitlane.

'What's the problem with Driscoll?' she asked when they were outside.

'The lads are used to me giving the orders, and they don't like a newcomer doing it. They'll just have to get used to it, but I think I'll go back and give Steve some moral support.'

'Sure. I'll take a look at the opposition.'

As Angelica turned to walk down the pitlane she found herself looking straight at Wolfgang Schnering. He was perched on the pit wall guardrail smoking a cigarette, and must have been watching them all the time. There was a bitter little smile on his gaunt face. In a moment of panic Angelica didn't know whether to smile back or pretend she hadn't seen him. Wolfgang settled it by jumping down off the guardrail and walking across the pitlane towards her.

'*Wie gehts Angelica?*' he said. 'I hear you've found yourself a good ride.'

'Yes, it's a really good car,' she said, trying hard to smile.

Wolfgang gave a questioning look at Michael who was just disappearing into the garage. 'I wonder how you managed that my darling? Poor Wolfgang hasn't had such luck.'

'Difficult car?'

Schnering gave a bitter chuckle. 'The teacher ends up with the problems, and the pupil with the answers.'

She laughed uncomfortably. 'You always were a pessimist, Wolfy.'

'So it is, so it is. Well, I must go to work. Maybe I see you later?'

'Maybe,' Angelica said, grabbing the chance to smile politely and walk away.

Michael blasted out of the Woodcote chicane and onto the pit straight with the Glaser V6 whistling and howling behind him. He changed up into third gear, then fourth, then fifth, with quick, precise little wrist movements. This first practice session they were going for a quick time to put them as far forward as possible on the starting grid. As he flashed under the pedestrian bridge Michael looked right for his pit signal. He spotted his maroon-overall leaning out over the guardrail, and read the bright red letters on his board.

61

One-minute-sixteen.

The C4 was quick all right, easily the fastest car he'd ever built. One of the Glaser engine's many advantages was light weight, and the car was nearly on the 800kg minimum weight limit.

Michael braked smoothly, changed down into third, and turned right into Copse corner. As he squeezed the accelerator down again, his front right wheel kissed the red-and-white castellated kerbing exactly at the apex of the bend. What was so good about the C4 was its balance – even if he accelerated to early or too hard through a corner it just drifted sideways; as soon as he feathered back it held its line again. It was so comfortable to drive.

Too comfortable? Michael suddenly wondered.

The Group C fuel regulations had made endurance sports-car racing a battle of tactics. A flat-out lap in practice might earn you a good starting position, but it didn't predict the outcome of the race. The real question was what pace could each car keep up for 1,000 kilometres without going over the 510 litre allowance and running out of fuel.

Michael was back in fifth gear, and took the left-handed Maggotts kink without lifting. Then he braked really hard and changed down into second for the tight right-hander at Becketts. Rows of metre-high catch-fencing were meant to slow you down if your brakes failed there. At that approach speed they'd have a hell of a job to stop a car before it smashed into the railway sleepers beyond them.

Down Hangar Straight he topped 200 miles-an-hour, flashing past slower cars before braking for Stowe corner at the southern end of the circuit. Again, Michael could feel the power biting into the Tarmac in immediate, continuous response to the pressure of his right foot. *Fabulous!* But something was nagging away in his mind now.

Club corner was similar to Stowe, and then he was climbing uphill towards the *Daily Express* Bridge. Michael took the Abbey kink flat out, shot under the bridge, and then braked hard for the Woodcote chicane. Ahead of him, a long line of grandstands followed the curve of the track and then continued parallel to the pit straight. As he boomed past them to complete the lap an official was waving the chequered flag to signal end of first practice.

He did one more slowing down lap and then, just after the *Daily Express* Bridge, steered right onto the pit lane. It snaked about on the infield before straightening and widening out at the garages. Angelica, Conrad and Steve Driscoll were standing outside theirs, and he braked to a halt beside them. But where the hell where the mechanics? Undoing his safety harness Michael climbed out of the car and spotted them lounging about on the pit wall.

'Well?' Angelica asked.

Michael took off his helmet and balaclava. 'Just what you said – handles perfectly. How do our times compare with everyone else's?'

'We're definitely in the top five.'

'Let's fill her up and find out what the consumption was,' Michael said to Driscoll.

The team manager nodded, and walked across the pit lane to fetch his men.

Conrad's face was hard and tense as he turned to Michael. 'That lot don't like being organised, but by Christ they need it! Mind if I have a word with them?'

'Perhaps I should.'

'The idea was to take the worry of this side of things off you. Let me do it,' Conrad said. This time it was a statement, not a request.

Dennis Morrell had had a rotten week. Sharon had nagged him constantly after he'd told her that he was taking another Friday off work as well as the weekend to go racing. Then on Thursday, when he'd asked for his pay a day early, his boss had turned him down. That evening Sharon had made a comment about it and he'd slapped her – well, punched her in the eye was nearer the truth. She'd driven him to it, but Dennis felt bad about it . . . something about the way she'd slumped down against the wall crying quietly, like a miserable whipped animal. Also, he had left home at six o'clock on Friday morning without even saying goodbye to her.

After all that, when he'd arrived at Silverstone the team had been taken over by some little Hitler called Driscoll. Dennis liked to touch the C4's electrical systems whenever he wanted to. That way he could sometimes tell if something was about to go wrong – nothing more complicated than feeling dirt or damp on the wiring, or getting a bloody good belt of electricity from it! But this Driscoll said no-one was to touch the car unless he told them to. He worked for Conrad Church, and had been on some training course or other at Glaser's. That apparently gave him the right to barge in on the regulars and treat them like idiots.

So they'd had a little word about it. If you weren't allowed to touch the car until Driscoll said so, fine; but then he'd have to give each of them a direct order for every little thing he wanted done.

Now they were refuelling the car, and Dennis was having the most fun he'd had all week. The lads were like puppets – you had to move them from position to position. Driscoll was bright red in the face and shouting his head off. It wasn't enough for him to tell one of them to stick the refuelling hose into the valve on one side of the car: the bloke with the over-flow bottle waited for an order before connecting that to the outlet valve. Then they just stood there until Driscoll yelled at them: 'For Christ's sake, open the valves.' Conrad Church was getting the message too. His face was like an over-ripe cherry!

Finally the job was done, and the lads were exchanging smirks. If Driscoll had learnt his lesson they'd soon pack the game in and cooperate. Then Conrad barked out an order.

'Right! Everybody into the garage.'

The sly smiles disappeared as they shuffled into the grey-walled garage. Conrad came in last, switched on the fluorescent lights, and then slammed down the door with a metallic clang.

'You all know who I am,' Conrad started in an icy tone. 'My car distributorships employ over 100 mechanics. And yet you lot don't seem to think I'd know what was going on or what to do about it.'

With its doors closed, the garage was beginning to smell of exhaust fumes. To that was added the sweaty smell of tense human beings. Conrad let a silence build as he looked from face to face.

'Steve Driscoll here's an experienced team manager, who knows the Glaser engine. Everything I've seen this morning proves to me just how badly you need him. If you can't accept that you'd better clear off now.'

'Bloody hell!' Dennis burst out. 'Some of us aren't even getting paid for this!'

'Look!' Conrad snapped at Dennis. 'My firm's put as much as it can stand into this project, and so have I. If that's not enough for you, I'm sorry. But after tomorrow Alex Fitch is going to recommend who Glaser should back at Le Mans. If we get that additional money, you'll all be on top rates. And all you can do is stage a go-slow in front of him!'

There was a subdued murmuring.

'We all know what we want, and we all know how we can get it. Now I suggest you put your backs into your jobs, or you're out anyway.'

As he finished speaking Conrad was staring straight at Dennis.

In the motor-home Michael and Angelica sat side by side at the dining table. Michael stabbed the buttons of his calculator, and checked the read-out against the numbers on the pad beside it.

'Shit! *Just* too high,' he said.

'So we can't go that fast without running out of fuel?'

'Right.'

'Can the Porsches and Lancias?'

Michael bunched his fists and punched them together. 'If only we knew.'

'You know,' Angelica said quietly. 'That car handles so well, maybe we don't need all the downforce we've got.'

'*That's* what was in the back of my mind,' Michael said. 'I think a smaller rear wing would get rid of enough drag to do the trick.'

'Won't it upset the balance.'

Michael was already sliding off the seat. 'We'll soon find out.'

Just then the door halfway down the motor-home opened, and Conrad and another man came in.

'Hope we're not disturbing you,' Conrad said. 'I just wanted you to meet an old friend of mine, Alex Fitch.'

'Well *hallo!*' Fitch said, ignoring Michael and taking Angelica's hand. 'I've been looking forward to meeting you, my dear.'

His palm was clammy, and he reminded her of a fish, but Angelica smiled at him coquettishly. 'And I've been looking forward to meeting you, Mr Fitch.'

'For heaven's sake call me Alex,' he said, his fat face beaming.

Dennis Morrell walked out of the back of the Church Team's garage, and headed across the paddock towards the toilet block. His chubby face was grubby and sweaty, and he looked thoroughly fed up. As he trudged across the tarmac someone called his name. Looking over his shoulder Dennis recognised Ralph Cambell. The Lomax team's chief mechanic was jogging to catch up, and he stopped and waited for him.

'Hi Dennis. How's it going?'

'All right,' Dennis said unconvincingly. 'Just off for a pee.'

'Me to. What's up? You don't look too cheerful.'

'Oh . . . nothing.'

'Well I've got some news that'll put a smile on your face. You know what we talked about at Snetterton, you joining us full-time. Well, I've had a word with the boss, and it may be on.'

Dennis's head came up in surprise. 'Yeah? You mean . . . you know . . . paid?'

'Two-hundred-and-fifty quid a week minimum. Our team's not run on charity, like some I know.'

'Too bloody true!' Dennis said.

They reached the brick-built toilet block, and turned into the entrance. To their left was a long tiled wall with a trough running along the bottom of it. Cambell walked right to the end of the wall before facing it and unzipping his overalls. Dennis followed suit.

'When could I start?'

Cambell waited for the only other person in the urinals to walk out before answering. Beside him, Dennis's stream was splashing noisily against the wall, but he seemed to be having difficulty in getting started.

'Sometime before Le Mans, but there is a little job you could do for us straight away.'

'Oh? What?'

Cambell looked round again before speaking. 'Make sure we beat your lot tomorrow.'

Dennis's eyes widened, and urine splashed down his overalls as he stared at Cambell. 'You mean nobble our car? I couldn't do that!'

'Why not? We're going to beat them in the end anyway. All you'd be doing is speeding up the process a little.'

'Christ! You're serious.'

'It's a serious business,' Cambell said. 'We've got the money and we've got the jobs. We're waiting to see how keen *you* are on getting a share of them.'

'I don't . . . I'm not . . .' Dennis stammered.

But Ralph Cambell had already zipped himself up, and was walking away.

'Think about it,' he said over his shoulder.

Seven

THE TWO flag marshals had been at their post on the banking between Stowe and Club corners since eight o'clock that Saturday morning. Now it was tea-time, and the second Group C practice session was nearly over.

'Who d'you fancy?' the taller, younger marshal asked.

'Her for a start!' Bill said, pointing at the maroon sportscar rocketing along Hangar Straight. He looked about ten years older and one stone heavier than his spotty-faced companion. 'To win the race I mean.'

'That's what I meant, Eric. It's just your dirty little mind again, isn't it.'

Both of them turned to watch the C4 negotiate Stowe corner. It powered through, visibly gaining ground on the brown-and-beige Glaser-Lomax about 200 yards ahead of it.

'D'you really think she's got a chance against the Porsches and Lancias?' Eric asked after both cars had howled past them.

The teasing grin disappeared from Bill's floppy face as he watched the C4 turn into Club corner. As a volunteer marshal he had closely observed every conceivable type of racing machine over the last decade.

'It's not handling as well as it was this morning,' Bill said. 'Probably running full tanks. But she's still about the quickest thing on the track, and the car's reliable.'

When the two sports cars reached Hangar Straight again just over a minute later, the C4 was within striking distance of the Lomax.

'Steady-blue-flag him,' Bill ordered.

Eric selected the 'car-closing-on-you' signal, stretched it taut between his hands, and held it over the guardrail.

As the brown car reached its braking point for Stowe corner its nose dipped and its tail twitched about. Suddenly the maroon car was closing right in on it and diving to the right to claim the inside line. It was almost alongside when the Glaser-Lomax chopped across its bows, slamming the door on the overtaking manoeuvre.

'Wave the flag at him!' Bill snapped as the cars accelerated out of Stowe nose to tail.

A tidal wave of sound rolled towards the marshals, battering their eardrums as it swept past them.

'Oyyy! That's my girlfriend you're carving up!' Bill screamed into it.

Angelica glared through her windscreen at the brown-and-beige car ahead of her. Harvey Trip had been way off the pace in the morning practice session, so it had to be Wolfgang driving it now. Hadn't he seen her back there at Stowe, or had he deliberately carved her up? Whichever, she had to avoid dicing with him because she was doing the critical fuel consumption test.

With a small rear wing fitted, the C4 was more nervous than it had been that morning, but still no problem to drive. That was more than could be said for Wolfgang's dramatic progress ahead of her. Whenever he braked the Glaser-Lomax's twin-boomed tail started a lazy fishtailing movement. By the middle of a corner that had developed into a frenzied twitching, like a hooked trout being lifted out of the water. It was obvious that Wolfgang was making a do-or-die effort for a good time because he was fighting the car all the way. They flashed under the *Daily Express* Bridge, still nose to tail, and rushed towards the Woodcote chicane.

Maybe he didn't see me, Angelica told herself.

On the banking, marshals were frantically waving blue flags at Wolfgang. Even so she moved her car so that its centreline was pointing straight at the Lomax's right wing-mirror. If he looked in it he couldn't possibly miss her. Just before she braked Angelica steered further to the right and then drew alongside him. She had the inside line for the chicane. There was no way he could go for it without ramming her.

The brown car shuddered under late braking. It wasn't dropping back. Suddenly Angelica realised that Wolfgang intended to fly the red-and-white-painted concrete semicircle they were meant to steer round. She turned right to take the chicane, but he headed straight for it. The Glaser-Lomax slammed into its ramp-like leading edge and took off like a wingless jet fighter, flew through the air for thirty yards, then crashed down onto the track ahead of the C4.

'You stupid prick!' Angelica shouted.

Of course he'd seen her! How could she have thought otherwise? Wolfgang never could stand her beating him.

They had met six years ago when she was training with the Austrian Women's Olympic Ski Team at Kitzbühel. Wolfgang was a professional racing driver who had come there for a winter holiday and liked to hang around with them.

At first, Angelica hadn't taken much notice of him, although he obviously fancied himself and had a brand new Porsche Turbo road car. He was twenty-eight years old, a little bit short and a little bit ugly. Then Wolfgang started telling her how impressed he was by her skiing, her speed, her balance – she really ought to try his single-seater racing car because he was sure she would make a natural racing driver. That won Angelica's attention all right, because she knew a downhill racer only had so many seasons, and she couldn't imagine life without it, or something pretty similar.

It was all a beautiful dream, until one evening Wolfgang walked her to her bedroom door and made it quite clear what he expected in return. Angelica told him exactly where to go. She knew from bitter experience what that game had done to her parents' life, and she was utterly determined that she wasn't going to play it. Somewhere along the line Fraulein Hofer would meet Prinz Charming, marry him, and be faithful for life.

And then one morning she caught Wolfgang creeping out of her bitter rival's bedroom. For three days Angelica had to listen to her boasting about the Formula Three test drive she had been promised, the lucrative backing a girl driver could attract, and the golden second career that stretched ahead of her.

On the team's last day in Kitzbühel, Angelica walked into Wolfgang's hotel and knocked shyly on his bedroom door.

It hadn't been as hard as she'd imagined to sleep with him. In fact it was quite a relief to lose her virginity after playing the ice maiden for five years. And having done it once . . .

Three months later, Angelica watched him come third in a Formula Three race at Hockenheim, and was quick to explain how she would have done better. Wolfgang couldn't wait to get her in the car and prove how much slower she was. A fortnight later they were back at the German track for a test session. Angelica *was* slower, but at this stage she didn't care a bit – Wolfgang was giving her just what she wanted.

For two seasons he remained her lover and her motor racing mentor, introducing her to entrants and backers into the bargain. One of these was a wealthy sports racing car owner who asked her to drive for him. That wasn't all he wanted from Angelica, and the resulting split with Wolfgang was as bitter as it was inevitable.

All that was four years ago. Now as they hurtled along the pit straight Angelica tucked into Wolfgang's slipstream and wondered how the hell she was going to get past him.

To her relief her pit sign said IN, so she hung back for the rest of the lap and pulled off onto the pit lane just after the *Daily Express* Bridge. She switched off the engine as early as possible and coasted to a stop in front of the Church Team's garage.

'Had to slow down a bit on the last two laps,' she reported as she stepped out of the car and pulled off her helmet.

But Michael was walking to the back of the C4 with a concerned look on his face. 'Christ, look at this!' he said, pointing to the rear wing.

It was an unpainted aluminium one, which had been hastily fitted to the maroon sideplates between practice sessions. The centre of the aerofoil had buckled slightly under the massive downforce, but that was enough to have nearly torn it away from the sideplate nearest Michael. Steve Driscoll and Conrad hurried over to see what he was looking at.

'We'll have to do better than that for the race,' Michael said coldly, and started to explain what needed doing.

The team only had one small wing with them, so somebody would have to drive to the Reading workshop and bring another one back to Silverstone. Then they would have to strengthen it, and mount it more securely. By now the mechanics had gathered round as well, and there were weary sighs at the prospect of another six or seven hours at the circuit.

Michael took Angelica and Conrad to one side. 'I'm staying to see the job's done right and to buck the lads up a bit, but there's no point in us all hanging around.'

'I'll keep you company,' Angelica said.

'*You* need a good rest before tomorrow.'

'Quite right,' Conrad intervened. 'You take my car and go back to the hotel. I'll stay with Michael.'

Angelica smiled at the brothers. 'All right. I can't fight you both.'

She kissed Michael on the cheek, and then followed Conrad through their garage into the paddock. Her suitcase was in the team's motor-home, and when she came out with it Conrad had unlocked the hatchback boot of his black Glaser 822.

'Very smart!' Angelica said, 'but where are we staying?'

'The Saxon Inn in Northampton. Very easy to get there.'

Conrad was explaining the route when, out of the corner of her eye, Angelica saw Wolfgang walking towards his Porsche Turbo parked a few yards away. She turned her back to him, but suddenly Conrad was trying to catch his attention.

'Excuse me, excuse me; you're staying at the Saxon aren't you? I saw you there this morning.'

Wolfgang glanced uneasily at Angelica before answering. 'Yes, that's right.'

'Could you show Miss Hofer the way?'

An amused smile formed on the German's lips. 'Of course. It would be a pleasure.'

'Very kind of you,' Conrad said, opening the Glaser's door for Angelica. He waited for her to start it, waved, and then walked back towards the garage.

In her rear-view mirror, Angelica watched Wolfgang driving his white Porsche out onto the paddock's exit lane. It was the same one that had so impressed her six years ago. Like its owner it was beginning to show its age. Then Angelica caught sight of her own face in the mirror. The girlish softness it had when she first met him was gone now, replaced by a harder more angular look.

They're not the only ones who've aged, Angelica thought.

She found reverse, and backed the Glaser out behind Wolfgang's car. He led the way out of the paddock, over the *Daily Express* Bridge, and onto the road to Silverstone village. There they turned right towards Northampton.

Until Towcester the traffic was heavy, but most of it turned left or right onto the A5. The Porsche and the Glaser carried straight on at the traffic lights. Ahead of them the A43 climbed straight towards the horizon about a mile away. Angelica had never driven an 822, and she was interested to know how it performed. Changing down into third, she accelerated hard. The V8 engine responded with a smooth surge of power that carried her effortlessly past the white Porsche. Angelica pulled into the left again.

The brow of the hill was close now, but behind her she heard the urgent whine of the Porsche's engine. Then Wolfgang shot past her. Angelica smiled to herself – still the same overgrown child who had tried to race her on skis a lifetime ago. Well, she had no intention of playing games on the road.

Then Angelica saw the chance.

Wolfgang's charge had swept him over the brow of the hill and right up to the tail of a slow moving lorry. The road curved left, and in his left-hand-drive car he couldn't see what was coming even by edging out a little. Angelica, further back, could. Judging an oncoming car carefully, she changed down again and blasted past the Porsche and the lorry in one smooth surge.

'Just follow the road all the way to Northampton,' Conrad had said. She didn't need Wolfgang just yet. But now he was overtaking the lorry and closing on her as though it was the last corner of a ten lap sprint.

Screw you! Angelica thought. Here's some of your own medicine.

On the left of the road was a red-ringed 30 mph sign at the beginning of a village. Angelica stamped on her brake pedal and changed down at the same time, smiling as she heard his tyres shrieking behind her. The road twisted and turned between weathered sandstone houses with absolutely no-where for Wolfgang to pass her. Angelica slowed right down and crawled through the village. As she came to the final bend she squeezed the accelerator hard and took the rev-counter to its limit before changing gear. She looked in her mirror – Wolfgang was struggling to catch up, but there was traffic ahead of her in both directions.

Angelica slowed down, but left plenty of space to the car ahead. Wolfgang had closed right onto the Glaser's tail. Slowly she reached her hand up to the light switch. As a chance to overtake presented itself she flicked on the side-lights and floored the accelerator at the same time. Wolfgang saw red tail-lights again and slammed on his brakes.

Angelica kept it up all the way to the outskirts of Northampton before remembering that she didn't know where to go. She slowed down, and Wolfgang overtook her, mouthing a sarcastic 'very clever' as he did so. She fell into line astern, wondering if he was childish enough to try and lose her, but Wolfgang seemed to have had enough of the game.

The eight-storey Saxon Inn jutted up between a seedy old part of the town centre and a brave-new-world car park. Its grey-blue concrete and glass facade was topped by a distinctive roofline like a row of white shells. Wolfgang led the way past its covered entrance and turned into the car park in front of it. Angelica parked beside him. They climbed out, trying to avoid each other's eyes, and Angelica opened the Glaser's hatchback boot.

'I suppose I deserved that,' Wolfgang said sheepishly.

'You sure did! You nearly had me off at Woodcote.'

Wolfgang walked over to her and reached for the suitcase. 'I was on my hot lap. Here, let me take that.'

'Hot lap? More like a bomb about to explode! Whatever happened to all those theories about smooth driving?'

'Smooth is fine when you have a racehorse. When you have a donkey you have to kick shit out of it.'

'I knew I smelt something, but I thought it was in *my* pants!'

Wolfgang roared with laughter and started to walk towards the hotel's awning. At the reception desk a girl handed him his key and then turned to Angelica.

'Ah yes Miss Hofer, we were expecting you,' she said, handing her another one.

'Nothing to sign?'

'It's all taken care of.'

Wolfgang glanced at her key. 'Fourth floor. I'll carry your bag up.'

'I can manage,' Angelica said, but he had already grabbed it and turned away.

They walked past the lobby, furnished with dark brown chesterfields to soften the modern architecture, and stopped at the lift. Wolfgang pressed the call button and they stood in silence until it came. When its doors hissed open it was empty. He waited for Angelica to enter it first, then followed her in and pressed the fourth floor button. Someone had been smoking a cigarette inside it, and its stale smell added to the claustrophobic atmosphere as the doors closed. The lift began its swishing, unearthly climb.

'It's good to see you again,' Wolfgang said. 'As a matter of fact I've been looking forward to this.'

'You've got a strange way of showing it!'

'I've already apologised, and you've had your own back.'

As the lift slowed for the fourth floor Angelica turned to him and smiled. 'All right, Wolfy.'

'*That's* better.'

She stepped out first and started down the corridor, hunting for her room number. When she found it she unlocked the door and half opened it before suddenly stopping. Wolfgang was right behind her.

'Thanks,' she said, one hand on the doorknob and the other reaching for her suitcase.

'I'll bring it in. Maybe I could send for some drinks . . . like old times.'

'I don't think we should do that.'

'Don't be ridiculous, Angelica! One drink won't hurt us.'

'I didn't mean that,' she said quietly, still blocking the doorway.

Wolfgang pushed past her. A yellow-walled corridor led past the bathroom. At the end of it was a square, brown-carpeted room. Its twin beds were covered by gold-patterned bedspreads.

'Look, I won't eat you without your permission . . .' He stopped as he reached the bedroom and stared at the wooden armchair beyond the second bed. Michael's jacket and trousers hung over it.

'So it is,' Wolfgang said quietly.

'Well what did you expect? We've been apart for four years. Did you think I'd be saving myself for you?'

Wolfgang laughed unpleasantly. 'I suppose *this* is just what I should have expected.'

'What the hell does that mean?'

He dropped the suitcase on the carpet and looked straight at her, his eyes cold and cruel now. 'You know your problem Angelica? Despite all my help you couldn't make it on talent alone. You had to screw your way into drives.'

She bunched her fists as though she was going to punch him. 'Well I certainly paid you back then!'

Wolfgang snorted and looked at the armchair again. 'And now there's someone else you're . . . paying back.'

'Get out!' Angelica spat at him. 'You're still a mean little sewer rat.' She pressed back against the wall of the corridor as Wolfgang stalked past her. 'And if you get in my way again tomorrow don't expect me to sit there and take it!'

Outside the door Wolfgang spun round and stabbed his finger at her. 'So you still think you're better than me. Maybe you need a little reminder.'

She slammed the door in his face.

Angelica woke up with a start. Someone had turned on the corridor light and was moving toward her. She sensed as much as heard him.

'Who's that?' she hissed.

'Just me,' Michael said, sitting down on the edge of the bed and bending to kiss her cheek. 'Sorry I woke you. It's nearly midnight.'

'Finished?'

'Everyone's in bed now except your electrician friend Dennis. He's cleaning up.'

Angelica yawned and rolled onto her back. In the half darkness Michael looked shadowy, handsome and utterly lovable. She lifted her hand and stroked his cheek. 'You can come to bed too, then.'

'Didn't you find someone nicer whilst I was away?'

Angelica tensed.

'What's the matter.'

'Nothing, nothing.'

'Tell me.'

'Well . . . your brother asked Wolfgang Schnering to show me the way to the hotel. When we got here we had a bit of an argument. He and I . . . we were once . . .'

'You don't need to tell me,' Michael said softly, brushing a strand of hair away from her cheek.

Angelica pushed herself up in the bed and the bedclothes dropped below her naked breasts. 'All right, but watch out for him tomorrow,' she said in a quiet, almost frightened voice. 'He's a jealous little boy with a vicious temper.'

But Michael wasn't listening. He bent forward and took one of her nipples in his mouth. As his tongue tasted her salt skin he stroked his hand down her body, pushing back the bedclothes.

And soon Angelica had forgotten Wolfgang as well.

A slight figure stepped out of the hotel into the chill night, turned up the collar of his brown-and-beige anorak, and zipped it right up. Wolfgang couldn't sleep. He walked into the car park, unlocked the door of his Porsche and climbed in. Starting the engine with the minimum possible noise, he drove off into the darkness.

Eight

TEN MINUTES to twelve on Sunday morning. Low clouds
floated above Silverstone circuit like great grey whales about
to spout. Below them two parallel lines of sports cars
stretched back from the start of the pit straight to Woodcote
corner, curving with the track. They were still silent, and
mechanics and officials swarmed around them. From the
packed grandstands walling in the track came an expectant
murmuring.

Five minutes to twelve. The trumpet-like loudspeakers
blared out a bugle charge, and seconds later thirty-four racing
engines snarled into life. As if in retaliation a few drops of
rain spattered down from the leaden clouds. Marshals
frantically cleared everyone off the grid.

Three minutes to twelve. The dark green Jaguar S-type at
the front of the grid moved off to start the pace lap, and the
field moved away jerkily to follow it. As they accelerated
along the pit straight the sportscars began to weave from side
to side to put heat into their cold tyres. In the front row were a
works Porsche and a works Lancia, their white bodywork
striped with the different colours of their sponsors. Behind
them, nearest the pit wall, was the second works Porsche,
with the maroon C4 outside it. Michael's helmet was just
visible through its sharply curved windscreen. Three rows
further back, the Glaser-Lomax darted about aggressively.

At the end of the lap, the Jaguar pace car appeared under
the *Daily Express* Bridge and headed for escape down the pit

lane. Behind it the first cars were accelerating hard but holding grid order. Suddenly three of them flashed into view side by side, the brown-and-beige one in the middle bursting through between the others. At the start line the green lights were on, irrevocably signalling the start of the race.

As the Glaser-Lomax blasted past them it was already attacking the third row. It tucked into the slipstream of a yellow Porsche on the right of the track. There seemed less than a car's width between that and the breeze block wall, but the Lomax dived into the gap and forced its way alongside. On the pitwall a line of faces rolled back like a breaking wave as the two cars hurtled past them seemingly bolted together. Then as they reached the braking area for Copse the nose of the Porsche dipped but the Lomax kept going.

On the left of the track Michael braked just before his normal point. He glanced in his right-side wing-mirror – nothing near enough to stop him taking the ideal line through the corner. Looking ahead again he steered towards the red-and-white kerbing marking the inside of the corner. Then in his peripheral vision he was aware of a dark shape looming up. Michael's head jerked right. What he saw was like the climax of a nightmare.

The Lomax was bouncing across the kerbing towards him, its driver trying to shorten the corner. Michael could see bulging grey eyes through the slit in the helmet, but there was no panic in them – just madness. Desperately Michael floored the accelerator to provoke a slide, feeling the still cool tyres lose grip and move him to the left. It wasn't enough. The Lomax reached the end of the kerbing and took off. It crashed down onto the track and slammed into the C4 just behind its cockpit. The impact straightened out the brown car but punched the maroon one into an uncontrollable spin.

Michael fed on opposite lock and hit his brakes as the world revolved around him. When it stopped he was facing back the way he had come, with the rest of the field racing out of Copse towards him. He stared through the windscreen at the on-rushing cars, expecting one of them to smash through it and obliterate him at any moment. Two rounded Copse side by side, locked up their tyres and skidded towards him wreathed in tyre smoke. Just when collision seemed inevitable they climbed off their brakes and passed either side of the C4. He had to sit there whilst every last car went past. Michael opened his mouth to shout, but his throat was paralysed by fear and frustration.

God Almighty! his mind was screaming. In the first corner!

Suddenly a hard cold anger rushed up through his body like a sword drawn from its scabbard. It reached his brain and his hands and feet started their reflexive coordinated movements again. As the last cars flashed past him he restarted the engine, snatched first gear, then spun the C4 back round again in a cloud of tyre smoke and chased after them.

All Michael's senses were at supernormal levels now, their memory stores opened. Would he feel the vibrations that meant damaged wheels or suspension, or hear and smell fibreglass grinding on rubber? But even as he sensed for these warnings he was accelerating the C4 to full speed. Michael braked hard for Becketts and rushed out of it into Hangar Straight. The car seemed to be all right. He was nearly with the backmarkers now, but the leading cars were already taking Club, two corners away. As he glanced at them one car seemed to enlarge and stand out.

Schnering! Michael thought, glimpsing the brown-and-beige car exiting Club on the other side of the circuit. Angelica's warning flashed through his mind, and his anger intensified.

His left hand reached for the boost control knob and twisted it to the right – with the small wing they had a little fuel in hand, and he intended to use it. Already Michael was tearing past the much slower Group B cars, racing versions of road-going sports cars. On the banking blue flags were being waved at them to signal his progress. A fat-faced marshal between Stowe and Club was waving his as though his life depended on it. Michael was driving faster than he had done in practice as though he had suddenly acquired some sort of super control. He was overtaking cars in the middle of corners without slowing down at all, blasting past them with total confidence and commitment.

Halfway down the pit straight he overtook the leading Group B car. Angelica and the rest of the Team were leaning over the pit wall guardrail to see if the C4 was damaged, but Michael didn't even look for a signal. He was concentrating totally on taking each corner as fast as possible, as though he was in a sprint race.

As he accelerated away from Becketts for the second time he glanced at the straight beyond Stowe corner. The Glaser-Lomax was only halfway down it.

I'm coming you bastard! he swore to himself.

Michael curved left onto Hangar Straight and checked his instruments. The turbo boost gauge read one-point-five, and the tachometer's red needle was reaching peak revs in each gear noticeably earlier. Ahead of him on the right of the track was a Group C backmarker. Michael was gaining on it fast, but he stayed in its tracks to take maximum benefit from its slipstream.

He felt a vibration behind him, something like the flapping of a trapped bird, but then it stopped. The Group C car ahead of him grew until it filled his windscreen, and Michael flicked the steering wheel left to overtake it.

In that instant the C4's rear wing tore away from its left sideplate. In a nanosecond the loose end smacked down on the rear bodywork, then bent back at a diagonal to the side-plate to which it was still attached. Like an aeroplane rudder it forced the tail round, so that the maroon car was pointing straight at the railway sleepers lining the outside of the track. At over 200 miles-an-hour it smashed head on into them, the nose impacted into the cockpit, and the car flipped over into a sickening series of sideways rolls that ripped off its bodywork and suspension.

Even before it bounced to a stop at Stowe in a cloud of dust and debris, grim-faced marshals were sprinting towards it from all directions.

Dennis Morrell felt sick, guilty and lost. Four hours ago he had jumped into the back of Conrad Church's car with another mechanic, whilst Angelica had climbed into the front passenger seat. Conrad had rushed out of the paddock and along the old airfield runways to Stowe, leading a convoy of the team's roadcars. Despite the thumping and banging as they raced over the crumbling concrete there was an eery background silence, a familiar noise missing. When Dennis looked at the track he realised why – the only vehicles moving on it now where red rescue tenders and white ambulances. The race had been stopped. That told him the accident was as bad as he'd thought, when he'd first heard the clipped announcement on the loudspeakers, as though the commentator was for once lost for words. But it still didn't prepare Dennis for what he saw when they reached Stowe.

They stumbled out of the car in shocked silence, and began to run across the track towards the wreckage. Rescue marshals worked frantically round it, and they had to get close to see past them. The bodywork was gone. All that was left was compacted aluminium, bent steel tubes, and the mangled engine still attached at the back.

Michael's lower body was completely buried in twisted metal. Dennis no longer wondered whether Michael was dead – just how the hell they would get his body out of there.

He looked at Angelica. She was pressing against the rescue marshals struggling to free Michael. Suddenly she turned away and walked to the sleepers. For the second time in a week Dennis saw a woman's face collapse with dumb animal hopelessness and misery as she slumped down against them.

Less than an hour later, the race had been restarted. Conrad had driven Angelica away. All that was left for the team to do was pack up and go home. They were in the middle of that now, and it was a haunted process. There was no car to winch up into the transporter, but everybody instinctively acted as though it was still there. They loaded spare wheels and tyres into the racks first, only to realise that nothing would stop them doing so later. Without this disciplined order the process became even more of a distressing slog.

Snatches of excited commentary drifted into the garage, broken by the roar and scream of cars racing past on the pit straight. The mechanics worked on in a horrible atmosphere of guilt and suspicion. Everybody knew that the C4 had been hit at the start of the race – on the right side. But several marshals at Stowe had told them that the rear wing had let go on the left. That was what had nearly happened in second practice, and they were meant to have made sure it didn't afterwards. Could one of them have made a fatal mistake? Who had fixed on the wing's endplates, and had they drilled and riveted them correctly? Who had carried in the box of rivets? Who had fastened the wing onto the sideplates, and had they used the right fasteners in the right order?

Steve Driscoll stood behind the transporter ticking of the loading list, his eyes hooded and his bearded face dark with silent accusation. As Dennis climbed down out of the transporter he spoke to him gruffly.

'All right. You can go now.'

Dennis didn't argue. He just wanted to get away from the place. Nodding curtly to the others, he walked round the side of the transporter, still in his maroon overalls. The paddock was almost deserted, everybody watching the race, and he started to trudge across it towards the adjacent car park. As he rounded the cafeteria dividing the two he felt a tap on his shoulder. Dennis turned round and Ralph Cambell was right behind him.

The chief mechanic's face looked even more feline than usual – something about the coldly appraising eyes and knowing smile on his lips. Quickly Cambell stretched out his hand and tucked something into the breast pocket of Dennis's overalls.

'Here's something to be going on with, till the heat dies down,' he said.

For a moment Dennis stared at him blankly. Then his eyes widened and he started to protest. 'But . . . but I didn't do anything!'

'Sure, sure. A bit more dramatic than expected, but keep your cool and you'll be all right.'

As soon as he'd finished speaking Cambell brushed past Dennis and walked on as though they'd bumped into each other by accident.

'Hang on!' Dennis called out, putting his hand into his breast pocket. His fingertips separated folded paper. Dennis looked down as he pulled it halfway out of the pocket. Old tenners! A thick bundle of them! His eyes flicked up to see if anyone was looking, but there was no one in the car park except Cambell. He was just turning round the other end of the cafeteria. If Dennis shouted now he would still hear him. He opened his mouth and glanced down at the wad at the same time.

A strangled cry died in his throat. As Ralph Cambell disappeared Dennis swallowed and pushed the banknotes down into his overalls again.

It was gone ten when he finally parked his Escort outside the Battersea tower block. With infinite weariness he trudged inside and pressed the lift button. If it didn't come this time he reckoned he'd never make it up the stairs. For once it showed up, and carried him creakily up to the eighth floor.

As he fumbled to put his key into the doorlock he was suddenly overcome by a wave of guilt and remorse. How could he go in and face Sharon? He stood there trying to steel himself up to it before deciding that he couldn't stand there all night. Taking a deep breath he opened the door and stepped inside.

Silence. The lounge light was off. He felt panicky as he went to the bedroom door and opened it. Grey light filtered through the thin curtains, and he could just make out Sharon's shape in the bed. Breathing a sigh of relief, he tiptoed in and started to undress.

Now he could see Sharon's face and curly blonde hair on the white pillow. Something about her tugged at his heart and made him want to burst into tears. She looked so doll-like asleep, so innocent. He felt like a big ape who smashed and hurt everything it touched. As he stared at her, Sharon suddenly blinked her big blue eyes open.

''Lo Dennis,' she said in a small, sleepy voice. 'How'dit go?'

Dennis moved to the bed and knelt down beside her. Slowly he reached out his pudgy hand and touched her soft hair as if for the first time.

'We . . . didn't finish,' he said, almost choking.

'Never mind. Come to bed.'

He bent forward and rested his face on the bedclothes as if in childhood prayer. A hand began to stroke the back of his head, and he had to fight back his tears.

'Oh Sharon,' he said, 'I've been rotten to you, so bloody rotten, but I'll make it up. You'll see.'

Nine

NORBERT DÜRR walked to the other end of his all-weather tennis court, trying hard to control his breathing and his mounting excitement. Having just turned fifty, the Glaser finance director could have chosen to age gracefully. He was a tall, elegant man with a patrician face and a distinguished head of silvery hair: but the tension around his eyes and mouth and his ultra-fashionable tennis clothes betrayed a man desperately reaching back to his youth.

At the other end of the court Curtis Stockwell was moving into position to receive his service. Dürr loved tennis. It had always been *his* game. When the new vice-president had mentioned that he played as well, it would have been natural to challenge him to a match. But the American's physique had worried him, and mutual friends had later confirmed that he was an exceptionally good player. Dürr had managed to avoid the issue until Stockwell himself had suggested a match that Sunday, and done it so pointedly that he could hardly refuse to invite him.

Now, despite all his misgivings, Dürr was on the point of beating him. What was more, his wife was there to see him do it. He had taken the first and fourth sets, Stockwell the second and third. Dürr was five-four up in the final game, and serving for the match.

At the other end of the Court, Stockwell was crouching and shifting weight from foot to foot.

Dürr's fist tightened round the grip of his black carbon-fibre racket, and he wound up to serve. He hit the ball hard into the net. His second attempt was gentler, and Stockwell hit it back with a searing forehand that easily beat the older man. Both players looked equally concerned.

Dürr's next serve didn't seem much better than its predecessor, but Stockwell dived towards it and sprawled on the ground as it beat him.

'Good serve Norbert!' Frau Dürr shouted from the sideline.

'Quiet dear!' he snapped, secretly pleased by her support. Better than the indifference that Stockwell's wife, sitting beside her, was so obviously showing.

With conscious effort he wound up for his third service. This time the American returned the ball, Dürr hit it back and stormed to the net. As the ball came back he was perfectly positioned to batter it past Stockwell. Thirty-fifteen.

Dürr served again. Stockwell returned the ball, but seemed to be tensed up – possibly sensing defeat, Dürr told himself as he rushed the net and put the ball away again. Forty-fifteen!

Hardly able to breathe he served for the match and double-faulted! Forty-thirty. One more chance. In nervous agony Dürr served again. Now Stockwell appeared to be fighting like a tiger, dashing from one side of the court to the other, but never quite hitting a winning return. The rally went on and on, Dürr's face changing colour like a ripening plum. He couldn't hold out much longer. The American had positioned himself perfectly for his powerful forehand, was smashing the ball with tremendous force, but too high, too high! As the ball flew over the backline Dürr threw up his racket in triumph, and Stockwell pounded the red asphalt with his.

The finance director went to the net to meet Stockwell and put a consoling arm round his shoulder. 'You play well Curtis. Next time you'll beat me.'

'Only if I crowd you out a bit more. Your placing's uncanny Norbert.'

'You must come to my club. We'd make a good doubles pair, no?'

The mutual congratulations continued until they reached the side of the court, where the matronly Frau Dürr added more praise. Only Caroline Stockwell appeared unmoved. She was several years younger than her husband, with shoulder-length chestnut hair and a well-drawn face except for a pinched, almost bitter mouth. Her eyes were dark and cynical.

'A good match, no?' Frau Dürr twittered, irritated that she hadn't joined the flattery.

'Curtis is so inconsistent,' Caroline said coolly, ignoring her husband's glare. 'He played *much* better last time I watched him.'

Frau Dürr laughed falsely and turned away to offer Curtis a drink. Such a charming man. Too bad his wife was such a . . . The word that came to mind shocked her deeply.

Somewhere behind them an outside bell began to ring with a telephone's rhythm.

'Excuse me one moment,' Norbert Dürr said, leaving the court and climbing the steps to his house.

The rather pretentious white stucco building was meant to look like a miniature chateau. It was sited on a terrace above the tennis court, and its first floor windows overlooked the Zürichsee less than half a kilometre below.

Five minutes later he came back, but now his face wore a shocked expression.

'Something wrong?' Frau Dürr asked.

'That was Alexander Fitch phoning from England. Our car has had a terrible accident at Silverstone. The driver was killed instantly.'

She clutched her ample bosom. '*Schrecklich!* Terrible!'

'Were any spectators killed?' Stockwell asked.

'Spectators! My God, I didn't ask. Is it possible?'

'Don't you remember what happened at Le Mans in 1955? Nearly a hundred of them died in an accident. That's why motor racing's banned in Switzerland, isn't it?'

'That's right,' Dürr murmured, his face ashen.

'I'm sure Alex would have told you if that had happened.'

89

'He didn't mention it, but can you imagine what it would do to the company if . . .'

Stockwell nodded grimly. 'I've dreaded something like this happening. Does Rico know yet?'

'Fitch told me he tried to phone him first. He was out, so he phoned us.' For a moment Dürr wondered how the Englishman had known that Stockwell was there with him. He dismissed the thought as trivial compared with the main issue. 'I think you should call Fitch again to check this – he's left me a number. Then we should phone all the directors and warn them what to say to the press.'

'Right,' Stockwell said, pushing himself out of his chair. 'Please excuse us, ladies.'

Despite the tragic circumstances Frau Dürr smiled warmly at the American – such a gentleman to remember his manners even at moments like this.

The fourteen-year-old boy walked up to the blue fibreglass starting block at one end of the Olympic-sized swimming pool. Willi Glaser was wearing only a pair of orange-and-yellow-striped trunks, and he looked smaller and younger than the seven other boys moving up to identical boxes. Dark blue tiles on the pool bottom marked the lanes ahead of them. They seemed to wriggle about like live eels in the aquamarine water.

Willi looked up at the stepped benches running along one side of the pool, and spotted his father. Rico punched out both fists, thumbs up in a gesture of encouragement.

'Take your marks!'

Willi climbed up onto starting block number three, shaking and rolling his arms about to loosen them up.

'Set!'

His tough little face was deadly serious now, lips stretched over small white teeth, narrowed eyes fixed on the far end of the pool. In fact, he looked remarkably like his father had done at the same age.

The explosion from the start gun shook the transparent

panels covering the pool. Before it had a chance to bounce back off them, roars of encouragement rose to block the echo. Rico was yelling his head off.

'Come on Willi! Go, go, go!'

Below him, his son had made an excellent start and was lying third. His arms and legs threshed the water in a powerful crawl, making up in energy what they still lacked in finesse. As Willi somersaulted round to start the second length a well-timed push away moved him up to second equal.

Now his Zürich schoolmates were running along the poolside shouting encouragement. Rico jumped to his feet, pounding his hands together and screaming advice.

'Keep the style, keep the rhythm!'

In the final strokes Willi kept his face down and took second place by a touch. Rico dance up and down, clapping his hands above his head. His son looked up from the end of the pool and waved a weary hand at him. Realising that he was the only onlooker still standing, Rico turned to sit down. He was surprised to see Kurt Fontana and Hanspeter Brack on the bench behind him. What on earth were Glaser's production and personnel directors doing there at five o'clock on Sunday afternoon?

'Hallo you two,' Rico said. 'Come to watch?'

Kurt Fontana shook his bull-like head, his expression telling Rico that something was terribly wrong. Fear crawled across his scalp like a poisonous centipede.

'What's happened?'

'Norbert and Stockwell phoned us about an hour ago. They said they'd tried to call you.'

'Tell me what's happened!'

Kurt Fontana took a deep breath. 'One of the cars using our engine crashed at Silverstone. The driver was killed instantly.'

Rico sank down onto the bench. 'Which one? Which driver?'

'The Englishman, Church.'

Rico sucked in breath and closed his eyes as if in terrible pain.

'Norbert was in a complete panic,' Hanspeter Brack said. He was about the same age as the others but had a softer, more refined look. 'He told us to say nothing if journalists called, and that we'd decide how to limit our exposure from it tomorrow.'

'*Limit our exposure?* That doesn't sound like Norbert.'

'Nor to us. He did the talking, but I felt Stockwell was pulling the strings. We think he's going to use this to go for you tomorrow, so after we spoke to each other we phoned Eva to find out where you were.'

Rico looked into the eyes of his old friends and nodded his appreciation. 'There's a cafeteria in here. Let's go and talk this through.'

On Monday morning Alex Fitch sat in the Glaser boardroom mournfully recounting the disaster. Usually the powder-blue carpet and unstained beechwood furniture made it bright and pleasant despite its artificial lighting. Today the atmosphere was hard and funereal, maybe because of the way Fitch and the six directors seated at the round table had dressed.

Two chairs to his right, Curtis Stockwell was sombre and silent. It was crucial that he didn't appear pushy today, and everything he was wearing was chosen to that effect. His suit was a pinstriped grey, well-tailored, but not cut to show-off his figure, superb for a thirty-six-year-old. A plain white shirt and dark blue tie went with it. His lean, chiselled face was furrowed with responsibility and concern. But underneath the facade entirely different emotions boiled in a cauldron of ambition.

Win, win, win!

All his life seemed to have been a build-up to this, his first attempt to unseat the man at the top and take over his job. That was the essence of his long and expensive management training. The issue wasn't important anymore: war had been declared, and all that mattered was the result. That was how he judged his peers, and that was how he judged himself, and an overblown little Swiss mechanic wasn't going to beat him!

92

His distance from Alex Fitch was deliberate – Stockwell didn't want it known that he'd picked him up at Kloten Airport and briefed him before the meeting. Too much eye contact could have given the game away. The same went for Norbert Dürr and Francis Jaggi two and three chairs to his right. That put Rico Glaser opposite him where he could study his every twitch, and Kurt Fontana and Hanspeter Brack on either side of him in positions of implied alliance. Perfect placing. They hadn't just taught him to sharpen pencils at business school. The trap was set. All that remained was for Rico to jump into it feet first.

Alex Fitch had finished speaking. There was a shaking of heads, hissing intakes of breath, and the creaking of chairs as the directors shifted about uneasily. Stockwell glanced at Rico.

Come on man, blow your cool.

To his intense disappointment Rico stayed silent and let Norbert Dürr be the first to speak.

'Well, gentlemen,' the finance director said, looking round the table in an elder-statesman manner. 'I think we all share a deep sense of shock at what has happened. What we have to do now is minimise the bad publicity this has caused, and make certain it doesn't happen again by terminating our motor racing programme.'

Stockwell's eyes were fixed on Rico's. Still no reaction! Did he understand the game as well?

'What bad publicity?' Hanspeter Brack asked quietly.

All eyes turned to the personnel director.

'Good God, Hanspeter!' Dürr blustered. 'Can't you imagine what sort of questions we're going to be asked?'

'I can *imagine* them, but as press inquiries are referred to me I'm in a position to tell you who's actually asking what. Unless of course someone has been doing my job without telling me.'

Dürr looked nonplussed. 'Of course not Hanspeter. It would be most useful to know this.'

'I've had two phone calls this morning, both from specialist

93

motor sport magazines: circulation, five- and twenty-thousand respectively. Both asked if we would be withdrawing our engine as a result of the accident.'

'We agreed yesterday you wouldn't say anything until we'd discussed this!' Dürr said.

Stockwell grimaced at his clumsiness in giving the game away. This wasn't going at all the way he'd planned it.

'Don't worry,' Brack continued. 'I parried the question by asking what they were going to write. Both journalists told me that depended on our decision: if we didn't withdraw the engine, they wouldn't have a story. I told them I'd phone back this afternoon.'

'No story!' snapped Francis Jaggi, the young design director. 'It could have been as bad a disaster as Le Mans in fifty-five!'

'How? There were no spectators at that point.'

'You're sure of this?'

'In my job I'm used to emotional reactions,' Brack said pointedly. 'I know how important the facts are, so *I* did my homework.'

Jaggi pushed his enormous spectacles back up his nose with a petulant gesture.

'I know this sounds cynical,' Kurt Fontana broke in, 'but one racing driver got killed, not even an internationally famous one. That might rate a mention in the general press, and it's even possible they'll get the make of the car right; but the engine? Who cares? Even in the specialist press it's just a detail.'

Norbert Dürr coughed unhappily. 'I think we should discuss this a little more deeply,' he said, looking to Stockwell for support.

But the American was staring at Rico Glaser. The president still hadn't said a word. He didn't need to. He had already secured three votes to match his, Dürr's and Jaggi's, and in the event of a tie Rico had the casting one.

'I don't see any point in prolonging the discussion,' Stockwell said bitterly. 'It's quite obvious unchangeable positions have been taken on the racing project yet again. But I want a formal vote on it.'

Three hands went up for, then three against.

'In that case,' Rico said, 'I exercise my casting vote in favour of continuing the programme.'

Stockwell turned on him with ill-concealed fury. 'And I will report to the owners exactly what happened at this meeting, and that it was your casting vote that decided the issue. If another accident occurs, it will be entirely your responsibility.'

The two men glared at each other. Everyone else in the room was quite still, the silence only broken by the muted humming of some electrical appliance.

'I think I can live with that,' Rico said finally.

We'll see, Stockwell thought; we'll see!

Ten

SHARON MORRELL smelt tea. Still half asleep she sniffed to make sure she wasn't dreaming. It was tea all right, hot, sweet and milky. Blinking her big blue eyes open she saw a steaming mug of it on the crate that served as her bedside table. Dennis was just straightening up after putting it there.

'Morning love,' he said, smiling down at her.

'What's this?'

Dennis bent close to the mug, doing an impersonation of a policeman. 'I would say it's a cup of tea madam.'

'Clown!' Sharon laughed, wriggling up into a sitting position in the bed. 'I meant why did I get it this morning?'

'I've got the day off.'

'On *Thursday*? It is Thursday today, isn't it?'

'Yeah, well, I'm not taking any more Fridays off for a bit, so I thought I'd take you shopping in Oxford Street.'

Sharon wouldn't have looked more astonished if he'd announced they were flying to the moon. Then she narrowed her eyes suspiciously. 'Shopping in the West End? You haven't done anything wrong have you, Den?'

'Nah, the team paid us a bonus, that's all, and I told you I was going to make it up to you didn't I?'

'But how did you get the day . . .'

'Look, no more questions!' Dennis said sharply. 'If you want to come and spend it with me, drink up and get your Khyber out of bed.'

For a moment longer Sharon looked doubtful. Then she

96

giggled gleefully and reached for the mug of tea.

An hour and a half later, Dennis parked his old Escort just north of Marble Arch. He glanced up and down the pavement as he walked to the meter, then stuffed it with metal blanks the size of ten pence coins. He took Sharon's hand and helped her out of the car. In her schoolgirl's navy-blue raincoat she looked too young to be a mother, but the bulge underneath it was unmistakable.

'Come on,' Dennis said, leading her towards Oxford Street.

Sharon stopped and stared into every shop window, her expression a mixture of wonder and longing.

'We can go in you know,' Dennis said after the tenth one. 'They won't bite us unless we borrow something.'

Sharon squeezed his hand and smiled at him shyly. 'I know Den, and I know what I want. It's just that we haven't got there yet.'

'Name it gal.'

'You won't be angry?'

'Angry? Why should I be angry?'

'Because it's not something for me, not directly anyway.'

Dennis looked puzzled. 'Who's it for then?'

'The baby, things for the baby. Oh Den, that's what I really want.'

As he stared at his wife, Dennis's face began to pucker up. 'I have been a selfish bastard, haven't I,' he said quietly. Then a smile spread over his features. 'Come on then, lead on gal.'

The Mothercare store wasn't far away, and Sharon's eyes lit up as they entered it. But now they were buyer's eyes, narrowed and appraising, She walked along every row, touching, feeling, trying to make up her mind. After half an hour she had circumnavigated the store.

'I can't decide between a pram and a carrycot,' Sharon said exasperatedly.

'You don't have to: buy both.'

Sharon stared at Dennis, delight and doubt fighting for possession of her face. 'Are you sure Den? I mean, it is all right, isn't it?'

'Look,' Dennis said, stabbing a finger at her, 'I won't tell you again – get what you want before I go back to Selfridges and buy that windsurfer we saw in the window. I can just see myself sailing out through the surf, taking off over a breaker . . .'

But Sharon had gone. She was hurrying towards the prams and walkers section with an ecstatic look on her face.

Jonty stood in the Oxfordshire churchyard staring down at Michael's coffin. The priest's resonant voice had paused, and he could hear birds warbling irreverently in the warm spring sunshine. There was an overpowering smell of damp earth. Suddenly a shovelful of it exploded over the box, making an obscene brown splodge on the ebony wood.

'Forasmuch as it hath pleased Almighty God of his great mercy to take unto himself the soul of our dear brother here departed, we therefore commit his body to the ground; earth to earth, ashes to ashes, dust to dust . . .'

More earth splattered over the coffin, and Jonty jerked his head up from the unbearable spectacle. On the other side of the grave stood members of Michael's team, dark-suited and grim-faced. A bearded man's eyes met Jonty's, filled with guilt, and looked away.

You should feel guilty! Jonty thought, his mouth quivering with grief and anger. One of you stupid bastards killed him!

He stared at the downturned faces, wondering which of them had scored the aluminium, forgotten to put on a lock washer, or made whatever tiny mistake had led to the wing coming loose. Did one of them *know* he'd committed the fatal error, or were several of them tortured by the thought that they might have contributed to it? Conrad had told him the car was in such a state that the investigators would be hard put to find an exact cause. It was just one of those motor racing accidents . . .

Michael's death just one of those things!

They had been the closest of the brothers, even though Michael was nearer Conrad in age. Ever since Jonty could remember, Michael had looked after him and stuck up for him. He had started him motor racing as soon as he was old enough to hold a driving licence, lending him his racing car, paying the expenses, and telling anyone who would listen that his little brother was going to be the greatest thing in sports cars since Siffert and Rodriguez. But their ghastly fate had been reserved for Michael – Jonty shuddered as he remembered how nearly it had been his.

'We give thee hearty thanks, for that it hath pleased thee to deliver this our brother out of the miseries of this sinful world . . .'

Suddenly Jonty felt Angelica sag against him. Turning towards her, he saw that her eyes were almost closed – the eyes that had been wide and staring when she had first seen him an hour earlier as though she had seen a ghost. Her cheeks had turned a ghastly grey-green colour. Quickly he grabbed her under the shoulder, and on her other side Conrad did the same. The priest glanced towards them, then looked back at his prayer book and speeded up the Collect. At last it was mercifully over.

'Let's get her out of here,' Conrad murmured tensely.

Between them they turned her round and led her away from the grave. The churchyard was packed with mourners. Locals of all ages, family, motor racing people. The faces of the racing drivers stood out, stiff with shock, as though they had just watched their own funeral. Everybody tried to get out of the way as the three of them approached, tried not to stare at Angelica, but in the end were too fascinated to resist doing so.

'She came in Michael's car, but she's in no state to drive,' Conrad said across her back to Jonty. 'I'll take her to my place and call a doctor.'

'Right. I'll get someone to ferry her car over.'

'You bring it,' Conrad said firmly. 'I want to talk to you.'

The house was halfway between Nettlebed and Reading, set on its own at the edge of rolling woodland. Built in the thirties, its red brick facade would have been dull without the ornate wooden eaves and lintels, almost Viking in style.

Jonty followed Conrad's car up its rutted drive. The place was so familiar yet so strange. He had lived there with his parents until he was seventeen. When they'd died Conrad had inherited the house. Jonty hadn't been back since Karen had brought him there from Reading Hospital almost a year ago.

Karen – Conrad's ex-wife. She was a coarse version of Julie Christie, a bonier face, but the same lush blonde hair and sensual lips. Everything about her said 'bitch', yet Conrad had taken her on as a nineteen-year-old secretary and married her two years later. What had she done to catch his brother, Jonty wondered? Probably much the same as she'd done to him. She had slept around from the start, and the marriage had been a sick joke.

The cars crunched to a halt on the circular gravelled area in front of the house. Jonty jumped out and hurried to Angelica's door. When he opened it she looked up at him with the same shocked widening of her eyes that he'd seen when they first met. He gave her his hand, and she tried to smile at him as she climbed wearily out of the car. Conrad held onto her other arm and together they guided her into the house.

'I'll take her upstairs and call the doctor,' Conrad said. 'Wait for me in the lounge.'

Jonty gave an involuntary start. Did his brother know where it had happened? But Conrad's expression didn't change as he led Angelica up the broad staircase to the first floor. Jonty turned towards the lounge.

As he stepped through its door he felt as though he was entering a familiar dream. At the end of the long room French windows overlooked a lawn and beyond that woodland. A white-and-grey marble fireplace dominated the right-hand wall, with a plush sofa and matching chairs grouped round it. Jonty stared at the sofa. He was compelled to move towards it, to stretch out his hand and run it along the

100

upholstery. The purple velvet tickled his fingertips. A year ago . . .

Karen had come to collect him from Reading Hospital one summer morning. He had been stuck there for two months after his crash at the Nürburgring, and she had taken to visiting him regularly – the concerned sister-in-law. Somehow she had convinced Conrad that he must convalesce at their house. Jonty remembered hobbling into the lounge using a stick to support himself, and sinking gratefully down onto the sofa. Conrad was at work.

'Make yourself comfortable,' Karen had said in a voice with a teasing edge in it. 'I'll fix us a drink.' She brought them over and sat down right beside him. 'Cheers,' she said, holding up her glass and placing her free hand on his thigh at the same time.

At first Jonty ignored the contact, but then Karen moved her fingertips in teasing little circles that went higher and higher. She turned to face him and smiled provocatively.

'Don't,' Jonty whispered, beads of sweat breaking out on his forehead.

But Karen had just laughed. Then she bent over him, doing unbelievable, skilful, torturing things with her tongue and lips. Jonty lay back overcome by pleasure and shame, all the pent up frustration of eight weeks in hospital bursting out of him like a flood breaching a dam.

The stupid thing was that Conrad need never have known. After that first uncontrollable release Jonty had arranged to go back to his Fulham flat as quickly as possible. A few months later Karen had found another lover and moved in with him. Conrad had finally started divorce proceedings.

Then, during a slanging match in front of their lawyers, he had called her a whore. Karen had retaliated by saying that his family had nothing to be proud of, and told him about the affair with Jonty to prove it. The marriage was over, but from then on he was the scapegoat Conrad blamed for its final breakdown and the impossibility of a reconciliation.

Jonty was startled out of his reverie by his brother's voice in the hallway. Listening to the one-sided conversation he realised that Conrad was calling the doctor. After a while the receiver went down and he walked into the lounge. Jonty was still standing by the sofa.

'How is she?' he asked.

'About how you'd expect. Doctor Ryder's coming over to take a look at her. Drink? I need one.'

Jonty nodded. 'Anything I can do?'

'No, but there is something I want to talk to you about,' Conrad said. He carried two half-full brandy glasses to his brother, gave him one, and then put his free arm round his shoulder and steered him towards the French windows. 'There's been bad blood between us for too long Jonty. Now that Michael's . . . we've got to forget it now if we're ever going to.'

They had stopped at the windows and Conrad was staring into the distance. Jonty looked at him in surprise. He couldn't ever remember hearing or seeing him like this – brotherly, sensitive, like Michael used to be.

'That whole business with Karen,' Conrad went on. 'I can imagine how it happened now . . . the way she behaved. It was over between us anyway, but I was in a hell of a state about it.'

'You had every right to be.'

'Anyway, it's over now, forgotten. We've got to work together, and I didn't want it hanging over us.'

'Work together?'

Conrad looked at his younger brother as though surprised by the question. 'You know the family trust owns the garages. Well, we're the sole beneficiaries now. You'll have to get more involved with them. And there's the team of course.'

Jonty's head jerked back. 'What about the team?'

'We've got to keep it going. That's what Michael would have wanted. We've got his share of the trust to do it with, and I think we should finish what he started. He can never win Le Mans now, but with your help his car and his name can.'

Jonty's mouth hung open in astonishment. 'You must be

joking!' he said finally. 'One of those careless bastards forgot to screw up the wing or something. I wouldn't lift a finger to help them.'

'There's absolutely no evidence of that. Be reasonable Jonty – these things happen in motor racing.'

'You're damn right they do! I was nearly killed in one of those fucking things. Now Michael's bought it instead. And you're seriously telling me we should keep the team going?'

'It's what Michael would have wanted. It's the only practical help we can give to Angelica.'

Jonty shook his head disbelievingly. 'You can't be serious!'

Any remaining trace of brotherly love disappeared from Conrad's face as he turned on his younger brother. 'So what do you intend to do with your share of the trust? Spend it on yourself?'

'I don't know. I hadn't even thought about it until you brought it up, but not on motor racing – that's for very bloody sure!'

'Christ Almighty!' Conrad exploded. 'I've been grovelling about trying to make it up with you, thinking you might have changed a bit, but all I find is the same spoilt selfish brat you've been since the day you were born – me, me, me! What can *I* get out of it – fuck everyone else!'

'How you can think I'm being unreasonable . . .' Jonty had started to say when the doorbell rang.

'That'll be the doctor,' Conrad said, storming out of the lounge and slamming the door behind him.

For some time Jonty just stared at it. Then he shook his head and let out a great sigh of despair.

Eleven

ANGELICA WAS drowning in thick black mud. It had entered her lungs so that she could hardly breathe, and her head was hammering with blinding red pain. She fought to get to the surface. Why didn't Michael help her? Forcing her hands through the resisting sludge she tried to find him but couldn't. A terrible despair overwhelmed her – Michael had gone; what was the use of struggling? She might as well give up and let herself sink down after him.

But as Angelica relaxed she started to float upwards. The mud was changing from black to ever-lightening shades of grey. For a moment she glimpsed a concerned face looking down at her, so like Michael's but younger. Then it vanished into the solid greyness above her.

'Michael? Michael?' she called out, jerking up into a sitting position.

Blinking her eyes, Angelica looked around her. She was in a large bedroom, shadowy in the dim light filtering through two sets of curtains. Its walls were covered in vertically-striped wallpaper whose colours she couldn't quite make out. In places it was beginning to peel away. The furniture was old-fashioned and dark, and her clothes hung over the back of a chair in one corner. Running a hand down her sweat-soaked body Angelica found she was still wearing her bra and panties. How had she got there? She was quite certain she'd never seen the room before. And her head! Angelica put her hands up to stop it bursting.

Slowly blurred memories came back to her – Conrad helping her up some stairs – a doctor examining her and making her swallow some tablets. Where was the bottle? Maybe they would do her some good. She looked at the bedside table, but it only had a lamp and her watch on it. Angelica picked it up – 11.45. Day or night? Pushing back the bedclothes she walked to the first set of curtains and parted them. Bright sunshine shone on a vista of tall silvery trees, and beyond them rolling green hills.

And then Angelica remembered everything. She staggered back to the bed and sat down on it, weeping bitterly.

After a while she lifted her head. With the back of her hand she wiped tears and matted strands of hair away from her face. On it now was a hard, defiant expression. Looking round again Angelica saw that a doorway led to a white-tiled bathroom. She stood up and went into it.

Half an hour later she walked down the stairs in the same clothes she had worn at the funeral. Conrad came out of the lounge to meet her.

'I'm sorry to be such trouble.'

'Don't be silly,' Conrad said, taking her gently by the arm and leading her towards the lounge. 'Can I get you anything?'

'Have you some coffee? And something for my head maybe?'

'Coffee yes, but I don't want to give you any medicine until the doctor's seen you. He'll be here any time now.'

Conrad sat Angelica down on the sofa, and then left to make the coffee. She looked around. Such a *British* room – tall, leaded windows overlooking a lawn, hunting prints on the walls, and in one corner a small round table with decanters and glasses on a silver tray. Angelica stood up and tiptoed guiltily to the table. She lifted the tops off the decanters and sniffed until she recognised cognac. Quickly she poured a little into a tumbler and swallowed it in one gulp. Hot fire burned down her throat and into her bloodstream. That felt better – much better! She half-filled the tumbler and emptied it again in two swallows. As she hurried back to the sofa the ground seemed to sway under her as though there was an earthquake.

Conrad came back carrying a tray, and wrinkled his nose suspiciously as he sat down beside her.

'I must have stopped you going to work,' Angelica said as he handed her a cup of black coffee. 'I'll leave as soon as the doctor's been.'

'There's absolutely no hurry, but wouldn't you like me to drive you home? One of my men could bring your car over later.'

Angelica shook her head. 'No thank you. I want to go straight to the workshop. I haven't been there since . . . since the accident, and I want everyone to know we're going on as soon as possible. Le Mans is only five weeks away.'

Conrad stared at her in surprise, and Angelica looked down at her lap.

'I hope you don't think that's hard of me, I mean, not showing enough respect for your brother. I loved him you know. I loved him very much. He was the first man who meant more to me than . . .'

'Please don't think that,' Conrad butted in. 'I'm glad you feel that way because I do too. I *know* Michael would have wanted us to go there. Winning Le Mans was his life's ambition.'

'Then you'll help me?'

'Of course I will, but we've got a problem with my youngest brother.'

'Jonty? Michael hoped he would drive with us at Le Mans. Surely he will help now?'

Conrad sighed and put down his coffee cup. 'You know about his accident?'

'Yes. Michael told me about it.'

'Well, it's not just that he doesn't want to race any more. I'd better explain the whole thing. You see, Michael discussed his will with me after our mother died. I'd inherited this place, so we both thought it fair he left his house and personal estate to Jonty. Seemed a pretty theoretical exercise at the time.' Conrad paused and shook his head sadly.

106

'Go on.'

'The problem is the family trust. It owns all sorts of assets, including my garages, from which it paid the three of us an income. We all put our shares into the team, until Jonty had his accident, packed up racing and kept his for himself.'

'But I thought your garages sponsored us.'

'They do to some extent. They've bought most of the hardware, and we've put the sponsorship through their books as advertising and publicity. But the recession's hit them hard. It'll take at least a hundred thousand pounds to get you to Le Mans now, and there's no way the garages can afford that at the moment.'

'So it has to come from your family trust?'

'Unless we can find massive outside sponsorship at once, yes. And Jonty and I are the sole beneficiaries now. We're going to need his share of the income *and* some of the trust's capital. Even to request that from the trustees I'm going to need his full cooperation.'

'But we must talk to him. He *must* help us now.'

Conrad gave a disgusted snort. 'I've talked to him already and he doesn't want to know. He's either scared, greedy or both.'

Quite suddenly Angelica realised whose face she had seen in her dream – so like Michael's but several years younger. 'Let me talk to him,' she said quietly. 'Maybe its just a problem between you two.'

Conrad's head whipped round and his eyes bored into Angelica's. 'What d'you mean by that?' he asked sharply.

'Just what I said.'

For some time he continued to stare at her suspiciously. Finally he relaxed. 'Well, I suppose it's worth a try.'

Jonty drove his Lotus Esprit west along the M4 motorway. It was already dark, but a full moon and a clear sky made his headlights almost unnecessary. Two years ago he would have been doing a ton and hunting for speed traps. Now the speedometer read just over seventy, and he had other things to think about.

Why did Angelica want to see him? She had phoned him at his Fulham flat on Friday afternoon, the day after the funeral, and asked if she could visit him as soon as possible. As Lindsey had just moved in with him, Jonty wasn't too keen on inviting her there. So he had arranged to meet Angelica at Michael's house on Saturday evening.

Lindsey hadn't liked that. He had explained who he was going to see, but there was a flash of jealousy in her eyes as she'd told him *she* certainly wasn't sitting at home on her own on a Saturday night. Jonty wondered what she was up to now. Lindsey was too gorgeous for her own good. He might be in love with her, but he certainly wasn't sure of her.

After the motorway spur into Reading, Jonty had difficulty remembering which side street led to Michael's house. Since his accident at the Nurbürgring they'd met up much less frequently – how bitterly he regretted that now that it was too late to do anything about it. Eventually he found the road of terraced houses and parked outside Michael's house – *his* house now. What the hell was he going to do with it? He wasn't too happy about going into it, let alone living there. Jonty climbed out of the Lotus, pushed open the gate in the low brick wall fronting the road and walked towards the front door. In the moonlight he could see that the garden was as unkempt as he remembered it. A light was on in the hallway. He rang the bell and waited.

Angelica opened the door, and he stared at her in surprise. When he had first seen her at the funeral she'd looked grey and exhausted. Now her long face was carefully made up and had a sort of tragic beauty. Shining brown hair tumbled down over a silk wrap-around dress with long loose sleeves. For the first time Jonty could understand what Michael had seen in her.

' 'Lo Jonty,' Angelica said in a slurred voice. 'Thank you for coming.'

As soon as she opened her mouth he knew she was drunk. It wasn't just the way she had spoken – he could smell the brandy. 'That's all right,' Jonty said, stepping past her into the hallway and wondering what he had let himself in for. To his right was a framed photograph of his father in his Lister-Jaguar, and he stopped to look at it.

'It's yours now,' Angelica said, closing the front door. 'All of this is yours now. I'll move out as soon as . . .'

'Don't be silly. You can stay here as long as you need to.'

Angelica gave a drunken nod and walked past him towards the living room. She had to put out a hand to steady herself as she went through the doorway. 'Drink?' she asked.

'Errr, yes please – brandy and ginger, something like that.'

The living room stretched the full depth of the house. At the end nearest the road a tube-steel sofa and armchairs surrounded a television set. A round wooden dining table surrounded by chairs dominated the other end. Bottles of brandy, whisky and gin stood on top of it beside several packs of mixers. Jonty sat down in one of the armchairs whilst Angelica went to the table, bent to read the labels on the small bottles, and then tore at their shrink wrapping. It burst open, and the contents rolled across the table and thumped down onto the beige carpet. Angelica knelt down to retrieve them, knocking chairs noisily against the table. Finally she managed to pour two drinks, and carried them unsteadily over to Jonty. She handed him a tall glass with a fizzing amber mix in it.

'Well . . .' she said, sitting down on the sofa and lifting her glass towards him.

Jonty nodded back and tasted his drink. It was lukewarm and incredibly strong. He began to realise how hot the room was – the central heating must be on full blast. Both of them were giving each other embarrassed little glances as though not quite knowing what to say.

'Will you be going back to Germany?' Jonty asked to make conversation.

Angelica laughed explosively. 'As I'm Austrian, it's unlikely!'

Jonty coloured, and then suddenly he was laughing uproariously too, more from release of tension than because it was really funny.

'I'm sorry Angelica. I suppose that's a terrible insult.'

'Not really. You see, my father's Austrian but my mother's German.'

Jonty took another mouthful of his drink. It didn't taste so bad this time. 'I'll try again – are you planning to go back to Austria?'

Angelica looked straight at him. 'That depends on you.'

'On *me?*'

'Don't answer me straight away, just listen for a while. You see, I know you and Michael were close.'

'Very close,' Jonty said quietly. He looked down into his glass and then drained half of it in one swallow.

'He told me a lot about you – how he took you to a test session at Brands Hatch the day after you passed your driving test, how he let you drive his two-litre Lola sports racing car . . .' Angelica's voice drifted away and her eyes went out of focus as though she was picturing the scene. 'He told me he knew within a few laps that you had ten times his talent.'

'Ohhh . . .' Jonty went, shaking his head deprecatingly.

'Don't play the modest Englishman. Don't insult your brother's judgement. He talked a lot about your racing – your good points and what you still had to learn. I already knew something about you because, you know, you made quite an impression when you first came to Europe, the fast new boy . . .'

'Too fast!'

'It happens to all the top drivers,' Angelica said, her voice no longer slurred but sure and persuasive. 'You have to find your limit. You just can't accept to drive below it, not to find out where it is, and it's much higher than for most drivers. The only way to find it is to step over it, but most of you survive and learn from it, become better racers in the process. That's why I'm so confident you can drive with me at Le Mans. You will be a bit slower than before maybe, but wiser and safer.'

As she spoke Jonty's expression had changed from humility to anger. When he lifted the glass to his mouth again his hand was trembling. 'I wondered why you wanted to see me Angelica,' he said in a shaky voice. 'I didn't know exactly what you were to my brother, but I wondered whether you could possibly want to keep the team going, whether you'd ask me for money.' Jonty downed the rest of the drink in one savage gulp. 'I learnt all right – I learnt what a mad business motor racing can be, how it can take all your time, energy, money, and if you're unlucky . . . like my brother was . . .'

He lowered his head. Surely he wasn't going to cry. He hadn't been able to shed a tear since Conrad had phoned from Silverstone to tell him the shattering news, hadn't cried at the funeral or since then. An icy sense of fate, of inevitability had frozen his emotions and kept him from it, but now that seemed to be melting away.

'You're right – I was close to Michael,' he went on painfully. 'I loved him. And you know what? I wish to God he'd learnt the lesson too. I wish . . .'

Suddenly Jonty couldn't go on. His shoulders shook convulsively and he put his hands up to hide his eyes. Angelica slid off the sofa and knelt beside his chair. Gently she took his head and rested it on her shoulder.

'It's all right, I understand,' she whispered, stroking his hair and feeling his tears dampening her dress. 'We'll help each other. We need each other.'

Slowly she lifted his face so that she could look into his sparkling brown eyes. She wanted to cry out. It was like seeing Michael as a boy. His tear-stained innocence tore at her heart and made her start crying as well. She wanted him so badly, wanted to help him, to hold him again. Her lips parted to say something, but her throat was paralysed by emotion.

Jonty's mouth worked silently too. He felt giddy with strange feelings, and his eyes shone now with something more than tears. Slowly their heads moved closer. Their lips met and he tasted the saltiness of their mingled tears. The tip of Angelica's tongue touched his and he returned the pressure. He lifted his hands to hold her and felt the girlish outline of her breasts.

Again Angelica was floating upwards, released from the blackness of death into the light and love she had known with Michael. She felt with him again, held, loved, protected. Hands caressed her through her dress. Putting her own down to its opening she pulled it wider and let it fall over her shoulders. For a moment she felt cool air on her breasts, and then the warmth of hands cupping them.

Jonty stroked her nipples with his palms, feeling them pulse and grow. He was lost in the sweet comfort of it, the rightness of it. And then from nowhere a poisoned image flashed into his mind – another lounge, another woman's forbidden kiss. He whipped his hands up to Angelica's shoulders and pushed her away from him.

'What the hell are we doing?' he shouted. 'You were Michael's girl for Christ's sake!'

Jonty leapt up as though he'd been bitten, and stared down at her as though she was the serpent. She knelt on the floor looking up at him with imploring eyes. Tears began to cloud them.

'Please,' she murmured, reaching out to him.

'Jesus Christ!' Jonty said disgustedly, spinning away and making for the hallway.

She stayed on her knees until she heard the front door slam, and his car starting up and fading away into the night.

Then Angelica rolled onto her side, drew her knees up into a foetal position, and began to cry silently.

Twelve

SHARON MORRELL was vacuuming the living room carpet, trying to keep the sweeps in time to the pop record blaring out of the radio. She was humming the tune as well, but the curiously hypnotic dirge wasn't really the sing-along variety. The grin on Sharon's face showed that she was enjoying it anyway.

She paused to move the brand new carrycot that she and Dennis had bought exactly a week ago. It had a pram-like frame, and Sharon wheeled it carefully into the area of carpet she'd already hoovered as though the slightest brush against the furniture would damage its shiny chromework. Bending down, she stroked the tartan fabric that her baby would be lying on in three months' time. A strong smell of soap powder wafted off a clothes rack loaded with sheets and towels. Sharon had to move that as well, and perspiration formed on her forehead as she struggled to balance it in front of her bulging stomach. She didn't care – the cleanup was long overdue, and she'd felt like getting on with it ever since the shopping spree with Dennis.

When she had finished the carpet Sharon decided to take a coffee break, and danced into the kitchenette. Her nose wrinkled in disgust as she opened the cupboards – the insides looked as though half their contents had been smeared over them. How had she put up with it before? If her Mum had seen them . . .

Sharon made a mug of coffee and walked back to the

dilapidated three piece suite in the living room. She had already put the mug down on the coffee table when she decided to find out just how much dirt had accumulated under the upholstery. Bending over Dennis's favourite armchair, she lifted up its seat cushion. There was a tidemark of sweet papers and crumbs around the edges of the black support fabric, and a folded copy of *Motoring News* in the middle of it. What was that doing there Sharon wondered? It came every Thursday, but Dennis usually tossed it on top of earlier editions on the coffee table when he'd finished with it. She sat down on the sofa still holding onto it.

As she sipped her coffee Sharon glanced at the front page, paying as much attention to the David Bowie-soundalike groaning away in the background. Some poor driver had been killed at Silverstone. Suddenly her foot stopped tapping. She looked at the paper's date – last Thursday's edition, so the race was the weekend before that. That was the one Dennis had been at. Strange him not mentioning anything about the accident.

Then Sharon re-read the driver's name. Suddenly she felt terribly sick, and her faced turned a ghastly shade of grey.

'It's that Austrian woman isn't it,' Lindsey called accusingly from the bathroom.

'What?' Jonty mumbled.

He had turned the spare bedroom into an office, and now he was doggedly one-finger typing at the desk against one wall. On either side of him were ceiling-high piles of pastel-coloured sportswear in polythene bags. Jonty had first seen the range during a motor racing trip to Italy, and bought some for himself. After his decision to give up motor racing he was absolutely determined to start his own business. Conrad was right – he had been the family's spoilt baby so now he was going to show him that he could make it entirely on his own. Several flights back to Italy and a lot of fast talking had secured him an exclusive agency on the range. Jonty's company, 'Sportswear International', was still at the acorn stage, but it gave him a huge kick to see 'his' clothes in Lillywhites and Harrods already. He had sketched ideas for a collection of his own, which he was going to subcontract out to British manufacturers the following season. But the biggest problem at the moment was quality control.

Lindsey appeared in the doorway in a pink towelling dressing gown. Her face was smeared with cream, and her short corn-coloured hair hung around it in wet tangles. 'I said it's the Austrian girl, and we're going to be late for the party unless you start changing.'

The typewriter's painfully slow clacking stopped. There was a staccato zip as Jonty ripped out the paper, balled it up and flung it into the wastepaper basket to join his three previous efforts.

'Will you *shut up* until I've finished this!'

'See what I mean? You've been grouchy ever since you went to see her last Saturday.'

'For Christ's sake, Lindsey! I'm trying to write a letter to my main supplier telling him the colours run on his tracksuits if they so much as see a washing machine – that's what's making me grouchy.'

Lindsey pouted as she massaged the cream into her cheeks. 'Don't see why you want to be a clothes salesman anyway. You don't need the money.'

'That's not the point. I want my own business, and I've got to start somewhere.'

'I tell everyone you're still a racing driver. It sounds much more interesting.'

'Well I'm not, and I wish you wouldn't,' Jonty said, but Lindsey had disappeared.

Of course it had nothing to do with Angelica, Jonty thought, winding a fresh set of papers into his portable. It was just this bloody problem with the tracksuits, which meant retrieving the whole consignment and shipping it back to Italy. God knows how you squared that with customs at either end. All part of the joy of starting your own business, like having a girlfriend who looked down on what you were doing.

Suddenly he pictured Angelica quite clearly – that long, sad face with its hauntingly beautiful green eyes. Why did thinking about her arouse such a confusion of feelings in him? He couldn't help wondering what Angelica would think about his business. Probably she would understand what he was trying to do better than Lindsey did, but then Lindsey was eighteen years old and Angelica had to be nearer thirty. Not even his type. Much too old for him for a start. Determinedly Jonty forced her out of his mind. There was no way he was going to get involved.

He stared down at the blank sheet in front of him, trying to phrase a decisive letter. Maybe he should just send the whole lot back and tell them exactly what they could do with them. He heard rather than saw Lindsey coming back into the room as he made another start. Then he felt her hands beginning to massage his shoulders.

'Anyway,' Lindsey said softly, 'what's she got that I haven't got.'

'For God's sake . . .' Jonty started, spinning round on the chair. He stopped with his mouth wide open.

She was stark naked, not even a trace of makeup on her cute young face. A coppery tan covered the whole of her exquisite figure except for a provocative white triangle where her bikini bottom had been. It seemed to point at her bush of tiny blonde curls.

'Nothing,' Jonty whispered, pulling her down onto his lap. 'She's got nothing you haven't got.'

Sharon heard the front door opening just after six-thirty.

'Hallo love,' Dennis called out as he walked down the corridor towards the living room. 'I thought we might . . .' His voice trailed off as he saw his wife's face.

The Shirley Temple look had vanished. In its place were ice-cold eyes and a no-nonsense jawline. She was facing him with her arms crossed and the copy of *Motoring News* dangling menacingly from one hand like a rolling pin. Dennis glanced at it and reddened.

'What's up love?' he asked, trying to sound puzzled.

'This,' Sharon said, unfolding her arms and holding up the newspaper.

Dennis scanned the headline. 'Yeah? What about it?'

'You didn't tell me about it, that's what.'

'Oh come on, Shar!' Dennis said, casting his eyes up to the ceiling. 'We're not back to that, are we? I don't have to tell you everything, do I?'

'Don't bullshit me, Dennis Morrell! You don't have to tell me everything, but when you do tell me something I want the truth.'

Dennis stared at her, open-mouthed and wide-eyed. 'I . . . I thought you'd be upset. That's why I didn't say anything.'

'But you *did* say something Dennis. You told me the team had paid you all a bonus. A bonus! When your boss has been killed and the car's wrecked? What in God's name have you been up to this time?'

Dennis walked past her, slumped down in his chair and buried his head in his hands. 'Oh God, Shar!'

'Never mind him – *I'm* here and waiting to know how you got that money. Out with it, or I'll fetch my dad.'

'All right, all right,' Dennis moaned, rocking backwards and forwards with his head in his hands. 'I was going to tell you Shar, honest I was, but I didn't know how to . . . didn't know if you'd believe me.'

Sharon sat down on the arm of his chair, and put her hand on his shoulder. 'Just tell me the truth, and I'll believe you,' she said quietly.

For some time Dennis just gulped in air as though he'd been winded. Then he started to talk. 'It all started at Snetterton a month ago. Ralph Cambell came up to me . . .'

'Who's Ralph Cambell?'

'Chief mechanic of the Lomax team. They've been lent the same engine as us this season, so we're big rivals. Anyway, Cambell introduces himself at Snetterton, and says they might have a permanent job for me. I didn't think too much about it, but then he comes up to me again at Silverstone after

117

practice and says the job's as good as mine – two-hundred-and-fifty quid a week minimum!'

'But?'

'*But* all right Shar! There's a little job I can do for them right off, like nobbling our car to make sure they beat us.'

'Dennis! You didn't . . .'

'Of course not!' he said, looking at her imploringly. 'You can't believe I'd do that can you?'

'No. But where *did* the money come from?'

Dennis took a deep swallow. 'After the . . . accident . . . Cambell bumped into me in the paddock, accidentally on purpose sort of thing, and stuffed a bundle of tenners in my pocket.'

'Because he thought you'd fixed the car?'

'Must have done.'

'But why didn't you tell him you hadn't?'

'I tried to love, honestly I tried to, but he was walking away and . . . you know . . . the baby . . .'

'Oh *Dennis!*' Sharon moaned despairingly, closing her eyes.

'I'm sorry love, God I'm sorry. I'd been such a rotten sod to you, and I thought I could make it up . . .'

Sharon sat quite still, letting him ramble through the story for some time. Then suddenly she opened her eyes and looked straight into his. 'You've got to tell the police about this Dennis.'

'You must be out of your mind Sharon! With my form? I'd be inside so fast . . .'

'You've got to tell *somebody* Dennis. Suppose Cambell *did* get someone to do it. You might not be the only one he put up to it. Or suppose he tries it again?'

Dennis shook his head vehemently. 'There's no way I'm talking to the filth, no way at all!'

'Then talk to the garage owner, what's his name. The brother who sponsored the team.'

'Conrad Church! If he and that pet dog of his hadn't tried to push me out I'd never even've talked to Cambell.'

'What about the youngest brother,' Sharon persisted, 'the one who was driving last year? You always said you liked him. He was more our age.'

Dennis's face was a mask of anguish. 'I don't know, I don't know.'

'I do!' Sharon said sharply. 'You talk to him, or I'll do it for you!'

Thirteen

THE VAUXHALL estate car turned off the Great West Road at Hammersmith Flyover and pulled into the kerb in the Broadway. Angelica wound down the passenger window and tried to attract the attention of a pedestrian above the background roar of traffic. He marched past, resolutely refusing to look in her direction. So did a lady walking a white poodle. Finally a middle-aged man bent to look into the car, leered when he saw her, and came up to the window.

'Looking for something, deary?' he asked knowingly.

'Kensington High Street.'

'Straight ahead. Like me to climb in and show you the way would you?'

'No thank you,' Angelica said stonily, finding first gear and accelerating away. She felt cheap already, and the man's assumption that she was a cruising whore made her feel even cheaper. Wolfgang's taunt started up in her head again like an irritating record she couldn't forget.

'You have to screw your way into drives . . . screw your way into drives . . . screw your way into drives . . .'

She shook her head as if that would knock the needle out of the groove, and mentally went through the reasons why she had to carry on – she owed it to the team – the mechanics' jobs were in her hands now – she owed it to Michael.

Why lie? she thought suddenly. The real reason I'm doing it is for myself.

What was the alternative? Stop racing, go back to Austria

120

and do exactly what? And above all, more important than everything else, only racing relieved the pain. Without it she knew she would go mad.

As soon as she had talked down her guilt another anxiety rushed into her disturbed mind to take its place: a fortnight had gone by since the accident, and Le Mans was only three weeks away. This Saturday night she *had* to get what she needed.

Angelica spotted the turnoff just before an American burger bar in Kensington High Street – he had given her directions when she'd phoned him. She turned left off the main road and then first right into a street of Georgian terraced houses. Cream-painted porches protected their imposing front doors. Slowing to read the numbers painted on their columns, she found the one she wanted and parked a few cars beyond it. Angelica switched on the interior light and took off her anorak, the only coat she had with her in England. Underneath it she was wearing a silky pink wraparound dress with a plunging neckline. She adjusted the rear view mirror and checked herself in it, sweeping her shining hair back over her shoulders and rubbing away a smudge of glossy pink lipstick. Shivering as she climbed out of the car into the chill night air, Angelica walked back to the house and climbed the steps to the front door.

To the right of it were a series of bell pushes, with a flat number and owner's name beside each one. Alex Fitch's was number three. She pushed it and waited.

'Hallo-oh,' a distorted voice sang from the miniature loudspeaker under the buttons.

'Angelica Hofer here, Alex.'

'Angelica! Open the door and come on up.'

There was a loud buzzing, and when she pushed the door it swung open. Ahead of her was a wide flight of burgundy carpeted stairs. Angelica climbed them, running her hand along the elegant mahogany handrail. The stairs doubled back on themselves, and as Angelica turned round on them she saw Alex Fitch on the landing above her. His greedy eyes widened and ran over her body, giving her the sensation that he was mentally undressing her. She thought again how decadent he looked, tall but overweight, with a bloated, supercilious face. But Angelica put on a sweet smile and kissed him lightly on both cheeks as she reached him.

'What a pleasure to see you. Come in, come in,' Fitch said in his fruity voice. He pushed back the door of his flat and gestured towards a room on the left that overlooked the street. Angelica walked in ahead of him. The room was huge, a high white ceiling increasing the feeling of spaciousness. Leather covered chesterfields and antique furniture added a rich glow and an expensive smell of leather and polish.

'What a beautiful place,' Angelica said.

'Been in the family for years. Drink?'

'A small brandy please.'

Fitch opened a mahogany corner cupboard and clinked bottles and glasses. 'Didn't have a chance to talk to you at the funeral,' he said, bringing the drinks over to Angelica's arm-chair. 'So sorry about . . .'

'That's all right.'

Fitch nodded manfully, and sat down on the sofa. 'Anyway, you look much better. Terrific in fact. What have you been up to?'

'Getting the team ready for Le Mans,' she said matter-of-factly.

He looked at her in surprise. 'You mean you're going?'

'If we possibly can.'

'But I thought . . . I thought you and . . .'

'It happens to a lot of teams,' Angelica said quickly. 'They don't just give up, and neither have we.'

'But who's sponsoring you?'

'Conrad Church has given me his full support, and now I need yours.'

'Oh,' Fitch sighed. A look of disappointment crossed his face. 'So that's why you wanted to see me.'

'Only partly Alex,' she said softly.

Fitch frowned and studied her with his piggy eyes. There

was something unpleasantly calculating about them, but Angelica smiled back sweetly. He sighed again and shook his head.

'That's going to be difficult, very difficult. The Glaser board agreed to give official support for Le Mans to whoever did better at Silverstone. Under the circumstances, most unfortunate as they are, it's gone to the Lomax Team.'

'But we outqualified them at Silverstone. Ours is the faster car. The very least you should do is lend us engines for Le Mans . . . unless of course you don't have the authority to decide that.'

Fitch's eyes narrowed in response to the challenge. Suddenly his mouth twitched with amusement, as though he was laughing at some private joke. 'That depends,' he said.

'On what?'

'On many things. Why don't I take you to dinner and we'll discuss them.'

Angelica forced a smile. 'I'd really like that, Alex.'

Fourteen

THE NIGHTMARE was starting again. Jonty tried to tell himself he was dreaming, but then came the sickening certainty that he wasn't.

He and Michael were walking across a large dam made of rocks and boulders. To one side of it was a reservoir of pent up water surrounded by forest. On the other side, below them and beyond some meadows, was a village of Swiss chalets. As they looked down the dam one of the rocks suddenly moved. Water began to trickle round its edges. The brothers looked at each other, knowing that unless it was pushed back immediately the dam would burst.

'I'm so tired,' Jonty whined.

'I'll go then,' Michael said kindly, and started to climb down the rock face.

By the time he reached the loose boulder, water was spurting out of the cracks around it. Michael leant against it, straining to force it back into place, but the flow of water was growing. It sprayed all over him until Jonty could hardly see him anymore. And then the rock came right out of the dam flinging Michael out into space with it.

'Angelica's in the village! Angelica's in the village!' Michael screamed as the dam exploded.

Now Jonty was running with giant's steps, sometimes on the ground, sometimes through the air, making for the chalets. He looked over his shoulder and saw Michael, his face covered in blood, being carried along by a tidal wave of water. Desperately Jonty leapt out of its path. Then he was on top of the valley, watching the wave sweep past and hearing his brother's screams.

'Angelica's in the village! Angelica's in the village!'

He daren't go down there. How could he? He'd be drowned. Then a terrible guilt overwhelmed him – he was the youngest brother; he should have dealt with the loose boulder. And now he hadn't even got the guts to save Angelica. Something inside him snapped.

Jonty leapt off the valley side and landed right in front of the tidal wave again. He started to run towards the village. When he glanced back the water was catching up with him and he couldn't see Michael anymore. Jonty looked ahead, concentrating on running as fast as he could. He could feel waves lapping at his ankles. In the village an alarm bell began to ring. The water was climbing his legs, weighing them down, spurting through between his thighs. He wasn't going to make it.

'Angelica! Angelica!' he screamed out.

A blinding light shone in his eyes, and he threw up his hands to shield them. The ringing noise went on. As Jonty slowly adjusted to the brightness he parted his fingers and saw Lindsey staring down at him. She was very definitely real and very definitely furious.

'Do you know whose name you've been shouting in your sleep?' she demanded. 'That's the bloody limit! Well don't just stare at me, answer the phone!'

Jonty stumbled out of bed and made for his office. The telephone was vibrating away on the desk. When he picked up the receiver he heard a rapid-fire series of pips and then a metallic clunk.

'Mr Church? Jonathan Church?' A cockney voice asked.

'Yes. Who's that?'

'Dennis. Dennis Morrell. Hope I didn't wake you up, only I tried to ring you last night and I wanted to get you before you went to work.'

Jonty was trying to put a face to the name which rang a vague bell.

'I'm the sparks from Battersea. I helped you and your brother . . .'

'Oh yes!' Jonty said. 'What can I do for you, Dennis?'

There was a sharp intake of breath. 'I've got to see you as soon as possible, Mr Church. It's about your brother's accident. You see, I'm not sure it was an accident.'

The shop Dennis had told him about was up a side street off Lavender Hill. Its frontage was painted bright red, and fading white letters above the windows proclaimed EVERYTHING FOR IN-CAR ENTERTAINMENT. To the left of the shop was an archway of the same bright red, in stark contrast to the sooty yellow brickwork of the rest of the terrace.

Jonty climbed out of his Lotus, crossed the road and stepped onto the fouled pavement in front of the windows. Inside them, crude racking supported an assortment of car radios and speakers, some of them second hand. Dog-eared cards had prices written on them in black felt-tip. Most of these had been slashed through with a broad red stroke, with BARGAIN OFFER and a lower price sandwiching the old one. Jonty sensed eyes appraising him, and looked up. A sour looking man of about fifty was staring at him from behind the counter. Jonty opened the glass-panelled door and went in.

'Can I help you, sir?'

'I'm looking for Dennis Morrell.'

The shopkeeper looked at him suspiciously. 'Something to sell him have you?'

'No, no; just wanted some advice on quad speakers for my Lotus.'

'Oh, well, he's round the back,' he said, nodding at the archway.

Jonty went out of the shop and through the archway beside it. A cobbled lane led to an open-fronted garage at the back, roofed with corrugated iron. A newish Jaguar XJ6 and a scratched white Metro were parked inside it. Maroon-overalled legs stuck out of the front passenger door of the Jaguar.

'Dennis?' Jonty said.

The legs wrigged about, and then the rest of Dennis's body came into view as he sat up. 'Hallo Mr Church,' he said in a slow, uneasy voice. 'Thanks for coming. Mind if I just finish this off? The owner's coming for it any minute.'

'Go ahead, and please call me Jonty.'

Dennis nodded appreciation and laid down on his back on the floor of the Jaguar. The door of the Metro alongside it was open, and Jonty sat sideways on the driver's seat so that he could see Dennis at work. A tangled mass of multi-coloured wires and bits of tape hung down from the Jaguar's dashboard, but Dennis's stumpy fingers worked quickly and certainly, selecting one of them, circumcising the plastic protection, and connecting the exposed wire to a radio cassette player.

'I don't know how you do that,' Jonty said wonderingly.

Dennis raised his head. 'You're not taking the . . . making fun of me are you?'

'No way! Electricity's a complete mystery to me.'

'Lot of people say that, and I can't understand it,' Dennis said, carrying on with the job as he talked. 'The way I see it this job's made for a dummo like me. I mean, you don't even need to read – you get different colours to follow, and if you do something wrong you get a belt up the arm to make sure you know about it.'

Jonty laughed. 'Well I was reckoned to be pretty bright at school, and I couldn't wire that up to save my life.'

Dennis shook his head incomprehendingly 'D'you know what puzzles me? How you raced like you did, I mean absolutely balls out, when you didn't know how the car'd been put together.'

'I didn't want to! I reckon I'd never have got into the things if I had done.'

'I'd never thought of it that way, but I reckon you're dead right! But how did you get them to go so fast, you know, tune the chassis?'

'Because I could always *feel* what was happening, even if I didn't know why. I told Michael exactly what I'd felt, and he'd translate that into adjustments.'

Just then a hard-faced man in a flashy blue suit walked into the garage. 'Got it ready, Den?' he asked.

'Just about,' Dennis said, connecting a final wire, and then sitting up and inserting a cassette into the player.

Olivia Newton-John started to warble out of four speakers, and Dennis carefully adjusted the tone and balance. The tough looking man climbed into the driver's seat and smiled contentedly.

'Sound like she's in the motor with me,' he leered, bunching his fist and flexing his arm in a crude gesture. 'I'll go and square up with old misery guts.'

'See what I mean?' Jonty said as the Jaguar drove away. 'You under-estimate yourself. I reckon a lot of people would like to steal you away.'

From the thunderstruck look on Dennis's face he realised he'd hit a raw nerve. 'What did I say?' Jonty asked.

Dennis walked round to the passenger door of the Metro and climbed in beside Jonty.

'I'd better tell you the whole story,' he said quietly.

Dennis finished talking and hung his head in shame. Beside him Jonty stared into the distance, slowly beginning to comprehend what his nightmare had meant.

'So how *did* the wing come loose?' he asked finally.

'I dunno,' Dennis said in a mystified voice. 'Could've been deliberate, could've been an accident. You see, we'd lightened just about everything this year including the wings, so they didn't have a strengthening bar through them. The big'un had bloody great endplates, but the little ones' were dinky, not up to the job if you ask me. One of them pulled out when we tried it in practice. We beefed up the spare for the race, but it wouldn't have taken much for someone to weaken it – bugger up a couple of rivets, something like that.'

'But the Lomax hit your car at Copse, so it could have been an accident.'

'Or a bit of both.'

Jonty shook his head grimly.

'You do believe me don't you?' Dennis asked plaintively. 'I mean, that I didn't do it?'

'*I* believe you, but will the police when I tell them.'

Dennis's eyes filled with terror. 'Oh no Jonty, *please* don't go to the Bill.'

'What else can I do? You must have known I'd do something.'

'But not that. I'm begging you.'

Jonty's face hardened. 'You'll have to tell me why I shouldn't.'

'Because . . . because I've got form, that's why. I've been done for receiving.'

'Not those Sony Walkmans you sold us last year for a tenner? I thought that was too good to be true!'

'Fraid so, amongst other things. I've got a suspended sentence hanging over me, so if you tell them I took money . . .' Dennis sighed despairingly. 'I only missed a stretch because I'd got my girlfriend pregnant and had to marry her. She's having the baby in three months' time.'

But Jonty had a faraway look on his face. So that's what the dream had been about – to find out what happened to Michael he was going to have to face up to a towering wave of fear and pain. He was going to have to help Angelica. And to Jonty's surprise he felt strangely excited.

'Anyway, Cambell gave you used tenners,' Jonty said, almost to himself, 'so there's no link to him at all. We'd probably just warn him off, and I want to catch the bastard behind this red-handed.'

'So what are you going to do?' Dennis asked.

Jonty looked straight at him. 'What are *we* going to do you mean!'

Fifteen

MID-MONDAY MORNING Jonty drove his Lotus Esprit along the Towcester-to-Silverstone road. Around him the Northamptonshire landscape was a spectrum of vivid greens in the spring sunshine. He slowed as he entered Silverstone village, feeling as though he was going through a gateway into the past. Memories of club-racing Sundays came flooding back.

Michael had insisted that his younger brother start in a Formula Ford single-seater, even though Jonty's interest and ambitions centred round sports cars. Races on Silverstone club circuit were always memorable, invariably ending up in a frantic last corner battle at Woodcote. Jonty had his favourite line, but after a race or two there his rivals knew about it. The trick had been to bluff them that he was going to try something different, then dive for the inside at the last possible moment. It had worked surprisingly often. A trace of amusement played on Jonty's lips. Then he remembered why he had come back, and his mouth returned to its unhappy downward set.

Just after the village, a minor road to the left led to the Circuit. Jonty followed it, and after half-a-mile turned left again into the competitors' entrance. He parked outside the circuit office, a single-storey redbrick building, and walked into the tiny reception area. A girl came to the bank-like glass screen to one side of it.

'Can I help you?'

'Jonathan Church. I phoned first thing this morning about

coming to see . . .'

'Oh yes,' she said, obviously forewarned. 'I'll fetch Mrs Rydell for you.'

The girl disappeared and came back with a round-faced dark-haired woman in her early thirties.

'Good morning Mr Church,' she said in a sympathetic voice. 'I have checked the position on your brother's car. It's being held as evidence for the Coroner's Court and the MSA enquiry.'

'MSA?' Jonty asked.

'Motor Sports Association. That's what the RAC call their racing side nowadays.'

'When will the enquiries be held?'

'In about four weeks' time.'

After Le Mans, Jonty thought.

'You can see the car if you want to, but I've got to accompany you. It's silly I know, but it's just to make sure that nobody . . .'

'I understand,' Jonty said.

Outside the offices they climbed into the Lotus and drove off towards the circuit. They turned before reaching it, drove parallel with the track for a few hundred yards, and then stopped outside an old hangar. It looked like a relic from the last war, the thick tar on its corrugated panels crazed like a dried-up river bed. The two sliding doors at the front were closed, but Mrs Rydell unlocked the Judas gate in one of them and pushed it open. Jonty stepped into the hangar after her.

Shafts of pale light filtered into the cavernous interior through dirty windows set high in the walls. Dust swirled about in them like curling smoke. There was a strong smell of decomposing grass. Jonty peered around, gradually accustoming his eyes to the shadowy gloom. An old green-and-yellow tractor was parked just inside the doors with some sort of agricultural machine nose-down behind it. At the far end of the hangar he could see an uneven line of lumpy shapes covered by oil-stained tarpaulins . . . except for two exposed piles of debris.

'That's it,' Mrs Rydell said quietly, following his stare. She stayed where she was as Jonty walked across the crumbling concrete floor towards them.

His face whitened with shock. From a distance the chassis looked like the half-stripped carcass of some strange animal. The engine and gearbox were twisted at a crazy angle to the cockpit, and the wheels had been ripped off, leaving jagged silver veins behind them.

Jonty stopped beside the driver's seat and the full horror of the crash came home to him. What had once been in front of the windscreen was now concertinad into the dash. Deep scars in the aluminium showed where they had cut Michael out. Rust seemed to have stained the metal around them, but as Jonty bent closer he realised that wasn't what it was. He straightened up quickly and closed his eyes. The stench of decomposition filled his nostrils, like the death smell of the churchyard at Michael's funeral. Jonty turned away.

When he opened his eyes again he was looking at the second pile of wreckage. What was left of the fibreglass body-work was piled up into a stack. The rear wing leant drunkenly against it, battered and twisted into a propeller shape. Jonty picked it up. Part of one endplate was still attached by two stretched rivets. The others had been ripped out, leaving bullet-like holes in the thin aluminium. He turned the wing round. The other endplate was missing altogether. How was anyone, however expert, going to prove anything from that, Jonty wondered? Even if they somehow managed to do so, it would be after the Le Mans 24-hour race.

Slowly, Jonty turned back towards the cockpit. A chilling determination began to enter his brain, more powerful than his other emotions and strong enough to drive them out. He remembered the feeling from his racing days – Michael would have entered him for a race in some massively powerful sports car. Jonty would be standing by it feeling scared and out of his depth. Then Michael would start to talk to him in that calm, confidence-inspiring way of his, and Jonty would start to experience the feelings he was having now.

Quite suddenly, he felt he was no longer alone. Jonty looked up at a smoky shaft of light that fell just beyond the cockpit. Dancing dust was playing tricks in it.

'You've got the talent! You can handle it! Michael seemed to be saying to him.

Jonty's eyes glistened, and his mouth formed a silent question. And then his face hardened as though the steely emotion had taken hold of it.

'Let's do it!' he whispered fiercely.

Jonty took a deep breath as he reached the door of the Reading car showroom. He felt like a novice parachutist at the jump-hatch, all the doubts and fears he'd had about what he was doing gnawing away at his stomach, but there was no turning back now. He yanked open the plate glass door and stepped inside. Turning to his right he began to walk past a line of saloon cars towards Conrad's office. Its door was open but he couldn't see anyone inside.

On the phone from Silverstone Conrad had told him he'd be out most of Monday afternoon, but that they could meet at five. Jonty looked at his watch – ten to.

'Can I help you?' a beige-suited salesman asked, hurrying to intercept him.

'I'm Conrad's brother. He's expecting me.'

Now the young salesman was all smiles. 'He's just gone into the back. I'll tell him you're here.'

Jonty reached the open door of his brother's office and paused. This bit was like going into the headmaster's study for a caning. Then curiosity overcame him and he went in. It looked just the same as when he'd last seen it over a year ago – a collection of trophies and models on glass shelves behind his desk, a rosewood bookshelf full of motoring books and magazines, and on the other wall, framed pictures and photographs. Jonty's eyes widened as he saw the one of himself. Surely Conrad couldn't have kept that around after the trouble with Karen? But there it still was. Maybe he'd misjudged his brother.

'Jonty! Good to see you,' Conrad said from behind him.

He turned round, and Conrad grasped his hand and shook it enthusiastically.

'Hallo Conrad,' Jonty said sheepishly. 'Sorry it's taken me time to see sense.'

'Don't apologise!' Conrad said, putting his arm round his shoulder. 'It's me who owes an apology, flying off the handle like that the day of Michael's funeral. I should have realised how upset you'd be, and left it for a bit; stupid of me . . . tactless.'

Conrad had moved Jonty towards a chrome and black leather armchair. He pressed him down in it, then walked round to the other side of his desk and sank down heavily into his high-backed version. 'Anyway, the important thing now is to get to Le Mans.'

'Yes. As I told you on the phone, I've thought it over, and I'm sure Michael would've wanted me to drive his car there.'

'That takes a lot of guts, Jonty,' Conrad said, stabbing a finger at him, 'changing your mind after what you've been through. I really respect you for that.'

'So where do we start?'

Conrad opened a drawer underneath his desk and pulled out a light blue cardboard folder. 'Right here,' he said, extracting a double sheet of accounting paper. 'Angelica and I have done some preliminary costings, and to build up a new car and do the 24-hour race we're going to need about 100 grand.' He took another sheet of paper out of the folder and pushed it across the desk to Jonty. 'I've asked the trustees to release that to us from capital, so if you'd just sign at the bottom alongside my signature we can get the finance under way.'

Jonty read the document, uncomfortably aware of his brother's eyes studying him.

'Anything wrong?' Conrad asked.

'This asks for the money to go to the garages,' Jonty said in a puzzled tone.

'That's right. The trustees wouldn't consider giving it to a racing team. The deeds don't allow them to, for a start. So we've requested funds for capital expenditure on the garages, which the trust owns anyway. Once we've got the money, we'll channel it to the team as advertising and publicity.'

Jonty still looked dubious. 'I don't know, Conrad; this is pulling the wool over the trustees' eyes. I'd like a little time to think about it. Maybe there's another . . .'

'We don't have time!' Conrad snapped. 'Look Jonty it's the end of May; Le Mans is in three weeks' time. Angelica's told me that unless we place firm orders and put cash down for parts immediately, there's no way we can make it. I've told her to come here at 5.30 for a yes-or-no answer, so it's entirely up to you now.'

Jonty looked down at the paper again. For some time he studied it, his forehead creased in a frown. Then he reached for a pen and scrawled his signature alongside his brother's.

'Good,' Conrad said, smiling again. 'Why don't you take a walk round the showroom whilst I make a few calls. Angelica should be here soon. She's bringing Alex Fitch with her, by the way, Glaser's racing manager, so we'll find out where we stand on their engines.'

'All right,' Jonty said, pushing himself up out of the chair, and leaving the office.

In the showroom the beige-suited salesman was mooching about with his hands behind his back. He almost stood to attention when he saw him.

'Just looking,' Jonty said.

'Help yourself Mr Church.'

Jonty opened the door of one of the French saloon cars. The bodywork had a more rounded look than most current Euroboxes, but the instruments seemed to have been inspired by *Star Wars*. He closed it, and moved down the line of cars until he reached the wedge-shaped stand with the black Glaser 822 on it. That was more interesting. Mountaineering up the slope, Jonty opened the driver's door and climbed in. When he looked up from the instrument panel, a silver Alfa

Romeo was just stopping in front of the showroom's plate glass window. Angelica opened its passenger door and climbed out.

She was wearing a cream polo neck sweater and a tight suede skirt, and she tossed her head to flick errant strands of hair over her shoulders. Jonty sat quite still, confused emotions stabbing at his heart and brain as he watched her – embarrassment, sadness, and something else; something he couldn't put a name to so easily.

The man who emerged from the other side of the Alfa was tall, overweight and vaguely familiar – Jonty remembered seeing Alex Fitch at Michael's funeral. Now he hurried round the front of his car to pull the showroom door open for Angelica, who stepped past him and turned towards Conrad's office. She walked past the Glaser without noticing Jonty behind its tinted screen. Just then Fitch caught up with her and slapped a hand down on her firm backside. Angelica jumped, and for an instant her face flashed unmistakable anger.

'Sorry, darling; can't get enough of your sweet little arse,' Fitch leered.

To Jonty's amazement Angelica's expression changed to an inane grin as though he'd paid her a tremendous compliment, and she linked arms with him. When they reached the office they parted and Fitch knocked on the door. Conrad opened it, and there was a loud exchange of hearty greetings.

Quietly, Jonty climbed out of the Glaser and moved towards the office. The door was half open, and as he neared it he could hear every word of the conversation in the office.

Fitch was talking in a loud, plummy voice: 'So did that young prick of a brother of yours sign up, or not?'

'Yes, I did,' Jonty said, stepping through the door.

Fitch spun round, his face aghast. 'I . . . I didn't realise . . .'

'Great opening Alex, ha ha ha!' Conrad intervened. 'You two haven't been introduced, have you. Jonty, Alex Fitch.'

Jonty shook his clammy hand, trying to keep the instant

dislike off his face. He glanced at Angelica but she couldn't meet his eyes.

'I used to race against Conrad in two-litre sports cars,' Fitch said, recovering his composure. 'He was always blowing me off or pushing me off, so you'll have to forgive me being a trifle rude about you Church brothers.'

'Well you mustn't be rude about Jonty today,' Conrad said. 'He's not only agreed to help with finance, he's going to drive for us as well! Anyway Alex, when did I ever have to *push* you off?'

As the two men started a bantering argument about their racing rivalry, Angelica stared at Jonty in surprise.

'What made you change your mind?' she asked quietly.

'Something I have to find out.'

'About yourself.'

'Perhaps.'

Angelica studied his face, as though trying to read between the words. Then she turned back to Conrad. 'Well that really puts us back in business. You see, Alex has agreed to let us keep the undamaged engine we still have, and to get us two more for Le Mans.'

'*Try* to get them,' Fitch added hastily. 'I must say I thought the team was finished after what happened at Silverstone, Michael getting . . . you know. Angelica's convinced me otherwise though.' He turned towards her and leered at her again. 'I must say she's been *most* persuasive.'

Jonty looked at Angelica. She was doing her best to look happy, but he was sure he read something else deep in her eyes.

'That's great,' Conrad said. 'Now all Angelica needs is some day-to-day help to get everything organised in time. I'd love to do it, but I'm absolutely snowed under here. Could you lend a hand Jonty?'

'I'll need a few days to tidy up my own business first.'

Fitch looked puzzled. 'What business?'

'Jonty's Jockstraps Limited!' Conrad said condenscendingly. 'He sells sportswear.'

Both men threw back their heads and roared with laughter, but Angelica didn't join in. When Jonty glanced at her she was looking at Fitch, and the secret emotion was much nearer the surface of her face. He was sure he could read it now – *contempt*.

Sixteen

THE HARE bounded confidently across the grass, then stopped at the edge of the tarmac. He sat up on his haunches, twitching his nose and ears suspiciously. He could hear birdsong and smell the scent of other animals. This wasn't one of those days when the ground was shaken by a noise worse than thunder, and the air stank of something fouler than the strange powders that sometimes appeared in the fields. Yet he sensed *something*. Turning his head, the hare saw and smelt the wind rippling through the grass, carrying its rich odour to his quivering nostrils. There was nothing to fear. He turned back to the strip of grey tarmac and leapt out onto it.

Death scythed towards him at 150 miles-an-hour, a monstrous predator with sleek brown skin and a single huge eye. Desperately the hare turned away from it but then it was upon him, crushing him into bloody rags and tossing them contemptuously over its back like a charging rhino.

Inside the Glaser-Lomax Wolfgang Schnering ducked his head into his shoulders as he hit it. Damned hares! Damned Copse corner! he swore to himself. He couldn't see or feel any damage, but the impact brought back the memory of a much worse one – he had hit Michael Church's car there just over a fortnight ago, and then . . . and then . . .

Wolfgang forced the guilt-filled images out of his mind. This wasn't the time or place to lose concentration. They had hired Silverstone Circuit for the whole of Tuesday to test their modified chassis. It was better all right, much better, but during the morning he had blown up a Glaser engine, and nobody seemed to know why. He glanced down nervously at the oil pressure gauge. Its red needle was vertical – normal.

Ahead of him now was Becketts corner. Wolfgang braked, changed down into second gear, then accelerated hard towards Hangar Straight. He checked the oil pressure again. There it went! The needle suddenly dipped left, then jumped back to the normal position. Wolfgang slowed down immediately, cruising round the rest of the lap and pulling off the track into the pit lane just after the *Daily Express* Bridge.

Today the Lomax team had free choice of pit lane garages, and had taken one which the victorious works Porsche had occupied during the 1,000-kilometre race. Wolfgang switched off the Glaser engine as early as possible and coasted to a halt outside it. He pushed his door open, and Ralph Cambell crammed his foxy face and shoulders into the opening, blocking out Derek Lomax. The designer was forced to peer in over his chief mechanic's back.

'Hit a hare at Copse,' Wolfgang said. 'Front right hand corner.'

Cambell stepped back, pushing Lomax unceremoniously out of the way as he went to the front of the car. He shouted something, and one of the mechanics appeared with a roll of silver tank tape. They knelt down by the front wing as the chief mechanic started to explain what he wanted doing. Meanwhile Derek Lomax had taken his place in the open driver's door.

'The oil pressure went low again,' Wolfgang said to him.

Lomax sucked in breath. '*Must* be something wrong with the engine installation.'

He turned to one of the mechanics and asked him to lift the engine cover. Wolfgang undid his seat belts and climbed out of the car. They were both peering into the open engine bay when Cambell appeared beside them.

'What the hell are you two doing? We're running out of testing time.'

'Low oil pressure again,' Wolfgang said.

'How low?'

The German held up his index finger to represent the needle. 'It dropped, like this, then climbed back to normal again.'

'Probably just the gauge then. Now get back in the car and we'll carry on.'

'I don't think it's the gauge,' Lomax said. 'I think it's the installation.'

Cambell turned on him angrily. 'Look Derek; am I running this test or are you?'

'You are. But we've already lost one engine and I don't think we should just assume . . .'

'Are you blaming me?'

'I'm not blaming anyone. I'm just saying we should check the installation.'

Cambell put his hands on his waist. 'Look, I supervised the engine change, and I'm telling you there's nothing wrong with it. Now I suggest you let me get on with my job.'

Lomax shook his head unhappily.

'All right Wolfgang,' Cambell said in the mock-patient tone of a schoolmaster. 'Let's get back in the car shall we. Any changes you want made?'

'No, no. The chassis is much better. Just I am worried about . . .'

'I know, I know. Keep your eye on it then. We're going to put on some qualifying tyres now so that we can measure what kind of improvement we've made.'

Five minutes later, Wolfgang set off down the pit lane seething with impotent rage. A couple of seasons ago he would have told anybody who talked to him like Cambell had done where to put his car! But a couple of seasons ago half a dozen teams wanted him, and a works Porsche drive seemed just around the corner. Now all that was a fading dream.

Ralph Cambell was a type anyway, Wolfgang told himself. There were plenty of them in motor racing, the sort of team manager who changed the suspension settings of a gifted driver just to show who made the decisions. But there was some special malice about Cambell's attitude to Derek Lomax. He never missed an opportunity to belittle his boss or to make fun of him behind his back. And whereas Lomax was a better designer than Cambell liked to make out, Wolfgang knew that the chief mechanic wasn't as hot as he thought he was. For a few moments longer he wondered just what was eating Cambell. Then the pit lane curved right and merged with the track just after Copse corner, and his mind automatically tuned in to racing.

Now the Glaser-Lomax had qualifying slicks on, smooth tyres made from an ultra-sticky compound that would only last two laps at racing speed. Wolfgang warmed them up carefully, staying on the racing line he had effectively swept clean on his earlier laps to avoid picking up any debris that would misshape them. He braked delicately for the same reason. As he swept under the *Daily Express* Bridge he built up to racing speed.

Turning into the Woodcote chicane he felt the super-grip instantly. The car went exactly where he pointed it without the slightest suggestion of skidding at either end. A feeling of exhilaration and satisfaction surged through his body, just as it had when he'd felt the chassis improvement that morning. Was this really the same car he'd wrestled through these corners a fortnight ago? Derek Lomax *did* know what he was doing.

Wolfgang thundered down the pit straight, concentrating on finding the exact braking point for Copse. He was into a flying lap now, one of only two, and he intended to make the most of it. He braked slightly late, changed into third gear, and then climbed quickly back onto the throttle. The car swept through the corner as though locked into an invisible track. Wolfgang realised that his mind was lagging behind the car now – his brain was still programmed for the confidence-sapping handling quirks of the prototype. He would have to override his instinctive reaction if he was going to take the car to its limit in just two laps. Becketts was rushing towards him. He reached the braking point.

'*Ein . . . zwei*,' he made himself count out loud.

Then he hit the brake pedal. The car twitched about but then bit down into the track as soon as he squeezed on the power again. Fabulous! Fabulous! He was going onto Hangar Straight much faster than before. Wolfgang wanted to use every last rev, and he glanced down at the climbing white needle of the rev counter. As it hit the limit he changed into fourth gear and kept accelerating hard. Beside the rev-counter the smaller turbo-boost gauge read one-point-five.

Suddenly, from the corner of his eye, he saw a red needle dip. Almost instantly there was a violent explosion behind him and he was flung forward against his seat belts as though he'd slammed on his brakes. The straps cut into his flesh. There was the dreadful scream of tortured rubber and the back end of the car began to skid round. For a moment of total unreality Wolfgang couldn't work out what was happening, because his foot was nowhere near the brake pedal. Then instinct took over, and his left foot crashed down on the clutch, freeing the rear wheels from the seized engine.

Now the car was diagonal to the circuit and heading for the trackside, a ten metre wide strip of alternating patches of grass and rough concrete. Wolfgang didn't touch the brakes, trying to straighten out without sending the Lomax into an uncontrollable spin. If he lost it the sleeper-lined bank was waiting to crush him. For an instant he remembered the hare, saw again its blurred and bloody remains flying over the windscreen. He had almost straightened the car out when the left-side wheels drifted onto the grass. Immediately the back end swung right round, and he was crashing sideways along the trackside, his spine being battered by the seat and his helmet smashing repeatedly into the fibreglass roof. The car completed its arc, and suddenly he was back on the track again but facing the way he had come. Wolfgang stamped his foot down on the brake pedal, and the tyres began to shriek and gush smoke. The car spun round twice more and then lurched to a stop on the far side of the track.

Silence, except for the violent singing in his ears. A stench

143

of burnt rubber. Wolfgang realised he'd stopped breathing, and gulped in air like a drowning man breaking water. He looked back up the track. Blue-grey tyre smoke was drifting towards him, forming strange shapes. For a moment he thought he saw a face in it with a familiar lopsided grin. Wolfgang stared at him in horror. Michael Church had died right there. Then the image broke up, spiralling into oblivion.

Just the smoke of course, Wolfgang told himself. Just his imagination. He was drenched in sweat, but an icy finger ran up his spine.

Alex Fitch stared down at his gold Rolex chronometer with intense concentration. He pressed the stopwatch start button and let the hands tick round for a few seconds before zeroing them. Then he put a large brown egg on a silver spoon and lowered it into the pan of water boiling away on his kitchen hob.

'How d'you like your eggs, darling?' he asked, glancing at Angelica and restarting the stopwatch at the same time.

She was sitting at the tiled breakfast bar at one end of his large modern kitchen. Angelica was wearing a pink kimono, and she blinked her eyes in sleepy perplexity. 'Boiled,' she said, 'like you're doing them.'

'I know *that*, but for how long?'

'Three minutes . . . five minutes. I never really thought about it. You know I can't cook.'

Fitch rolled his eyes upwards. 'Boiling eggs is hardly cooking, darling, and this is most important I'm a four-and-a-quarter minute man, give or take fifteen seconds depending on the size of the egg. Get it wrong, and the soldiers won't sog up the yolk.'

'Soldiers?'

There was a smell of burnt bread as the toaster noisily ejected two slices. Fitch tightened the cord of his red silk dressing gown, and then plucked them out of the machine.

'Look,' he said, solemnly buttering one of the slices and cutting it into strips. 'You dip these in the yolk – soldiers.'

'Very interesting, darling,' Angelica said.

Fitch didn't seem to notice the irony. He continued to fuss round the cooker with a look of childish delight on his jowly face. Finally he brought eggs and toast to the breakfast bar and sat down next to Angelica. She glanced at her wristwatch.

'Timing me?' he asked

'No, darling. Zürich's an hour ahead of us isn't it?'

'Yes. Why?'

Angelica smiled sweetly at him. 'Would you phone the factory after breakfast and check on this engine deal? It would be so nice to know we can count on it.'

Fitch was absorbed in manoeuvring a broad soldier into his egg. 'Plenty of time for that. Do it some time today I promise you.'

'I'd like to know before I go to Reading,' Angelica said with a steely edge in her voice, a hint of favours that could be withdrawn as well as granted.

Fitch looked up with a worried expression on his face. 'All right darling. I'll call them whilst you're having your bath.'

Alex Fitch closed the double lounge doors, and for a few moments stood holding onto their elegant brass handles. He felt a nameles dread hovering over him, like the blade of a guillotine poised to swish down and chop off his head. But would the executioner be Curtis Stockwell or Angelica Hofer? He shuddered as he remembered the boardroom battle in Zürich after the Silverstone tragedy, and what he was about to ask his patron Curtis Stockwell for now. And Angelica! Fitch realised that she wasn't entirely attracted by his personality and looks – being Glaser's racing manager was obviously a big part of it. How would she react now if he couldn't deliver the goods?

Sweating profusely, Fitch locked the doors. He walked to one of the deep-brown leather armchairs, collapsed into it, and lifted a trim-phone off the small round mahogany table beside it. His dumpy fingers messed up the dialling twice, but at the third attempt he got through to the Glaser factory, and asked to speak to Stockwell. Half a minute later the New Yorker was on the line.

'Morning Alex. What can I do for you.'

'Good morning Mr Stockwell. I was just phoning in to . . . ahhh . . . report progress on the racing front.'

'Go ahead.'

Fitch swallowed. His throat felt as if he'd been stranded in the Sahara Desert for a week. 'Ummm, two main areas to report on really. The Church team seem to have made a most surprising recovery since the Silverstone disaster. Michael Church's two brothers have raised enough finance to rebuild their car and go to Le Mans. They've still got one of our racing engines and . . . ahhh . . .'

'Yes?'

'They were rather wondering if we would still let them use it and . . . ummm . . . possibly consider lending them another one.'

'Who's driving for them?' Stockwell asked.

'Angelica Hofer of course, and Michael's younger brother Jonathan. He was . . . *is* an exceptionally talented sports car driver.'

'And the second area?'

'The second area? Oh, ah, yes. Derek Lomax phoned me from Silverstone yesterday afternoon. They were doing some development testing up there, and apparently the car went marvellously . . .'

'But?'

'There was some sort of mistake with the oil cooler layout, and the result was that they blew up two of our engines.'

'No problem,' Stockwell said matter-of-factly.

An explosion of surprise burst out of Fitch's throat, something between a cough and a 'what?'

'No problem,' Stockwell repeated. 'I happened to run a stock control programme yesterday, and I noticed we'd got two built-up racing engines and enough components to make several more. I think the thing to do here is to run a batch of four. That way we'll ensure both teams make it to Le Mans,

146

and we'll have a couple on standby. That all right with you Alex?'

'Yes, Mr Stockwell,' he managed to say, something like ecstasy lighting up his face. 'Perfectly satisfactory.'

Upstairs in the bath, Angelica waited for the conversation to end before putting the wall-phone gently back on its bracket. What she had heard gave her something to justify her behaviour to herself, but it still left a bitter taste. She reached for a large sponge, soaped it up, and began to scrub herself roughly, trying to wash away the repulsive thought of Alex Fitch's flabby white body.

Curtis Stockwell opened the sound-proofed door from the reception area into the factory, and a mechanical cacophony battered against his eardrums. He looked around the shop floor until he spotted Rico Glaser. He and Kurt Fontana were peering into a metallic green car on the 822 production line. Stockwell walked over to them and tapped on Rico's shoulder.

'Could I talk to you . . .' Stockwell started to say, but his sentence was lost in a machine-gun like burst of hammering.

Rico pointed back towards the offices, cupped his hand over the production director's ear and yelled something into it, then walked towards reception. As the soundproof door swung shut behind them the noise of the factory died instantly.

'Robot welds!' Rico shouted, not realising he was still doing so. 'Trouble is you can't kick a machine. You wanted me?'

'Yes,' Stockwell said, climbing the stairs to the first-floor offices beside him. 'Alex Fitch just called me from England. The Lomax team wrecked two engines in testing; some oil problem. I didn't quite understand. I told him we had two in stock, and we'd freight them out right away.'

They had reached Rico's office. He paused to study the American's face, then opened the door and went in. 'Why are you telling me this?'

'Because we've got a problem,' Stockwell said, shutting the door behind him. 'It looks like the Church team are back in business. Fraulein Hofer has got Michael's two brothers to refinance their team, and the younger one's going to drive at Le Mans with her.'

Rico had sat down behind his desk, and his head jerked up in surprise. 'Jonty is driving again? That's interesting.'

'The problem is that after the Silverstone accident, they've only got one of our engines left. We've enough components in stock to make several more. I know it's outside budget, but do you think we could run a batch of four, two for the Church team and two on standby here?'

Rico stared at him. 'Do I understand you correctly Herr Stockwell? *You* want to build more racing engines?'

'Yes. Surely we can find a way to justify . . .'

'Of course we can. I'm just surprised that it's you suggesting this. You have never been exactly an ally of the project.'

A born again look creased Stockwell's face, almost one of repentance. 'No, Rico. I tried to kill it in fact. I just couldn't believe in it as a marketing tool, but now I know I was wrong.'

'Oh? What's changed your mind?'

'The dealers. As you know I've been very involved with them over the last few weeks.'

Rico nodded sourly. 'Yes. Another area that's been taken away from me.'

'This whole racing programme is more important to them than I realised,' Stockwell went on, as though he hadn't heard the snub. 'They see it as vital to the image of the marque, vital to their sales.'

'I could have told you that if you'd let me.'

Stockwell nodded. 'Well I'm listening now. I think my perception of the Silverstone accident was wrong, and I think we should revitalise the racing programme before Le Mans.'

The beginnings of a smile formed on Rico's lips. 'Well that's good to hear. But apart from supplying engines to both teams what do you propose to do?'

'Have *you* spell it out to the dealers. Many of them will be visiting us over the next few weeks. I want you to be the focus of their visit, and explain the racing project to them. We need your personality and prestige to motivate them.'

Now a beam parted Rico's mouth, revealing his big stained teeth. 'I would be delighted to help Curtis. You only had to ask.'

Fifteen minutes later Francis Jaggi sneaked into the American's office. Stockwell was back behind his desk, working on some papers.

'Well?' the design director asked.

Stockwell looked up at him. 'He swallowed it.'

'Swallowed what?'

'A little bullshit and a lot of flattery,' Stockwell said with a malicious grin.

Seventeen

ON WEDNESDAY morning Jonty cruised his white Lotus west along the M4, doing eighty miles-an-hour when he could, but blending in unaggressively with the rush hour traffic as he neared Reading.

Just before the turnoff he saw headlights blazing in his mirror and pulled into the middle lane. A familiar yellow estate car came rushing past, and as Jonty glanced right he saw a grim-faced Angelica driving it. She didn't appear to notice him. The Vauxhall dived left across horn-honking light-flashing traffic to make the turnoff, and he followed it. They were obviously going to the same place, but what had Angelica been doing in London that early on Wednesday morning, Jonty wondered? Or the night before?

Jonty stayed behind her until they reached Church Racing's workshop. It had been a Reading builder's yard until he went bankrupt in the late seventies, and Michael had bought the premises. Standing beside one of the main roads into Reading with a petrol station on one side and a row of shops on the other, its frontage still showed its origins. Breeze block and cladding buildings formed a three-sided stockade round a central concrete yard. A small office and an open-fronted store faced each other, whilst at the end of the yard was what had been the builder's main depot. That had a large black metal sliding door in the middle of it.

Angelica turned off the main road and thumped the Vauxhall across the pavement into the yard. Jonty followed

150

more slowly, and parked his Lotus under the lean-to beside her. As he climbed out of the car he met her eyes. They reflected his own embarrassment. This was the first time they'd been alone together since he'd visited her at Michael's house.

'Good morning Jonathan,' she said, walking towards the dark green office door.

'Morning,' Jonty said. *Jonathan!* That was what his Mother used to call him when she was angry, and in that tone of voice too.

Angelica unlocked the door and walked into the office. Motor racing posters were fixed to the cream-painted walls with yellowing strips of sellotape. There were two windows, one looking out on the yard, and the other onto the road. In front of this one was a secretary's chair and a plain wooden desk. Angelica sat down behind it.

'Errr . . . look, I'm sorry about the other night,' Jonty said, still standing.

'That's all right.'

'I was . . . you know . . . it was difficult . . .'

'Forget it,' Angelica said curtly. 'If we're going to work together I think it's better we don't talk about it.

'Yes,' Jonty said, pulling up a cheap wooden chair and sitting down on it. 'How can I help you then?'

'In just over two weeks' time the car must be ready and on the way to Le Mans. This is what we still have to do.' She pushed a stack of papers across the desk and paused to let him look at them. 'The chassis arrived here yesterday. Fortunately we already had it on order as a spare. As you can see we need to buy just about everything else. Nearly all the parts on the crashed car were badly damaged, and anyway we're not allowed to touch it.'

'I know,' Jonty said quietly. 'I saw it on Monday.'

Angelica looked up at him curiously. 'You did? What were you doing at Silverstone?'

'Never mind. Just tell me what you want me to do.'

She studied him for a few seconds longer before answering.

'I can order the parts, and the men can pick them up. Our big problem is fitting them on the car and paying for them.'

'Fitting them?'

'Yes. I've kept the full time fabricators, Ian and Alastair, but not the part-timers or the volunteer mechanics.'

'Why not?'

'Because I didn't think you'd want anyone around who could have caused Michael's accident.'

'I want the team back together *exactly* as it was at Silverstone,' Jonty said firmly.

Angelica stared at him in surprise. 'You don't mind that? It doesn't bother you?'

'Whether it bothers me or not, we'd be lucky to find the skilled men we need in a fortnight. And anyway, we don't *know* one of them made a mistake. Not having them back is like finding them guilty without a trial.'

'Well, it would certainly solve a lot of problems,' Angelica said. 'We're completely stuck on electrics, for example. We had a boy who was really marvellous at that.'

'Dennis Morrell. He'll come back.'

'How do you know?'

'I saw him the other day, and he said he was keen to carry on, if we'd have him.'

Angelica narrowed her eyes. 'That's odd, you just happening to meet him.'

'Dennis helped the team when I raced for them. We've stayed in touch because he repairs my car radio.'

'I see,' Angelica said, but doubt lingered in her eyes.

'What's the finance problem?'

'Finance?'

'You said there was a problem with payments.'

'Oh yes. Conrad promised me sponsorship, but I don't know when it's coming. Most of our suppliers want cash on delivery, and we don't have time to argue with them.'

'Leave it to me,' Jonty said. 'Give me a list of names and addresses and I'll round up the lads, then clear up the finance with Conrad.'

Angelica rummaged around in the desk's drawers, and finally produced a sheet of paper. 'Here they are,' she said, handing the list to Jonty.

'Mind if I take a look in the workshop first.'

'Help yourself,' Angelica said, picking up the old-fashioned black telephone, and dialling a supplier's number.

Jonty walked out of the office, crossed the yard, and pulled back the black metal door of the main building. In contrast to the weathered brickwork the inside was immaculate. The floor was painted with glossy grey concrete sealer, and the walls with matt white paint. Wooden workbenches and Dexion racking lined the walls. In the middle of the floor the bare aluminium chassis sat on two tressles, looking more like a wide bobsleigh than the frame of a racing car. Jonty winced as he remembered the crumpled wreck in the hangar at Silverstone.

Two men were working on the chassis, and they looked up as Jonty stepped into the workshop. He recognised Ian Mottram, the taller one, who had been the ace spannerman when Jonty was with the team, and quite a joker. Now he looked embarrassed and uncertain.

'Hallo Jonty,' he said quietly. 'I hear you might be driving for us again.'

Jonty smiled. 'If you pull your finger out and finish this thing I will be.'

The lanky mechanic beamed with relief. 'This is Alastair Prior,' he said, introducing the stockier man, also in his late twenties. 'Used to be with the grand prix circus, but he chucked it up to come and learn from me.'

'You haven't changed a bit,' Jonty said cheerfully, 'and nor's your line of bullshit!'

As they bantered away Jonty began to feel an inner glow, as though he'd come back to somewhere he belonged. After a few minutes he looked down at his watch.

'Better go and rustle up some help for you two, otherwise I'm going to have to listen to Ian moaning for a fortnight.'

The sendoff the lanky mechanic gave him was friendly but obscene.

153

Jonty parked his Lotus outside his brother's Reading showroom, and walked through it towards his office. Conrad came storming out just before he got there.

'Make yourself comfortable,' he called. 'Back in a minute.'

Jonty went into the office and sat down in one of the black leather armchairs. He waited patiently for a few minutes, then stood up and moved to the rosewood bookshelves that almost covered one wall. Conrad seemed to have kept every motoring book and magazine he'd ever had. Jonty pulled out a children's book from the fifties. The racing driver on its cover looked not unlike their father. And Conrad was still collecting – the stacks of periodicals were right up to date. Most people who packed in racing tended to let it go all together, Jonty thought. Conrad's interest didn't seem to have flagged at all. But then he had been forced to give it up. The beginnings of an uneasy idea formed in Jonty's mind, but then his brother marched back into the office.

'Sorry to keep you waiting,' Conrad said, going round his desk and crashing down into his executive chair. He began to file through a stack of papers. 'What can I do for you?'

'Ummm, I've been at the workshop this morning, and Angelica's got things well under way. The big holdup seems to be money. Do you know when the sponsorship will be coming through?'

Conrad looked up with an expression of mild irritation on his face. 'Give it a chance, Jonty! We only signed the request to the trustees on Monday. I gave it to Rupert Fisher yesterday, but it's going to take him a few days to get approval from the others.'

'Oh,' Jonty said. 'What do we do in the meantime?'

'Same as you do in any business – delay your payments for a bit. I thought you said you were running one yourself.'

'But Angelica says the suppliers want cash on delivery.'

'Have you checked the company's bank account?'

'Which company?' Jonty asked.

Conrad gave a despairing sigh. 'Church Racing *Limited*. That means it's a limited liability company. Now go back and ask Angelica for the bank statements. You do know how to read one don't you?'

'Yes.'

'Thank Christ for that! So work out what cash you've got in hand, make a list of the payments you've got to make, and if you haven't got enough to meet them ask the bank manager for an overdraft.'

'But that takes time as well.'

'So bridge it yourself,' Conrad said impatiently. 'Christ knows what you do with your trust income since you stopped racing. It must be coming out of your ears. Now if you'll excuse me I've got to sort out this little lot.' He nodded down at the papers in front of him.

Jonty stood up to leave. As he reached the door Conrad called out to him.

'Oh by the way, I've given Steve Driscoll three weeks paid leave to help the team. He'll be with you tomorrow morning.'

The sidestreet off Lavender Hill was as dark and fouled as Jonty remembered it. An essence of dog droppings wafted down towards him as he climbed the pavement towards the red-fronted shop. He had left his car at the bottom of the road, hoping to reach the garage at the back unnoticed, but as he came level with the shop's front door he felt eyes glaring at him.

Jonty turned quickly under the red-painted arch, and began to walk down the cobbled alley. Then the sour old shopkeeper opened the side door and called out to him.

'Come for some more advice on your speakers have you?' he said sarcastically.

'Is Dennis down there?' Jonty asked coolly.

'He don't need any more trouble you know. Neither do I.'

'What makes you think I'm trouble?'

The man gave a derisive grunt. 'You must think I was born yesterday! I can smell it a bloody mile off, son!'

He stepped back into the shop, slamming the door so hard that the smeared glass rattled in the frame. Jonty stared through it at his departing back. When he looked down the alley again Dennis had come out of the garage to see what the fuss was about.

'Afternoon, Dennis,' Jonty said. 'I'm afraid I've upset your boss.'

Dennis laughed. 'Doesn't take much doing. How've you been getting on?'

Jonty walked into the open-fronted garage beside him before talking. 'We're back in business. I've just phoned or visited all the lads, and they're coming back.'

'Including bloody Driscoll?'

'Yes. The only one left is you.'

'Well count me in,' Dennis said firmly. 'I've been thinking it over, and I want to know what's been going on as much as you do.'

'What's old misery guts going to say?'

Dennis shrugged. 'Not too much. Last time he fired me it cost him two grand – the comedian he got to replace me burnt out a brand new Cortina!' His pudgy face beamed maliciously at the memory. Then suddenly it darkened. 'It's not him I'm worried about. It's my missus.'

Jonty arrived back at the Reading workshop late on Wednesday afternoon. When he walked into the office Angelica was sitting at the plain desk, telephone cradled between head and shoulder, and hands sorting through a pile of invoices. He pulled up the wooden chair and sat down opposite her.

'I know you don't know me,' she was saying exasperatedly into the mouthpiece, 'but it's exactly the same team you supplied before. Yes. No. All right . . . *all right!* Cash on delivery, but we must have them first thing tomorrow morning.' She put down the receiver and looked at Jonty wearily.

'How are you getting on?' he asked.

'You heard,' she said, nodding at the phone. 'How about you?'

'Steve Driscoll's joining us tomorrow morning, on permanent loan until after Le Mans. All the part-timers are available when we want them, including Dennis Morrell. He's coming over tomorrow afternoon.'

'That's good. What about the sponsorship?'

Jonty shifted uneasily on the hard plywood seat. 'Yes, well, Conrad's put in our request to the trustees, but he says it'll take a few days for the money to come through.'

'There's no problem is there?'

'No, no.'

'Because if there is, it's better you tell me straight away. It will be tough, but I can still try to make other arrangements elsewhere.'

'I don't want you to do that,' Jonty said quietly.

'Do what?'

'You know what I mean . . . Glaser.'

Angelica slapped her pen down on the pile of invoices. 'Look Jonathan, if you don't come up with money I've got to get it any way I can. Glaser have already agreed to loan us engines. Maybe they will give us some extra backing.'

'It's not the factory I'm talking about. It's . . . it's Fitch.'

'What about Alex?'

'You know what I mean.'

'No, I don't know what you mean,' Angelica said, her Austrian accent suddenly very strong. 'I think you had better tell me just what you are saying.'

'That bastard's using you!' Jonty blurted out. 'Making you pay for everything he gives us.'

In the last few weeks Angelica's tan had rapidly faded, and now it wasn't deep enough to hid the livid flush on her cheeks. 'Don't you *dare* talk about Alex like that! He has been really helpful to me . . . to us.'

'Don't give me that! I know bloody well what sort of creep he is!'

'And don't you forget I came to you for help first,' Angelica said bitterly.

Jonty reddened and looked down at his knees. 'Well I don't want you to ask him for anything else. Just show me the account books, and I'll make sure we've got what we need until the sponsorship comes through.'

'Here!' Angelica said, pulling out some ledgers, and slamming them down on the desk.

'I'll take them home and look at them,' Jonty said, avoiding her eyes as he picked them up and walked to the door.

He had already opened it when Angelica called out to him.

'Jonty.'

'Yes?'

'What was the longest race you ever did?'

'Six hours.'

'Well listen to me,' she said gently. 'You must start training for Le Mans now. At least one hour running or cycling a day, building up to two hours next week. And try to get plenty of sleep; you must start storing it up now, like charging a battery.'

Jonty stood in the open doorway looking back at her. The window behind her silhouetted her head and shoulders in the late afternoon light. Her strong-featured face was shadowy, but he could read the concern on it.

'I'll remember that,' he said.

Just after half-past-seven Jonty unlocked the door of his Fulham flat and walked into the bedroom. Lindsey was sitting at the dressing table in her bra and panties. She carried on making up as he slumped down on the bed behind her.

'Where've you been?' she demanded without turning round, her petulant blue eyes staring at him in the mirror.

'In Reading, trying to put the show on the road.'

'We're meant to be at Lloyd and Amanda's at eight.'

Jonty stripped off his pullover and dropped it on the bed beside him. 'Listen, would you mind if we didn't go out tonight? Their dos always go on till breakfast, and there's something I've got to look at before tomorrow morning.'

Lindsey spun round, her baby face suddenly hard with anger. 'Christ, you come back at God knows when with some cock and bull story, and then say you're too tired to go out. Well I've got a pretty good idea what's going on in Reading! I'm going out whether you're coming or not!'

A few minutes later she flounced out of the bedroom, and slammed the front door behind her.

Eighteen

RICO GLASER walked down the office corridor with his middle-aged secretary fussing along beside him.

'But this is the *regular* mid-week board meeting,' Frau Rabensteiner said exasperatedly, handing him several cardboard folders.

'Yes, yes, but I can't remember everything,' Rico said, taking the files in one hand and opening the boardroom door with the other.

The five directors seated round the circular table turned to look at the latecomer. Then to Rico's amazement a smiling Curtis Stockwell stood up and began to clap enthusiastically. The others followed suit. Rico stared at them, wondering what the hell he had forgotten now – his birthday?

'Congratulations!' the American said.

'Brilliant!' Norbert Dürr added, advancing to meet him and giving him a bear hug.

Rico smelt an unpleasant mixture of toothpaste and cigar smoke as the suave finance director gave an impersonation of a Russian leader's greeting. He held his breath until Dürr let him go and went back to his chair. Rico sat down too.

'By this agreement with the German distributor,' Dürr went on pompously, 'you have brought unprecedented security to our company.'

Now Rico knew what they were talking about. Stockwell had produced a new agreement for the Glaser distributors. They had to accept a minimum quota of cars over a three year period, and if they didn't take them they could lose their dealership. The German importer who had just visited the factory had been horrified by it, but Rico had pointed out a clause making the penalty discretionary. He, Rico, gave his old friend his personal word that they would not be unreasonable. And the German, their second biggest customer, had signed. Rico hadn't thought it such a big deal, but Stockwell and Dürr obviously did.

'I want to tell you Rico,' the American said, 'honestly and sincerely, that I believe only you could have achieved this. There's a high level of initial resistance to minimum purchase quotas which can only be overcome by personal confidence. *You* provided that vital ingredient.'

Rico knew it was gross flattery, but he felt his lips bending upwards into a smile. What a turnaround Stockwell had made in his attitude towards him in the last few weeks.

'Now for the American!' Dürr said with relish.

'The American?'

'Darrell Rosenberg's coming over in ten days' time,' Stockwell said. 'If you can get him to sign a similar distributor's agreement for the States we'll have pre-bought production runs large enough to put us in profit from those two deals alone. Can you imagine what that means?'

'Yes,' Rico said, still trying to put the management jargon into plain German.

'Subject to a comparative population multiple of course.'

'Of course.'

Norbert Dürr leaned forward over the round beechwood table. 'This is the big one, Rico. If you can pull it off . . . but perhaps we are putting too much responsibility on your shoulders?'

'Rosenberg is an old friend of mine,' Rico said expansively. 'Just leave it to me again.'

'Oh don't worry,' Stockwell said quietly, 'we will.' A strange smile flickered across his lips.

A sudden thought struck Rico. 'Ten days' time?' he asked. 'Isn't that the week of the Le Mans 24-hour race?'

'Why yes, I believe it is,' Stockwell said. 'But this is *much* more important. And you needn't worry – Alex Fitch and I are going to represent the company there.' The malicious smile reappeared on his lips and stayed there.

'Now wait a minute!' Rico said angrily. 'Every year I go to the 24 Hours.'

'But this year you are needed here,' Dürr said stonily. 'We have all seen that. Surely there can be no argument?'

Rico shook his head unhappily. 'I suppose not.'

Jonty parked his Lotus under the lean-to, and grimaced as he climbed stiffly out of the low-slung car. A week of morning and evening runs had made him immeasurably fitter, but there was a price to pay. He shook his legs to loosen his aching thigh and calf muscles, and then walked towards the workshop.

Inside it, the car looked totally different from the stark aluminium tub he had seen just over a week ago. Now the engine and gearbox were attached behind the cockpit, and suspension arms and brake pipes sprouted from all four corners. Five mechanics were working on it, including Dennis. He was lying on his back inside the cockpit with his legs poking out of the door. Ian Mottram looked up and grinned at Jonty.

'All right, all right; what d'you need now?' Jonty asked with mock weariness.

The lanky mechanic was just about to reply when Steve Driscoll butted in.

'I'll deal with this, Ian. You get on with the fuel lines,' the bearded chief mechanic said abruptly, hurrying round the car and blocking Jonty's path to it. 'We're all right at the moment. Bit of a sweat on over bodywork, but Angelica's dealing with it, thank you very much.'

Jonty peered round his shoulders at the car, but Driscoll's stance made it quite clear he didn't want any interference.

'All right,' Jonty said, turning round and walking back into the yard.

161

He hesitated outside the office. After a week of working with Angelica he thought the embarrassment would have eased between them; but whenever he saw her, a complex of emotions that he couldn't put into words clutched at his heart and brain. He opened the door and felt them again as he looked at her. She was sitting behind the desk, telephone cradled between head and shoulder as usual.

'Promises, promises!' she exploded, slamming down the receiver. 'They told me they would deliver the bodywork yesterday, and still it is not here!'

'Will we have it in time?' Jonty asked.

'For sure! They make us pay in advance, so now if they don't deliver they are thieves!' She pushed a pile of invoices across the desk. 'Five more payments to make today I'm afraid. Have we enough money?'

Jonty looked through them. 'Yes, we can pay these,' he said, pulling a chequebook out of his bomber jacket pocket.

Angelica narrowed her eyes suspiciously, and strained to read the name over the space for his signature. 'But that's your own chequebook,' she said.

'Errr, yes, that's right. I'm bridging Conrad's sponsorship. No problem.'

But Jonty didn't fill in the balance on the cheque's stub. He didn't have a red pen anyway, and he'd have needed one to fill it in correctly.

As Jonty left the office and crossed the yard, he heard the door scrape open behind him. He turned round to see Dennis sneaking out of the lavatory.

'Could I 'ave a word with you?' the chubby Londoner hissed, hurrying up to him.

'Sure. What's the problem?'

Dennis sighed. 'It's Sharon, my missus. She's been fantastic about me coming here and helping again, but she flat refuses to let me go to Le Mans.'

'Is money the problem, because we're going to pay you all that week you know?'

162

Dennis shook his head. 'No, it's not that. She's scared. I haven't heard from that nutter Cambell since Silverstone, but she still thinks he's going to do something to me.'

'Would it help if I talked to her? Told her we'd hold your hand there?'

'Might do. Would you mind Jonty?'

'No problem. I'm going into town now to see my accountant. Tell me where you live, and I'll go and see her after that.'

The Italian restaurant Rupert Fisher had suggested for a lunchtime meeting was near his offices on Chiswick High Street. Rupert's father had been one of the original trustees. When he died his son, a partner in his accountancy practice, had taken his place in the trust, while doubling as the Church family accountant.

Jonty arrived five minutes early and eased his aching muscles under a corner table by the front window. He pushed back the green-and-red curtains a little so that he could watch the pavement, and shortly afterwards saw Rupert Fisher striding towards him. He was a tall man in his early forties, with an almost permanently concerned expression on his bespectacled face. It brightened up as he entered the restaurant and spotted Jonty, and he greeted him with genuine warmth. An Italian waiter rushed to their table with menus, and waited for their orders.

'Well, what can I do for you,' Rupert said when they had been left alone.

'Give me some advice,' Jonty told him. 'You may have heard I'm winding up my sportswear business.'

Rupert Fisher nodded. 'Yes. Conrad told me you'd decided to work with him, and I must say I'm delighted.'

'Work *with* him?'

'Yes. You haven't changed your mind have you?'

'No, of course not,' Jonty said quickly. He picked up some ledgers from the seat beside him, and put them on the table in front of the accountant. 'The thing is I've been trading for under a year, and I'm showing a profit. Will I have to present accounts to the revenue people, and pay tax on them?'

Rupert Fisher thumbed through the books for a few minutes. 'My compliments,' he said in a mildly surprised tone. 'Right up to date, and just how I advised you to keep them. Any outstanding debtors and creditors?'

'Yes,' Jonty said, handing him some typed sheets of paper. 'There's also a list of undelivered orders, but I've found an import agent who'll complete them and split the commission with me. The final figure on the debtors' list is an estimate to cover that.'

'Hmmm,' Fisher went. 'We should be able to . . . ummm . . . *avoid* unnecessary taxation. Give me a day to look at it more closely though.'

The waiter returned with their first course, and they let him serve them before talking again.

'I must say,' Fisher said, spooning out avocado and prawns, 'I'm delighted you're joining forces with Conrad. *Relieved* might be a better word.'

'Oh? Why's that?'

Fisher chewed thoughtfully before answering. 'The business badly needs some fresh thinking.'

'The garages?'

'What else are we talking about?'

'Nothing. I'm just not quite clear what you mean.'

'Of course, you've hardly been involved with them at all until now have you. Well, they're just not producing the turnover to support their overheads.'

'And what d'you think needs doing about that?'

Rupert Fisher wiped his mouth with his napkin. 'I don't know the trade well enough, so I can't say whether a new range would solve the problem or not. But in my opinion the time has come to sell at least half of the outlets. Some of them are pretty dilapidated, but your father bought prime sites, and I don't think there'd be too much difficulty in finding buyers, even in the current economic climate.'

Jonty stared at him in astonishment. 'Sell half the garages! I knew the business had been hit by the recession, but are things really that bad?'

'I'm afraid so. Without some drastic action pretty soon you might well go under.'

'But why hasn't Conrad done something already?'

Fisher pursed his lips. 'You should know your brother better than I do. He seems to think that doing what I suggest would be an admission of failure, proof that he's not as competent as your father was. That's not necessarily true of course. Times change, businesses have to change with them, but he seems to see it that way.'

'And what about the request we put in to the trustees?'

'We granted £100,000 immediately, because we know there are structural improvements that have to be made. Why are you staring at me?'

'Immediately?' Jonty asked.

'Yes. After all, the trust owns the properties, and we've enough confidence in their value to feel we're not just throwing it away. Didn't Conrad tell you?'

'Aaah . . . yes,' Jonty said. 'There's so much going on at the moment that I'm getting a little confused, that's all.'

The first time the doorbell rang Sharon glanced at her wristwatch and then carried on ironing in the living room. Midafternoon. Dennis was in Reading helping the Church team for the day, so it couldn't be him. Probably the delightful gang of little boys who liked to get her to the door, and then scream obscene suggestions as they fled down the stairs.

When it rang again, Sharon propped up the iron and walked down the corridor, massaging her swollen belly with both hands.

'Who is it?' she demanded through the closed door.

'Jonty Church. Dennis is helping us . . .'

'Oh Christ!' Sharon said in a panicky voice. She fumbled with the latch and yanked the door open. 'What's he done now?'

'Nothing. He's fine. I just wanted a chat with you.'

Sharon breathed a sigh of relief. 'Come in,' she said, smoothing down her maternity smock as she led the way back to the living room. 'Like a cup of tea or coffee?'

'Love some coffee,' Jonty said, sitting down on the battered brown sofa.

After a while Sharon carried in a tray and sat down in one of the armchairs. 'Sorry about that. It's just that living with Den I'm always expecting trouble.'

'Is that why you don't want him to go to Le Mans?'

Sharon's big blue eyes assessed him shrewdly. 'So that's what you've come about.'

Jonty nodded. 'I'm not going to lie to you. I want to find out what happened to my brother. That's why I've put the team back together exactly as it was, including Dennis.'

'I know,' Sharon said, handing him a cup of coffee and a plate with a slice of sponge cake on it. 'It was me who made Dennis tell you what happened at Silverstone, and I'm really grateful to you for not going to the police. I can take him working for you at Reading. It's just the thought of him going off to France for a week . . . me sitting here wondering what he's up to, *knowing* if there's trouble he'll be mixed in it. He's so bloody *stupid!*'

'No he's not,' Jonty said. 'Your husband's a really talented electrician, and I'm not saying that just to get round you. Everyone in the team knows it, except him.'

Sharon smiled almost shyly. 'It's nice of you to say that, want me to be proud of him I mean. But I know Den too well. I really don't think I could stand him going off like that without me.'

Jonty nodded understandingly. Then he bit into the buttery sponge cake, and an ecstatic look came over his face. Strawberry jam and cream squidged over his fingers, and he licked them greedily.

'Like it?' Sharon asked.

'Oh God, I'm meant to be on a diet to get back to fighting weight! Where did you learn to bake like this?'

'My dad runs a pub, and I helped with the food since I was twelve.'

Jonty stopped munching and his eyes widened with sudden inspiration. 'Did you now. Well we're looking for a cook for

166

Le Mans. D'you think you could feed a dozen hungry lads for a week?'

'Dealt with more than 100 a day in the pub,' Sharon said confidently.

'Then how about coming with us to work *and* keep Dennis out of trouble. We'd pay you of course.'

Sharon clapped her hands together and beamed at him. 'You're on!'

Nineteen

ANGELICA WILLED herself to push the accelerator to the floor as the maroon Church C5 arced through Coram Curve. The G-forces built up relentlessly, trying to force her head down onto her left shoulder, but two months of neck exercises have given her the strength to fight back.

Two months, Angelica thought. Was that all it was since she had raced here with Michael? So much had happened since then. *Concentrate!* she told herself – halfway through Coram Curve at 150 miles-an-hour was no place to lose concentration.

Behind her, the turbocharged V6 Glaser engine gave a continuous roar of aggression like a soldier starting a bayonet charge. Then as the track straightened out the sound changed into a series of explosive coughs, as though machine gun fire had ripped through his guts.

'*Verdammte scheisse!*' Angelica snapped, dipping the clutch and blipping the throttle.

What the hell was wrong with the car? This was the last Thursday before Le Mans week, their only chance to test it before it was loaded up on Sunday. For the first twenty laps or so the new car had gone fine, handling as well as or better than its predecessor. The C5 was more responsive to rear end adjustments – probably something to do with the revised and strengthened wing arrangement. But then the misfire had started and defied all attempts to cure it. And Jonty hadn't even had a chance to drive it yet.

Jonty. She could feel herself blush as she thought about him. What the hell was wrong with her? Had she turned into a baby snatcher? Just because he looked like a young Michael, talked like him. Just because . . .

'Concentrate!' Angelica shouted into her helmet. She was way off line and had just passed the braking point into Russell bend. If the misfire hadn't slowed her right down she'd have been in the banking.

Angelica flicked the steering wheel left. Suddenly the engine gave a roar of rude health again, and the back end skidded wildly out of line. Instantly she fed on opposite lock and lifted her foot sharply off the accelerator. The tail rebounded back, effectively aiming her into the second part of the S-bend, and the C5 drifted out onto the uphill pit straight. As soon as the G-load was off it, the misfire set in again.

As she passed the pits Angelica looked right. Her despairing mechanics were standing by the Armco barriers, but she saw only one face clearly – Jonty's. Those eyes! Those same deep brown eyes! A terrible feeling of *déjà vu* stabbed into her, and she looked away quickly, forcing herself to concentrate on the track again.

Jonty walked through the back door of the pit lane garage and climbed into his Lotus parked just outside it. He slammed its door shut and gave a deep sigh of frustration. Having talked himself up to driving a racing car again for the first time since his crash, he had had to stand by whilst attempt after attempt to cure the misfire had failed. Angelica insisted it was unfair and dangerous to let him try the C5 in that condition, but now it was mid-afternoon, and the problem didn't seem to be any nearer solution.

Hearing the muffled sound of an engine, Jonty turned his head. A black Glaser drove through the paddock towards him and parked alongside the Lotus. Conrad climbed out and started towards the pits. Odd, Jonty thought – when he had tried to arrange a meeting with his elder brother over the last few days he had always been too busy to see him. Yet he could take a weekday afternoon off to drive up to Norfolk and watch them test. Jonty felt anger welling up inside him. He jumped out of the Lotus and called out to Conrad, who turned round and smiled at him.

'Hallo Jonty. Couldn't resist popping over to see how it was going.'

'Got a bloody misfire we can't get rid of. I haven't driven it yet.'

'Ah well, bad dress rehearsal, good first night and all that crap,' Conrad said, starting to walk towards the pits again.

'Just before you disappear there's something I want to discuss with you,' Jonty said firmly.

Conrad's smile looked forced now. 'I'm not *disappearing* anywhere Jonty.'

'Well, it's been pretty hard to get hold of you for the last few days, let's put it that way.'

Conrad put his hands on his hips. 'I'm not going to rise to this, but you'd better tell me what's on your mind.'

'Money. I've been trying to get some out of you for a fortnight, and there's still no sign of it.'

'Oh Christ Jonty!' Conrad said, raising his eyes. 'We've been all through this before. These things take time and . . .'

'The £100,000 we requested from the trust was granted almost immediately. Rupert Fisher told me.'

A sudden dark anger showed on Conrad's face. 'What were you talking to him about?'

'Winding up my sportswear business. We talked about the trust as well.'

Conrad shook his head and tried to laugh. 'Jonty, Jonty; you really don't understand the first thing about business do you. Do you think Fisher brings round banknotes in a suitcase? It takes several days for a transfer to clear through into our bank account. Then we've got to make deductions and process the balance through the books as sponsorship.'

'Deductions?'

'Well, who d'you think's paying for Steve Driscoll? And next time you're in the workshop take a look at how much of the stuff has come from us.'

'But Driscoll and the equipment are on loan!'

'So how's the loan repaid? God you're naive!'

'Come on Conrad, I'm getting tired of this game. I've put up *all* the money so far, and I'm badly in the red.'

Conrad lifted his hands despairingly. 'Well don't blame me for that, Jonty. I told you to go and see Church Racing's bank manager and sort out an overdraft.'

'That would have taken time, and you know it.'

'So what's the bank account number?'

Jonty looked puzzled. 'Church Racing's bank account number? I don't know it offhand.'

'Jonty, Jonty,' Conrad laughed, 'I can't take you seriously. You're moaning on about us not getting money to you, but you haven't even given us the account number. If you can bring yourself to phone it through tomorrow we'll transfer some funds to you.'

'Sure?'

'Of course. Even if it's not quite Kosher yet I'll find a way to get you something. Now let's take a look at the car.'

Conrad put a conciliatory hand on his shoulder, but Jonty still looked unhappy . . .

The intermittent sound of the Glaser engine had died altogether. Just then Angelica appeared through the back of their garage, looking thoroughly dejected.

'I'm afraid you're not going to get a drive in it,' she told Jonty. 'We could easily blow the engine if we run it any more. We'll have to take it back to the workshop and strip it down to find out what's wrong.'

Late that afternoon Jonty drove back to London, alone and deeply depressed. He kept asking himself how he had been sucked back into motor racing just one year after his crash, a year in which he'd decided never to race again.

Conrad had tried to persuade him that financing and driving for the team would be some sort of personal tribute to Michael. Jonty could see an element of truth in that, but Rupert Fisher's revelation about the Garages had shaken him. Now he wondered what Conrad's real motives were. He had used Jonty to obtain £100,000 of trust money. On the other hand he was now insisting that he would pass it on to the team as agreed – or part of it.

Then there was Dennis's fantastic story about Ralph Cambell's behaviour at Silverstone. That was what had really drawn Jonty into the whole thing. But there had been no contact from the Lomax team's chief mechanic since then. Why not? Or was it all being saved for Le Mans?

And there was Angelica. What was her interest in all this? At the simplest level, probably a desire to stay in work. Losing a drive must be as soul-destroying as losing a job in any profession, Jonty thought. But there was more to it than that – much more. Why did he think about her so much, yet feel so uneasy when he was actually with her? And why was he so bitter and suspicious of Alex Fitch?

Whatever the answers were, he was going to Le Mans on Tuesday, to race an unknown car on a shatteringly fast circuit he didn't know. It had become a classic setup for a disaster, and just thinking about it made him sweat with apprehension.

Jonty turned the Lotus off Fulham Road. Halfway down the sidestreet of terraced houses he could see Lindsey's yellow Fiat Panda. Its tailgate was up in the air, and as he passed it Lindsey staggered out of the house carrying a large cardboard box. He parked two cars further on and walked back up the pavement towards her.

'Let me help you,' Jonty said, as she struggled to force the box into the overloaded boot. 'Where are you off to?'

'I'm leaving,' Lindsey said. 'Don't try to stop me. I've made up my mind.'

He looked at her without saying anything. An increasingly familiar hardness had taken over her girlish features.

'I mean, what kind of fun is this?' Lindsey went on. 'You come home late every night, go for a run, crash out. We used to have fun, go to parties and things all the time.'

'It's not a game,' Jonty said quietly. 'I haven't raced for a year, and I've got to be fit.'

'Well I'm not hanging around until you get yourself killed,' Lindsey blurted out as she went on ferociously repacking the Panda.

'I thought you wanted me to start racing again.'

'I didn't know it'd be like this.'

'What did you expect?'

'Well . . . you know, going to races, having fun.'

Jonty gave a great sigh and shook his head.

'Anyway, it's not *just* that,' Lindsey added. 'I know what's going on with that Austrian cow.'

'Angelica? Nothing's going on with her.'

'You must think I'm daft or something! And even if it hasn't happened yet, I'm not waiting around for that either!'

Lindsey slammed down the Panda's tailgate, marched past Jonty and threw herself into the driver's seat. Two cars had sandwiched her in, and she had to manoeuvre furiously backwards and forwards to extricate herself. Finally she drove away, leaving a cloud of exhaust fumes behind her.

Jonty stood watching her go, amazed how little it affected him. Lindsey's departure seemed strangely irrelevant. Only Le Mans was important now. The answers to all the questions that were tormenting him had to be there.

And as he realised that, Jonty's courage returned. He *was* right to have become involved. He *had* to have those answers, whatever the cost.

Twenty

THE HARD rock tape came to an end and ejected from the Lotus's cassette player with a sharp click. With his left hand Jonty immediately pulled it out and picked up another one.

'You never told me why you decided to race again,' Angelica said from the passenger seat.

Jonty's hand hovered in front of the cassette slot. He had collected her from Michael's house that Tuesday morning, and driven on to Dover. There they had caught the midday hovercraft across the Channel to Calais, and now they were arcing south-west through France towards Le Mans. So far the music had provided an alternative to conversation, but now he put down the tape.

'Michael,' he said without looking at Angelica. 'I think it's what he'd have wanted.'

'I think there's a lot more to it than that, but I'm not going to push you. I know it's difficult for us to talk. I don't really know why, and maybe you don't either.'

Jonty shook his head.

'Anyway, if you want to tell me about it at any time, I'm ready to listen.'

Jonty glanced at her as though trying to make up his mind about something. Then he changed the subject. 'You never told me how *you* got started in motor racing.'

'Ohhh . . .' Angelica said dismissively.

'Tell me. I'm really interested.'

'Well . . . I was a ski racer.'

'In the Austrian Olympic team.'

'Yes, that's right, but also long before that. I won my first race when I was four.'

'Four!'

'Sure!' Angelica laughed at the memory. 'That was nothing unusual. My father was a ski instructor, so I was on skis as soon as I could walk. I wasn't very happy at home, so ski racing was my escape, I suppose. I was crazy about it, being special, everyone watching.'

'So why did you pack it in?'

'My speciality was downhill,' Angelica said. 'You know, not in and out of lots of gates, but racing down the steepest course they could make. I loved it, but I broke my left leg when I was twenty-one, then twice more the next year. After that I wasn't so fast anymore.'

'Afraid?'

'No, angry that I couldn't do what I'd done before. Girls I'd beaten easily were beating me.'

'And the motor racing? You still haven't told me how that came about.'

Angelica studied Jonty's face as though checking for innuendo. 'I met a young German racing driver. He came to watch the ski races at Kitzbühel. Afterwards he was telling us how difficult car racing was. We were meant to say how wonderful he was, but I told him I could drive much faster, no problem!'

Jonty laughed. 'And he let you try his car?'

'Not right away,' Angelica said with an edge of bitterness in her voice. 'But when he finally did I knew I could be as fast as him, maybe faster. And he was, you know, a rising star.'

'Who was he?'

Angelica glanced at Jonty in the same questioning way before answering. 'Wolfgang Schnering.'

Jonty's foot slipped off the accelerator. 'Schnering! The driver who hit Michael at Silverstone.'

Angelica met his eyes, and nodded.

As they reached the outskirts of Le Mans, Jonty realised that they'd been talking for almost an hour, easily the longest conversation they had ever had. Ahead of them the twelfth-century cathedral dominated the old city, an area of medieval buildings on a high point overlooking the River Sarthe. They crossed a bridge to the south bank, and then the road climbed steeply, passing under the city's massive ramparts.

'You know,' Angelica said, 'it's good we talk like this, because this race is not easy. I can help you if you let me. Maybe we can even be friends this week.'

'I'd like that,' Jonty said quietly.

The road emerged in a large square with the cathedral to one side, and a large fifties theatre ahead of them.

'The Place des Jacobins,' Angelica said. 'We must bring the car here tomorrow for scrutineering.'

She directed Jonty round a one way system that at first led them away from the square, but then turned back towards it. Both sides of the final street were walled in by weathered stone houses, their rooflines enlivened by dormer windows. Angelica pointed to a three-storey building with a square archway in the middle of it. Moulded white letters above it read HOTEL DE LA PAIX.

Jonty drove the Lotus into a courtyard and parked under the shade of a towering elm tree. They walked back to a small door under the archway that opened into the hotel's reception area. An ancient staircase led to the first floor. Tall windows overlooked the courtyard.

A tiny Frenchwoman walked through the doorway behind the reception desk and smiled at them. She had short, wiry hair and a determined face, but as she looked at Jonty her head suddenly jerked back in shock.

'*Ahhh . . . je suis* Jonathan Church, *et c'etait* Madamoiselle Hofer,' Jonty said with an atrocious accent. '*Nous avons reservées les chambres . . .*'

The birdlike woman came round the counter, her jaw twitching with emotion. '*Mon pauvre! Mon pauvre!*' she said, and embraced him.

Her head only came up to Jonty's stomach, and she started to cry and babble in French at the same time. He turned to Angelica in bewilderment.

'What's she saying?'

Angelica put her hands gently on the woman's shoulders as she translated. 'She says your brother stayed here every year for five years. She and her husband became very fond of him. They were looking forward to seeing him this year, and then her husband read . . .'

Suddenly Angelica started to cry as well, and the French-woman let go of Jonty and turned towards her. Angelica made some explanation, and then the two of them clung together, weeping piteously. Jonty stared at them, not knowing quite what to do. An old man had joined them in the reception area. He advanced towards Jonty and shook hands gravely.

'I am Paul Chaumond,' he said in slow, heavily accented English. 'This is my wife Yvette. We were so sad to read about your brother's accident.'

'Thank you Monsieur Chaumond,' Jonty said. 'What shall we do about these two?'

'Leave them for some moments. Let me show you your room.'

Jonty had been put on the second floor overlooking the courtyard. The corridor and the rooms on the other side of it separated him from the road, so that only the occasional rumble of a heavy lorry reached him. There was a bottle of Vichy water and a bar of chocolate on the table beside a huge old bed. The room had obviously been larger until a third of it had been partitioned off to make a modern bathroom.

Fifteen minutes later there was a knock on the door, and when Jonty opened it Angelica was standing outside.

'I'm sorry about that,' she said.

'Don't be silly.'

'It was just when Madame Chaumond started crying, it reminded me . . .'

'Don't apologise. I was rather moved by it,' Jonty said, putting a reassuring hand on Angelica's arm.

At his touch the atmosphere between them changed completely. It was as though the contact had created an electric tension so powerful that neither of them could speak.

'Let's go and see if the team's arrived safely,' Angelica managed to say finally.

Outside the hotel they climbed into the Lotus again and joined the late afternoon traffic. Angelica directed him to the ring road that circled the southern outskirts of Le Mans, and they drove slowly round it until she told him to turn left onto the Route Nationale to Tours. It rose uphill through bland suburbs and then, as they gave way to a vista of flat wooded countryside, the route dipped under a flyover.

'Tertre Rouge,' Angelica said, pointing to their right.

Jonty glanced out of his side window. Barriers closed off what was clearly part of a motor racing circuit, but they were still driving down an ordinary two lane road. The Lotus was right behind a petrol tanker, so he backed off the accelerator and hung back to get a better view. The Route Nationale dipped gently downhill and then curved out of sight after about half a mile. On their left was a long line of tall, stark elm trees. So this was the famous Mulsanne Straight, Jonty thought. Not so special after all.

Then as they took the curve the tree-lined road stretched unbroken to the horizon, mile after mile of it like an artist's exercise in perspective. Jonty caught his breath.

'Stay off the white lines,' Angelica warned, pointing to the roadside. 'If you try to cut the corner there you'll tear your tyres and they will blow.'

Beyond the broken white lines was a yard of tarmac at a slightly lower level – obviously the remains of a previous surface. After that there was another yard of rough hardcore, and then double Armco barriers. Jonty was hypnotised by the grey strips of cold steel. It would be bad enough slamming into them at seventy miles-an-hour, but what would it be like at two or three times that speed – 210mph? Add another twenty miles-an-hour to that, and you'd got the C5's top speed down the straight.

'Lift off the accelerator twice along here to let the turbochargers release pressure and cool down,' Angelica said.

'Twice?'

'Sure. It's six kilometres long, and you're running absolutely flat out most of the time. Just two quick lifts or the turbochargers will explode.'

Jonty did a mental calculation – six kilometres at 360 kilometres-an-hour. That meant he'd be on the Mulsanne Straight for a minute. Sixty long seconds running flat out, dead straight, in which he could check the instruments . . . or start to imagine what would happen if something did go wrong. And he'd be taking it a couple of hundred times in the race. Suddenly the unique challenge of Le Mans was a nerve-jangling reality.

For several more minutes they drove straight towards the horizon. The road undulated over a series of crests, only the occasional restaurant or factory interrupting the thick tree-lines on either side of it. It came as a shock when he crested a rise and found a sharp right-hander immediately after it. Jonty's bulging eyes must have given his thoughts away, because Angelica gave a metallic laugh.

'The Mulsanne kink, and yes, you do take it flat out – but not the first time!'

The Route Nationale crested another brow, and then a series of arrow-shaped boards behind the Armco barriers pointed to Mulsanne corner.

'Touch your brakes with your left foot as soon as you're over that last rise,' Angelica said. 'That warms the discs. Then brake at least three hundred metres out or you won't make the turn – it's *much* slower than you think, and you've got to read your pit signal immediately after it.'

Red-and-white castellated kerbing made the right-angled corner look more like part of a racing circuit. Immediately after it on the right hand side was a low white wall with a row of open-fronted concrete stalls behind it.

'The Mulsanne signalling pits,' Angelica said. 'They're connected to the main pits by telephones. *If* they're working you get a signal from someone standing on the wall.'

Jonty looked ahead again. A series of straights and gentle

right-handed curves worked the circuit back towards Le Mans. This section was still a two-lane road though, and didn't appear to be much slower than the Mulsanne Straight. In a few places the Armco barrier was further back from the track. Finally it dived right and left through a banked section and slowed dramatically at Arnage corner.

There, Jonty turned sharp right and started along yet another straight tree-lined section. Suddenly Angelica pointed to a series of white plastic bollards blocking a turn that curved away to their right.

'Don't follow the road – drive between those.'

As Jonty steered through them, the circuit changed character completely. From one second to another he was off the country roads and onto a smooth-surfaced track that looked much like any modern motor racing circuit. One neatly radiused turn led to another.

'Faster than it looks, but stay off the kerbs,' Angelica said. 'And watch out for grass here.'

'Grass?'

'From the drivers who go over the kerbs and mow the tracksides!'

As the track straightened out, Jonty could see grandstands ahead of him. There was a final double chicane to make absolutely sure the cars slowed down, and then they were on the pit straight. Grandstands towered up on their left, whilst to their right a low concrete wall separated the track from the pit lane. Beyond that was a long run of open-fronted pits topped by viewing boxes and galleries.

'Turn right at the end of the pit wall,' Angelica said. 'There's a way up to the paddock.'

'But where's the Dunlop Bridge and the funfair?' Jonty asked. 'They're the only bits I'd recognise, and we haven't seen them yet.'

'Just round the next corner on the final stretch to Tertre Rouge. Don't worry, you'll be sick of the sight of them soon!'

Jonty turned at the end of the wall and crossed the narrow pitlane. A road curved up to the paddock, a long rectangular strip as wide as a football pitch behind the pits. Already it had been turned into a motor racing caravanserai. Transporters and their awnings, motorhomes and caravans, and bungalow-sized tents covered every available space leaving only constricted access roads around them. This end of the paddock was on a grassy slope, and seemed to have been allocated to the less well-heeled teams. As they reached the flat, tarmac lower section, there was a distinct increase in opulence. Here the teams seemed to have colour-coordinated every piece of equipment down to the monkey bikes they used for speeding round the paddock.

A smell of hot pasta wafted through Jonty's open window – the Lancia team mechanics were taking a meal break at a long table, complete with wicker-wrapped Chianti bottles. Almost the whole of the far end of the paddock was taken up by the works Porsche team, with precisely organised areas for working, resting and eating. Jonty wrinkled his nose with distaste at the sour vegetable smell coming from their mobile kitchen. Then as they turned up the access road that ran parallel to the pits he sniffed appreciatively again.

'Fried bacon! Bet that's our lot!'

Twenty yards further on they spotted their maroon transporter, its cream side-awning protecting the C5, and half a dozen maroon-overalled mechanics working round it. Beside that was the team's motorhome. A taped up notice on its open door said FRYING TONIGHT in big red letters.

Jonty parked the Lotus opposite their encampment, and as he and Angelica walked across the access road the British-fry-up smell grew stronger and stronger. Steve Driscoll looked round, and then stood up to greet them, a smile on his bearded face for once.

'Hallo Steve. How's it going?' Angelica asked.

'We'll have the car ready tonight,' the chief mechanic said cheerfully. 'All we've got to do tomorrow is take it into town for scrutineering.'

Jonty was acknowledging the handwaves and calls of the mechanics. He spotted Sharon through the open door of the

181

motorhome, and she turned round and grinned at him. 'I've never seen this lot so happy,' Jonty said.

'We've got Dennis's lass to thank for that,' Driscoll told them. 'First decent grub I've ever had here!'

They were inspecting the immaculate C5 when Alex Fitch breezed in with Curtis Stockwell.

'So there you are Angelica!' Fitch called out in his plummy voice. 'Let me introduce Curtis Stockwell, Glaser's vice-president.'

Angelica shook hands and studied the smartly-suited American. He was smiling down at her, but there was a hint of amusement in his dark eyes, almost of mockery.

'All set for scrutineering?' Fitch asked. 'We want both our teams over the first hurdle without any falls.'

'I'm sure Miss Hofer's taken care of that as well, Alex,' Stockwell said. 'After all, she twisted you round her finger to get here didn't she.'

Fitch's fat face went a brighter shade of red as he spluttered denials. Angelica looked coldly at the American.

'Just a joke Miss Hofer. We're delighted to have two teams here instead of one. It gives us a much better chance of achieving the result we're after.'

'Which is what?'

'Why, winning the race of course.'

'Of course,' Angelica said coldly.

Alex Fitch began to back away. 'Yes, well, we'd better go and see how the others are getting on. See you later Angelica.'

Jonty waited until Dennis climbed into the transporter to fetch something, and then intercepted him as he climbed out of it again.

'Anything happened yet?' he asked in a low voice.

The stocky Londoner shook his head. 'Quiet as the grave so far.'

Further up the paddock, Ralph Cambell made a useful discovery. He could walk round the back of the Lomas team's transporter, past the adjacent caravan, and see the front half of the Church Team's C5. More importantly he could see the mechanics working on it. One of them was Dennis Morrell.

He wanted a word with him. In private.

Twenty-One

FOR THE second time in a week Jonty stood around waiting to drive the C5; but this time the fierce afternoon sun made him sweat inside his quilted red race-suit.

The car had been scrutineered near the Place des Jacobins in Le Mans that Wednesday morning. After two hours of checks on everything from weight and dimensions to fuel tank capacity, it had been passed as complying with Group C regulations. The vital sticker was attached to the maroon bodywork, and then the mechanics brought it back to the paddock to ready it for Wednesday evening's practice session.

At exactly six o'clock Angelica had been in the middle of a fifty-five car train leaving the pitlane and thundering out onto the circuit for the first time. The whole team waited on tenterhooks. Would they have another utterly frustrating repeat of the Snetterton fiasco? But four minutes later the maroon car roared past them already well up with the leading bunch, and Angelica started her first flying lap. She completed that in three minutes thirty-eight seconds, and suddenly the Church pit was full of grinning faces. Angelica proceeded to come into the pits for a series of minor adjustments, and then better her lap time until it was down to a superb three minutes thirty-one seconds – within sight of Jacky Ickx's qualifying record in a Porsche 956. After an hour she came in again to hand over to Jonty.

He felt ill at ease even as he was inserting himself legs first

184

into the cramped and unfamiliar cockpit. The seat felt lumpy and nothing seemed to be in the right position. Steve Driscoll leant into the cockpit, and together they struggled to move the seat back a bit. When the team manager pulled the safety harness tight, a crutch strap trapped one of Jonty's testicles. The spasm of pain nearly made him vomit into his balaclava.

'You all right?' Driscoll asked.

Jonty tried to answer, but only managed a nod. Driscoll stepped back and slammed down the driver's door, leaving him alone. He felt as though he was trapped in a tiny green-house. The struggle to adjust the seat had added to the intense heat in the stationary car. Stinging sweat dripped into his eyes, blurring his vision as he tried to remember the hot-engine start procedure. When he looked up from the instru-ments Driscoll was standing in front of the car, whirling his index finger round in the start-engine signal.

At the second attempt he managed to fire up the Glaser engine. Jonty ground the short gearlever into first gear with his right hand. Then he let his foot off the racing clutch too quickly and the C5 lurched forward and stalled. Blinking sweat out of his eyes he tried again. This time he gave the engine more revs, but the short travel of the clutch pedal caught him out for the second time. In front of the car Driscoll closed his eyes as if in prayer and flopped his hand round in a weary parody of the start-engine signal. At last Jonty managed to get the car away from the pit in a series of kangaroo hops.

After the pit lane the track curved right and climbed gently uphill. Ahead of him he could see the Dunlop Bridge, like an oversized tyre straddling the track. As Jonty drove under it the circuit dipped sharply downhill. At that moment a red-and-white blur screamed past on his left at about twice the speed he was doing. He hadn't even seen it coming! He jerked the steering wheel right and almost collided with a green car that he hadn't spotted either. As the two cars shot down the hill ahead of him Jonty's frightened eyes checked his wing-mirrors, and found they weren't properly adjusted for him.

At the bottom of the hill a fast S-bend led him to Tertre Rouge, and then he was accelerating cautiously onto the Mulsanne Straight. Jonty moved to the right of the track and let car after car overtake him. Two low and brutal looking Porsche 956s came past, and then one of the more sculptured works Lancias. Halfway along the straight even a Group B Porsche went by, looking more like a wide-wheeled road car than a racer. With a guilty start Jonty realised he hadn't even got his right foot hard down.

He glanced at the Armco barriers, just a blurred silvery-grey line at this speed, and his imagination went into over-drive – what if . . .

The C5 crested a brow and suddenly the kink was right in front of him, looking so tight that it seemed he must fly off into the trees ahead of him. Jonty snatched his foot off the accelerator and the back end twitched in protest. He gave the brake pedal a panicky stab and tried to move over to the left of the track. Then he was in the kink, off balance and veering from side to side as he fought to balance the car. A yellow car flashed past on his right, its driver shaking his fist at him furiously.

Jonty braked at the 500 metre arrow-board before Mulsanne Corner. He was going so slowly by the time he reached the 200 metre marker that he speeded up again, only to misjudge the bend and force a Lola onto the grassy track-side.

'What the hell am I doing here?' Jonty asked himself out loud, as he accelerated away from the corner behind another fist-waving driver. He was there for all the wrong reasons – to play amateur detective, because he felt guilty. But motor racing was a cruel sport that made no allowances. The truth was he just didn't belong on the track anymore. Thoroughly demoralised, Jonty carried on, trying at least to find some rhythm and keep out of everyone's way.

Four laps later he pulled off into the pit lane. It was only about three cars wide, and each pit had just enough room for theirs in front of it. Mechanics, photographers and hangarson swarmed around any car that came in. Marshals, blowing whistles and waving flags like demented linesmen, struggled vainly to keep them inside the yellow centreline. Across the track the spectators in the grandstands and terraces were calm, but the pits gave the impression of a football pitch invasion.

Jonty slowed to walking pace and hunted for his pit, more like an open-fronted concrete stall. When he found it he had to park at a diagonal because the car in front of the next pit was taking up too much space. Angelica opened the driver's door.

'What sort of times was I doing?' he asked miserably.

'Never mind that. All you should be doing is getting used to racing again. The times will come later.'

Jonty opened the safety harness buckle over his abdomen with a savage twist. 'Come off it – I was bloody hopeless!'

'What are you doing?' Angelica asked. 'Stay in the car! You *must* have more car time!'

But Jonty was already levering himself out of the cockpit. 'You carry on,' he said, pushing her aside and stepping onto the tarmac. 'Maybe a quiet think'll do me some good.'

Three pits further up, Derek Lomax stared unhappily down at his stopwatch as the brown-and-beige Glaser-Lomax wailed past with Harvey Trip at the wheel. The two drivers on either side of him looked equally unimpressed. Trip and Schnering had been joined for the 24-hour race by a tough looking professional called Helmut Hahn. His flat and scarred face looked as though it had been punched through a windscreen, which was exactly what had happened to it.

'What time?' Wolfgang Schnering asked.

'Three minutes fifty,' Lomax said.

Wolfgang muttered German obscenities. 'So now we have two handicaps.'

'Two?'

'The car handles fine, but it's just not fast enough on the straight. And Trip is going to cost us twenty seconds a lap when he's in the damned car!'

Lomax turned to glare at his number one driver. 'Look Wolfgang, we've been all through this before: no Harvey Trip, no money, so for Christ's sake change your tune will you? There's nothing we can do about it now.'

'Yes there is,' Wolfgang hissed. 'Tell him the truth, break his leg; I don't care how you do it, but keep him out of the damned car! What do you say Helmut?'

The German shrugged his shoulders. 'You're paying me the same whether I drive eight hours or twelve. But if you want a good result you better listen to Wolfgang. I was behind the Glaser-Church on the Straight one time, and it ran away from me.'

'Ah yes,' Derek Lomax said, 'with Angelica Hofer driving. Jonathan Church is nothing like as fast.'

'Yet,' Helmut Hahn said. 'I raced against that boy before he had his accident and he was incredibly fast, *too* fast. A good crash was just what he needed. Now he will be just a little slower and a thousand times safer.'

'He still looked scared when he got out of the car just now,' Lomax said, glancing down the pit lane.

Helmut Hahn's eyelids formed thin slits, and he seemed to be seeing something far away. 'I was right behind him when he tried to fly at the Nürburgring. I don't know how frightened he was, but I had to throw away my pants afterwards.'

There was a guffaw of laughter from behind them, and they turned to see Alexander Fitch chortling at the story. 'Judging by young Church's performance this morning, he still hasn't got over it!'

'Give him a few laps,' Hahn said coldly.

'He's had them, and he's doing about as well as Harvey! That was my problem when I last raced here you know, a slow co-driver.'

'When was that?' Hahn asked. '1930?'

Fitch's answer was drowned by shrill whistle blasts as another car came up the pit lane. For some time it was obscured by the crowd, but then the Glaser-Lomax appeared trailing oily smoke. Harvey Trip steered it in front of their pit, switched off the engine and opened the door.

'Some kind of oil leak I think,' he said, pulling off his helmet and balaclava. As Derek Lomax hurried to the back of the car he turned to his co-drivers. 'Sorry I'm not faster, you guys, but I'm beginning to get the message. If one of you could talk me round the circuit I think I could find ten seconds.'

Wolfgang opened his mouth to speak, but Alex Fitch jumped in first. 'More welly!'

The Californian turned toward him. 'I beg your pardon.'

'I said more welly. That's all you need old boy. I was watching you in the Esses, and you're just not giving it enough stick. The whole secret's to get your boot in good and hard as soon as you turn in. Then you've go to . . .'

Fitch's right foot pumped an imaginary accelerator and his hands twirled an invisible steering wheel as he talked. Helmut Hahn caught Wolfgang's eye, and their cheeks ballooned as they fought to suppress laughter. Harvey Trip wasn't so amused. He looked coldly at Fitch, waiting until he'd talked his way down the Mulsanne Straight. Despite his cream race-suit the Californian no longer looked like a middle-aged amateur racer out of his depth, more like a self-made millionaire used to demolishing people who got in his way.

'Someone did tell me your job at Glaser,' Trip drawled, 'but I've clean forgotten. As far as I'm concerned though you're their Sexual Director.'

'Sexual Director?' Fitch asked in a puzzled voice.

'You got it, Fitch – when I want your *fucking* advice I'll ask for it!'

By 9.30pm the molten sun had burned a hole through the horizon, and the sky had softened to a misty royal blue. Halfway down the pit lane, the famous Le Mans clock topped a set of traffic lights. Now the purple one flashed on, signalling all cars to light up. Even in the half-light their incredibly powerful headlamps hurt spectators' eyes if they looked straight at them.

Quarter of an hour later, Angelica brought the C5 into the pits and climbed out. 'Check the front discs,' she said to Steve Driscoll. 'I think one cracked when the sun went down. Where's Jonty?'

The chief mechanic nodded towards the crowded pit, and Angelica pushed her way through the small opening between the tressle table and the end wall. Jonty was sitting disconsolately on a tyre, and she stopped in front of him.

'They're just checking the discs. When they've done that I want you to finish the session.'

'You carry on until it's set up right,' Jonty said. 'I'll have another go tomorrow.'

'But you've got to have more car time.'

He shook his head dejectedly. 'I'm sorry Angelica, I really am, but whatever I had before my accident's gone. Maybe it's not too late to find another co-driver.'

Angelica looked round to check that no one was listening. Then she squatted down in front of him and put her hands on his shoulders. 'Come on Jonty! What did you expect? That it would be easy, getting used to 650 horsepower? You *will* find your talent again, I promise you, but you have to give it time. Now get back in the car and work at it.'

Jonty lifted his head and tried to smile. 'All right. I'm sorry I'm being so wet about it.'

'You're not. I *know* what it's like to come back after an accident.'

In the last hour of practice the sky turned midnight-blue with a flamingo pink line along the horizon. To Jonty's surprise, his first experience of night racing was easier than he'd expected. The powerful Cibie headlights bored a well-lit tunnel through the traffic – their reflected lights flashed a repeated warning in his wing mirrors as they closed in. Jonty was still braking too early for every corner and squeezing on the power too late, but gradually he was developing a rhythm.

In the pits Angelica looked up at the timekeeper sitting on top of the tressle table at the front of the pit, and asked for his lap chart. He handed it down with a grimace of disappoint-ment, but when Angelica read Jonty's times she gave a little smile. They were still relatively slow, but each lap was about a second faster than the last.

So the fire is still there, Angelica thought, the racer's basic need to go faster, do better. She remembered Michael describing Jonty's driving style before the Nurbürgring crash – the frightening aggression of a twenty-year-old com-bined with staggering car control. Maybe Jonty was maturing into a different kind of driver. Or maybe something would suddenly make the fire flare up again, and he would drive the way he had done before. Suddenly fear gripped Angelica's heart. That mustn't happen. She had to convince him that his steady progress was the right way to go.

At eleven o'clock the chequered flag was shown to signal end of practice, and after a slowing down lap Jonty drove the C5 up the pit lane and back into the paddock. Angelica was waiting for him when he parked it under their transporter's side awning. He climbed out of the hot cockpit in his sweaty race-suit, and began to shiver in the chill night air.

'Good! Really good,' Angelica said.

'What was the best time?'

'Three minutes forty-five.'

Jonty gave a disgusted snort and shook his head.

'Come on,' Angelica said, taking him by the elbow and steering him towards the motorhome. 'Let's change out of our race-suits before we catch pneumonia.'

The motor-home was divided into two sections, the front half nearest the paddock access road for cooking, and the back half for the drivers to change and rest in. Sharon was preparing supper for the team, and Angelica went up to the younger girl and kissed her on the cheek.

'Are you all right? I think you're working too hard.'

'I'm loving it!' Sharon said, waving over Angelica's shoulder at Jonty. 'Should have done something like this months ago.'

Angelica turned and followed Jonty into the back section,

191

closing the concertina partition behind her. Beyond it there were two double bunks on either side of the central corridor. Then a lavatory cubicle and a storage cupboard narrowed the access to three couches arranged in a U at the very end of the motor-home.

'Which bit do you want?' Angelica asked almost shyly.

'Oh . . . ummm . . . you change at the end. Promise I won't look,' Jonty said.

He sat down on one of the lower bunks and began to untie his boots. Angelica walked past him and disappeared from view.

'That was much better,' she called out. 'You were taking off a second a lap, nice and steady, doing just what I hoped you'd do.'

Jonty muttered something but it was lost in his vest as he tugged it over his head.

'What?' Angelica asked, stepping back into the corridor.

'I said fifteen seconds a lap slower than you is hardly . . .' His words trailed off as he looked up at her.

Angelica had stripped down to her bra and panties. Her bronzed skin glistened as though she had just stepped out of the sea. Her muscles were unusually developed for a girl, but her breasts and buttocks were small and firm. Quickly she stepped back out of sight, but not before the stunning, arousing vision of her had burnt itself into Jonty's mind.

'Maybe . . . maybe I can go faster,' he said throatily.

'I *know* you can.'

'Maybe . . .'

'Yes?'

'I was just thinking, maybe we could go and eat somewhere together. Not here I mean – drive into town and find a restaurant.'

Angelica came back into sight, but now she was wearing slacks and a white rollneck pullover. 'That's sweet of you,' she said gently, 'but I'm afraid I've already been asked out to dinner.'

'Oh? Who by?'

She turned away from him before answering. 'Alex Fitch.'

The Church team ate at a long wooden tressle table under the end of the transporter awning furthest from the access road. Dennis was attacking his second helping of plums and custard when Steve Driscoll suddenly snapped his fingers explosively.

'Anyone bring back the cracked discs?'

There was a negative murmuring and a shaking of heads.

'Would you go and fetch them Dennis,' Driscoll said. 'I'd like to take another look at them.'

At the end of the table Dennis grunted and shovelled in the lurid-coloured remains of his pudding. As the youngest mechanic he tended to be used as the Team's Gofer, unless there was an electrical job to be done.

'Cup of tea, two sugars when I get back, love,' he yelled as he scraped back his chair.

Hearing the shout Sharon turned round just in time to see him go.

So did Ralph Cambell three sites further up the paddock.

Dennis crossed the access road to the pits, and walked along the concrete wall separating them from the paddock until he found a gateway. At this time of night there was no official on duty to demand his pass, and so he walked straight through it, across a muddy path and into the passageway behind the pits. This really was the backside of Le Mans. Its muddy, litter-strewn floor ran the full length of the pits, giving access to each stall through a grey metal door. Every few yards large red letters on its damp concrete walls declared DEFENSE ABSOLUE DE FUMER, but the smell of cigarette smoke hung in the air. There was another unmistakable odour – the passageway was too convenient to avoid being used as a urinal.

The overhead lights had been turned out, and Dennis stumbled along it, bumping into support pillars and oil drums, and cursing Steve Driscoll. Finally he found their pit and pushed open its grey metal door. There were still some lights on in the pit lane, and they dimly illuminated the concrete stall. Dennis peered around the shadowy interior and spotted the brake discs in the front left corner. Somebody had slung them under the fuel hose and forgotten them. He crossed the pit and bent to pick them up.

'Hallo Dennis,' a familiar voice said from behind him.

Dennis whirled round. Ralph Cambell was standing sideways on in the doorway so that he could keep his eye on the passageway. In profile like that his face was even more fox-like, with its cunning eyes and pointed nose.

'I don't know if I want to talk to you,' Dennis said.

'Why not? What've I done?' Cambell asked, all injured innocence.

'Not been near me since Silverstone for a start. Not a bloody word! Where's this famous job then, £250-a-week and al! that crap?'

Cambell looked up and down the passageway before answering. 'What did you expect after that crash Dennis? A telegram of appointment for services rendered?'

'I get it. I've done my bit, and now you don't want to know anymore.'

'Not at all, Dennis. It was just a matter of discretion.'

'And I don't know many long words, but that sounds like a polite one for piss off.'

'A grand says it's not.'

Dennis eyes changed from anger to suspicion. 'We are using the same language are we? A thousand notes?'

Cambell nodded. 'That's right Dennis. And all you have to do to earn it is to bring your car to a grinding halt again. It doesn't matter how you do it, sugar in the petrol, loosen an oil bung, only . . .' Cambell grimaced and looked straight at Dennis, 'do me a favour, make it a little less dramatic this time will you?'

Jonty picked up his dirty plates and cutlery and carried them over to the motor-home.

'Thanks Sharon, nice meal,' he said.

'Cup of tea, coffee?'

'No thanks. I'm going back to the hotel. Night all,' Jonty said.

He hardly heard the cheerful response from the table. There was nothing else to do now but go back to the hotel. Bloody Alex Fitch had arrived to claim his prize half an hour earlier, leering with pride at his conquest. His whole attitude towards Angelica made Jonty feel physically sick.

As he trudged disconsolately across the access road, Jonty met Dennis carrying a brake disc in each hand.

'Anything happened yet?' Jonty asked him.

Dennis seemed about to say something, but then he shook his head. 'Quiet as the grave.'

'I wish you'd use another phrase,' Jonty told him.

Twenty-Two

JONTY WAS awakened on Thursday morning by a faint tapping on his window. He threw back the bedclothes, walked to the full length curtains and parted them. Outside sullen grey clouds drifted across a bright blue backdrop. Jonty looked at his wristwatch – 9.30. Angelica had told him to lie-in as long as possible, but he didn't feel like it this morning. He shaved, dressed casually, and left the bedroom.

'*Bonjour Monsieur Jonasan!*' Madame Chaumond sang like a cheerful dawnbird.

He did his best to smile as he walked past her into the breakfast room just off the reception area. Ian Mottram and Alastair Prior were sitting at a table with two of the mechanics he didn't know so well.

'Can I join you?' Jonty asked.

'Sure,' Ian Mottram said, shuffling along the bench seating against the wall.

Jonty sat down beside him. 'Angelica up yet?'

Mike Thomas, one of the newer mechanics, gave a dirty laugh. 'Shouldn't think so. Probably still with Fitchy boy!'

'What d'you mean?' Jonty asked, staring at him.

'He reckoned he was on to a good thing.'

'Leave it!' Ian Mottram hissed.

'No, go on Mike, what d'you mean?' Jonty insisted.

The mechanic's long face split into a knowing smile. 'Well, Fitch was going on about her in our pit yesterday. Said she

196

was the fastest lady in the world, *off* the track as well as on it!'

'Shut up, Mike!' Alastair Prior said.

For a few seconds Jonty just stared at him. Then he stood up and made for the door. 'Think I need a walk before breakfast,' he mumbled as he walked away.

'What did I do? What did I say?' Mike Thomas asked.

'You came last in the European Tact Contest!' Ian Mottram said.

Just before six o'clock that afternoon, Angelica climbed into the C5 in front of the pits to start the second practice session. Fat clouds still sailed across the sky, but they were white and unthreatening.

'Any sign of Jonty?' she asked Steve Driscoll. 'I haven't seen him all day.'

'Ian Mottram has, and he says he'll definitely be here.'

'I hope so,' Angelica said, slipping on the safety harness. 'What the hell is he playing at?'

Alex Fitch was trying to squeeze into the doorway beside the team manager. 'Don't worry about him, darling. Let's see some real fireworks eh?'

Angelica looked away. The clown was trying to get in on everything now! If only he would stay in the background like his mysterious vice-president Curtis Stockwell. Steve Driscoll closed the driver's door and she thought she was on her own, but the great buffoon insisted on kneeling down and leering at her through the side window. A few minutes later, the practice session started, and she gratefully joined the multi-coloured train of cars pulling out onto the circuit.

When Jonty walked into the pit Alex Fitch was waiting for him. 'Where've you been hiding yourself, my lad? I want a word with you.'

Fitch pushed through the crowded stall towards him, put his arm round his back, and steered him towards the back wall. Jonty looked at the pudgy hand on his shoulder with obvious distaste, but Fitch wasn't going to be put off.

197

'I think you and I need a quiet little chat,' Fitch went on in what he obviously thought was a confidential tone. Half the people in the pit craned their necks to hear what was being said. 'If your brother was here, he'd probably be saying this to you, but as he's not I'll have to do it for him.' Fitch's face suddenly registered that he might have been tactless. 'Conrad I mean of course, not Michael. Bad show what happened to him at Silverstone, and no-one was sadder about it than I was, but that's part of motor racing. We've all had to learn to live with it you know, so don't think you're the only one.'

Jonty stared at him in astonishment, brushing Fitch's arm off his shoulder as he did so. 'No, you're going to listen to me,' Fitch said, spreading his legs to block the escape route from the back of the pit. 'At the moment you're proving to be quite a handicap to a certain lady racing driver. In fact I'd say you're quite a handicap to the whole team. And your attitude leaves quite a lot to be desired, if I may say so young man, turning up half an hour late for practice! So I'm suggesting you pull yourself together before you wreck this year's Le Mans for them single-handed. Do you read me?'

Half a dozen amazed faces were glued to the scene as Fitch finished his monologue. Jonty continued to stare at him with an ice cold expression. 'Well, what have you got to say?' Fitch demanded.

At that moment Angelica swung the C5 in front of the pit creating a momentary diversion.

'Get out of my way,' Jonty growled.

'Now wait a minute!'

'Get out of my fucking way, Fitch!' Jonty said, shoving him hard against the side wall and making for the pit lane.

Angelica was out of the car. 'Hallo Jonty. The brakes are much better, and I want you to take it out and . . .'

Jonty grabbed his balaclava and helmet and pushed past her. He almost threw himself into the cockpit, battered the seat back, and yanked the safety harness over his shoulders as though he was trying to tear it out by the roots. In the right-side wing-mirror he could see Angelica saying something to

198

two mechanics. They fiddled about with the rear wing. He turned his head to shout something at her, but Driscoll closed the driver's door on him. Then the chief mechanic went to the front of the car and gave him the start-engine signal.

Fuck Angelica! Fuck Fitch! Fuck the lot of them! Jonty thought, blasting the engine into life and punching the gear-lever into first. He set off down the pitlane in a smoky blur of wheelspin. Then he was out on the circuit and accelerating as hard as he could towards the Dunlop Bridge. What did they want out of him? The sort of performance he'd put on at the Nürburgring, where he'd wrecked the car and nearly killed himself? It wasn't so difficult to sling a car around, even this big bastard. What was difficult was trying to drive it with a control and mechanical sympathy that was alien to him. But if they wanted him to drive like a fucking maniac, who was he to argue?

Jonty shot under the bridge and rushed downhill toward the Esses. He braked deliberately late, feeling the C5 judder and twitch about in protest. Then he flung the wheel over and threw the nose towards the red-and-white kerbing on the inside of the first corner. The car didn't want to turn in, so Jonty booted the accelerator to skid the tail round.

He skated out of Tertre Rouge onto the Mulsanne Straight in a hair-raising slide, car diagonal to the road and smoke pouring off the rear tyres as he gave the accelerator 'welly'. As the word came back to him, he pictured Fitch. God knows what the performance was doing to the tyres, Jonty thought, but this is what the idiot seemed to want! And the exercise seemed to be scratching away at Jonty's frustrations like sharp fingernails relieving an itchy back.

Jonty charged down the Mulsanne Straight, overtaking cars for a change, and positioning himself for the kink. *Flat!* he told himself. I'm going to take it flat. Nothing to it. Just keep your foot hard down and . . .

Suddenly he shot over the final brow before it and the trees were in front of him, waiting for him. But the road went sharp right!

'Flat!' Jonty shouted at himself, but he lifted his right foot slightly just before he took the kink with two quick wrist movements. Just as well, because the back end of the car seemed to be pushing him straight on, fighting the front end's efforts to steer into the bend. Too much understeer. That was what Angelica had told the mechanics to do – put up the rear wing, the classic way of setting a car up for a novice so that it was virtually impossible to spin. Well fuck that too! Jonty thought.

At the end of the lap, Jonty tore up the pitlane past a succession of flag-waving whistle-blowing marshals trying to make him slow down. Steve Driscoll opened his door. Behind him Jonty saw Angelica and Alex Fitch peering down at a stopwatch with bewildered expressions.

'Flatten the wing!' Jonty yelled through his helmet.

Driscoll stepped back and said something to Angelica who came to the cockpit.

'It was meant to stabilise the car for you,' she said. 'I thought it would help.'

'Yeah, well, it nearly stabilised the fucking thing off the kink! Put it back where you had it before!'

Jonty looked ahead. The mechanics were checking the tyre pressures. Good. That meant he could put in some real flyers without coming back into the pits to have them de-pressured. As soon as Driscoll gave him the go signal he slammed the car into gear, built up the revs, and catherine-wheeled off up the pit lane. At the end of the concrete-slab wall separating it from the track was a stand just large enough to accommodate one marshal and a set of traffic lights. Suddenly they changed to red. Jonty slithered to a halt and waited whilst a yellow-and-blue Porsche 956 screamed past on the track. It was already dissappearing from view as Jonty rejoined the circuit, but now he had a target to aim at.

He slung the C5 into the bends with redoubled fury. It wasn't just Fitch who was treating him like a prize prat – Angelica was babying him too. Two laps, Jonty thought, and they'll have my answer. As he reached the Mulsanne Straight

200

the Porsche was several yards ahead of him. Jonty reached for the knurled aluminium boost control knob under the dash. As he twisted it to the right he glanced at the turbo boost gauge – one-point-four, one-point-five. Behind him the turbo whistling had changed into something more like a jet scream. So the engine might blow – that would really give Fitch something to think about!

Jonty's eyes locked onto the car ahead as if he was hypnotised by it. He stayed in its tracks, shadowing it across the track, as though he could already feel its slipstream sucking him towards it. As the Restaurant des Hunaudières flashed past on his left, Jonty realised he *was* gaining on it. The two cars wailed on down the straight with the maroon C5 gradually closing in on the yellow-and-blue Porsche. With a sudden thrill Jonty realised he was going to catch him somewhere near the kink. That would make it interesting, because no way was he going to lift this time!

And then they were going over the final brow, the kink was ahead of them, and Jonty realised that unless he did lift he would have to overtake the Porsche *in* the Bend. A mad grin split his lips as he concentrated on the manoeuvre. At 230 miles-an-hour, he closed right up on its tail, then dived out to the right and aimed for the apex of the kink. He knew he'd have them both off if he took the conventional line. Ignoring Angelica's advice, Jonty went right over the dotted white lines so that the grey Armco was swishing past his side window like a continuous blade. He felt cornering forces loading up the car. The rough ground was destabilising it, and suddenly he knew he was going to hit the other car. There was nothing he could do about it now. The C5 was swept back across the white line, out onto the final section of the straight side by side with the Porsche on its left. Then it kissed it – just a touch, but enough to frighten the life out of its driver. Jonty laughed out loud as he began to pull clear.

I laughed at that! Jonty realised in amazement as he raced towards Mulsanne Corner. So that's not what he was afraid of. Why should he be? He had always found car control easy, a natural ability he was lucky enough to have been born with. So just what was he afraid of?

And suddenly revelation filled his mind, as blindingly clear as if it had been carved into his brain cells and illuminated by lightning – it's not the bloody car I'm afraid of. *It's me!* The madness that makes me pull a stunt like that at the kink, the madness that made me lap the Nürburgring far faster than I needed to. If I could control that . . . If I could learn to control *myself!*

He was on the pace now. What he needed to do was back off to one he could keep up all day and all night, a pace that would satisfy him yet keep him away from that kind of dangerous high. But how could he find that? By keeping inside the white lines for a start, Jonty decided. By not ramming the kerbs and sliding over the edge of the track. He began to drive with deliberate precision, braking slightly earlier, squeezing on power only when he knew he could stay within the lines.

When he went past the Mulsanne signalling pits for the second time, his sign told him he'd done three minutes thirty one seconds on that first standing lap. The board also ordered him IN. Well sod that. No way. Not when he was learning so much.

And then came the second revelation, in its way even more mind-blowing for him than the first – as he went past the signalling pits for the third time the signal board read three minutes twenty five seconds! How was that possible? After that hairy moment at the kink, he'd kept the C5 strictly on the racing line, only straying off it to overtake slower cars or slip-stream someone down the straight. How could that be faster than his half-crazed effort? The signal repeated the IN message, but Jonty ignored it, concentrating even more fiercely on steering a precise route round the circuit.

This time he picked up another superb tow along the straight, and a lap later he read the result on the signal board – three minutes twenty-three seconds! And IN again, this time with the signaller stabbing his index finger at it. Jonty gave him a curt nod.

As he drove back to the main pits waves of realisation and satisfaction surged through him. So that was what Michael had meant – 'You've got incredible car control, Jonty,' he'd often told him, 'and when you add smoothness to that you're going to be really quick!' Jonty had just smiled at him because he was setting pole position by miles in club races and qualifying at the front in international ones. Who needed smoothness? It hadn't meant anything to him then, but now that he had finally learnt its vital significance he could never be rough again.

Jonty steered the C5 into the pit lane and stopped at his pit. Angelica and Driscoll were waiting for him, but Fitch seemed to have disappeared.

'Why didn't you come in when we signalled you?' Driscoll demanded.

'Wasn't I doing well enough?'

'That's not the point. How d'you know we couldn't see something seriously wrong with the car?'

'Was there? What *did* you want anyway?'

Angelica tried a conciliatory smile. 'We were a little worried because you'd speeded up so much. What did you find out there?'

'The turbo boost knob!' Jonty said aggressively. 'Wound it up to one point seven!'

Driscoll put a hand to his forehead.

'My God!' Angelica said. 'How could you do something so stupid? This is final practice. Now we won't know what shape the engine is in for the race.'

'So you drive the fucking car!' Jonty shouted, smashing open the harness buckle and wriggling out of the car. 'Everything I do seems to be wrong!'

The practice session was divided into two halves with an hour gap between them. With just a few minutes of the first half left Angelica hustled the C5 round the circuit, trying to find out if Jonty's rough treatment had done any damage.

Nothing wrong in the engine department – the Glaser V6

was snarling aggressively and pushing her in the back as hard as ever. Nothing wrong with the handling either. Maybe she had been too tough on him. Why was it every conversation between them seemed to end in a shouting match, Angelica wondered bitterly? She had thought they'd made peace on the way to Le Mans, but now they were back to their old bickering ways. Yet she liked the boy so much, wanted to be friends with him.

Friends! Angelica thought. Is that what you call it. You know perfectly well what you really want him to be! Why, why, why did he affect her like that? Wasn't one brother enough?

She turned off the road part of the circuit and onto the smoother track section that led back to the pits. Angelica curved left into the first part of an S-bend, then started to take the flat-out right-hander that followed it. With horrifying suddenness she realised the car wasn't taking the corner anymore. It was straightening out halfway through it, heading across the track towards the Armco so close beside it. Angelica twitched the steering wheel right – no response. She had to be doing 250 kilometres-an-hour. Desperately she squeezed the brakes and slammed the gearlever into third. The engine screamed in protest and there was a stench of burning rubber as the rear tyres momentarily locked-up. The Armco rushed to claim her. Just before she hit it Angelica rammed the gearstick into second.

There was a deafening metallic clang as the front left wing hit the barrier. Then the whole car was flicked sideways like a toy, and its left side broadsided against it. Despite the safety harness, the seat smashed into Angelica's side, bending her ribs and winding her. She fought to slow down the rudderless car as it battered its way along the rippling Armco, finally stopping two hundred metres further on. Angelica slumped forward against the belts and was violently sick into her balaclava.

Minutes later, the loudspeakers boomed out news of the

crash within sight of the grandstands. The Church team strained to catch phrases of the report between cars howling up the pit straight.

'The back way!' Ian Mottram yelled, already running towards the passageway behind the pit.

Jonty sprinted to catch up with him, feeling sick and afraid. 'My Lotus!' he shouted as they emerged in the paddock.

The other mechanics were piling into the team's rented van, but Ian jumped into the sports car. Horn blaring, lights blazing, they tore round the access road to the paddock exit. A dirt track ran inside and parallel to the circuit, and Jonty stormed down it like a rally driver. The tail of the Lotus swung from side to side, shooting up clouds of red dust and sending the officials guarding the roadway scurrying for safety. Behind Jonty, the van was doing a passable imitation of a service barge racing to keep up with its car.

Suddenly they could see the crumpled C5. Marshals had helped Angelica out of it, and she was sitting on the bank with her head in her hands. Jonty was the first to reach her.

'You all right?' he asked.

She raised her head and nodded weakly. 'The steering let go. I broadsided it down the Armco. Hope it's not wrecked.'

Seconds later the mechanics had the nose off the car and Ian Mottram was bending down to examine the front suspension. He straightened up again, a shocked expression on his face, and walked up the bank to Jonty.

'The steering arm pulled out,' he said in a low voice.

'How the hell did that happen?'

'Without too much difficulty – looks as though it was only held on by two turns of a screw-thread!'

Jonty just stared at him open-mouthed. Then he nodded towards Angelica. 'Help me get her into my Lotus. I'm taking her straight back to the hotel.'

Twenty-Three

JONTY DROVE slowly out of the circuit, trying not to jolt the low slung Lotus over the bumps. In the passenger seat beside him Angelica grimaced with pain and massaged her left side.

'I'm sorry about today,' Jonty said. 'I've behaved really badly.'

'Don't blame yourself,' Angelica said. 'A track rod pulling out is nothing to do with the way you drove it. But how *did* it happen? Did someone forget to tighten the lock nut, or was the thread too short?'

Jonty sighed. 'There's something I think I should tell you if you feel up to hearing it.'

She stopped massaging her aching ribs and looked at him. 'Go on.'

They were almost back at the hotel when Jonty finished the story, starting with Dennis's phone call, and telling her why he had reassembled the team exactly as it was at Silverstone.

'Looks like I nearly got you killed in the process,' Jonty said.

'But the track rod – it could have been carelessness.'

'Like the wing at Silverstone?'

Angelica shook her head and winced at the pain the movement caused. 'You should have told me this much sooner Jonty. There's no way I would have dragged you into this if I'd known what you've just told me. Well I'm not having you killed as well. I'm releasing you from any obligation you feel

206

to me or the team, and calling the whole thing off. Enough is enough.'

'Is it hell!' Jonty growled. 'We're going to find out just what the hell's going on around here.'

For about five seconds Madame Chaumond listened to Angelica insisting that she was quite all right. Then she telephoned a doctor and insisted he come to the hotel *now*. Half an hour later a French surgeon confirmed that nothing was broken, but that Angelica was badly bruised and needed rest.

Madame Chaumond took charge, shooing everybody including her husband away from the room, and ordering absolute quiet on the second floor. Jonty was allowed a quick peek round the door. Angelica was lying in the bed with her wild brown hair spread out on the pillow.

'I'm all right,' she assured him. 'Just tired. How's the car?'

'Repairable,' Jonty said.

Steve Driscoll had driven over to find out how Angelica was, and had given him that information – the front and rear bodywork were scrap, but the chassis didn't appear to be distorted. The mechanics had started repairs right away.

Jonty went back to his room nearer the stairs and tried to read a motoring magazine. He didn't feel hungry. Maybe he'd eat something when the rest of the team came back. He must have dozed off.

Suddenly he was awakened by creaking floorboards. Somebody was walking along the corridor. There was a knock on one of the bedroom doors.

'Angelica. Angelica!' a familiar plummy voice said.

Jonty jumped off the bed and yanked his bedroom door open. Alex Fitch had his back to him and his ear against Angelica's door.

'Shhh! Don't wake her up,' Jonty said.

'Is she all right?'

'A bit bruised, but she's sleeping.'

'That's why I'm trying to wake her up!' Fitch said, as

though speaking to an idiot. 'I've organised a dinner tonight, and she's my guest of honour.'

'No dinner,' Jonty said. 'She's had one hell of a shunt and she needs to sleep.'

'Don't you tell me what she needs and doesn't need! She needs a decent co-driver for a start! If you hadn't slung that car around this afternoon this probably wouldn't have happened.'

'Oh, just get out will you,' Jonty said, taking him by the elbow and pulling him towards the stairs.

'Get your hands off me,' Fitch snarled. 'You don't seem to realise your whole half-baked team owes its presence here to me! My vice-president is expecting Angelica at dinner, and if I want to take her there I bloody well will.'

'You bloody well won't! You only own the engines, not her!' Jonty yelled.

The corridor was carpeted with loose rugs. Suddenly Fitch gave Jonty a violent shove, and one of them skidded out from under him as he fought for balance. As Jonty crashed onto his back Fitch ran back up the hallway to Angelica's bedroom and threw the door open.

'Angelica, you must have heard us . . .'

Jonty lowered his head and charged, ramming his head into Fitch's fat stomach. He felt a knee smash up into his face, heard a scream, and then he was kneeling on the ground seeing vivid flashes of lightning in front of his eyes.

'That'll teach you, you little bugger!' Fitch yelled.

Suddenly Jonty was aware of something like a miniature black tornado rushing past him.

'*Imbecile! Cochon!*' Madame Chaumond shouted, thumping Fitch across the head and shoulders with a heavy walking stick.

Inside the room Angelica had climbed out of bed in her nightdress. She was staring incredulously at the scene, and shouting at Fitch as well.

'Leave him to me Madame Chaumond,' Jonty yelled, grabbing Fitch's shoulder. His hand reached it just in time to be thwacked by Madame Chaumond's demonic stick. Jonty threw his fingers up to his mouth and sucked them whilst she drove Fitch back towards the stairs.

'You're finished, you little bastard!' Fitch screamed, trying to ward off the blows with his arms. 'You and your team! No engines . . . nothing! You'll do this race over my dead body!'

His threats receded down the stairs, drowned by Madame Chaumond's high pitched insults. Suddenly Jonty heard a laugh, and turned towards Angelica.

She put her hands in front of her mouth, but raspberries of laughter kept exploding through her fingers. 'I'm so sorry . . . I don't mean to laugh . . . it hurts so much . . . but when I opened the door and saw . . . with the stick . . . hitting him on the head . . . then you on the hand . . .'

It was too much for Angelica. She staggered back to the edge of the bed, sat down on it and began to cry with helpless laughter. And suddenly Jonty was doing so too. He didn't know why because his knuckles felt as though they'd been broken, but he laughed and laughed. Each time one of them thought they had it under control they only had to look at the other to break into agonising paroxysms again.

Slowly the tide of hysteria began to ebb away.

'He is such a *prat!*' Jonty said. 'What you ever saw in him . . .'

'Nothing,' Angelica said, 'except engines.'

Jonty was suddenly serious. 'But did you really have to . . . you know . . .'

'Make love to him to get them? I slept in the same bed, but there was always some way to get out of doing anything with him. Usually he was so full of gin *he* made the excuses.'

Jonty stared down at Angelica. Her nightdress was just one layer of filmy white material. Through it he could see the livid black-and-purple bruising on her side, the curve of her breast, the darkness of a nipple. 'Honestly?' Jonty said hoarsely.

'Did you really think that of me, so soon after Michael?'

'Don't talk about Michael,' Jonty said, looking away.

'Why not?'

'Because . . . because I think I'm falling in love with you, and it seems wrong somehow.'

Angelica looked up at him, her expression a mixture of surprise and happiness. She lifted her hand and took his. 'Look at me,' she said gently. 'I loved your brother very much. Surely I can say that without hurting you. And now I want to love you.'

'Because I remind you of him?'

'Perhaps, but also for yourself – the way you came back to help me even though you were afraid, because you loved Michael too. I love you for your courage.'

Jonty stared at her in amazement. 'You don't understand – I've always been the spoilt brat of the family; I've never had to fight for anything just had it put on a plate . . .'

'That's Conrad talking!' Angelica said sharply. 'I've told you what you are – a brave man I admire very much, a man I want to love if he will let me.'

'Angelica!' Jonty whispered, looking away again.

She increased the pressure on his hand so that slowly he sat down on the edge of the bed beside her. The heat of her body seemed to pass through her flimsy nightdress and burn into him. He turned towards her.

'Oh Angelica!' Jonty said, bending forward and kissing her lightly on the lips.

She put up her arms to hold him, and returned the pressure of his mouth. The kiss deepened, but then he pressed against her bruised side, and she winced and pulled back.

'All right?' Jonty whispered.

'My side.'

He put his hands to the neckline of the nightdress, spread it and eased it over her shoulders. It fell around her waist. Then Jonty bent to the bruised flesh and began to kiss it, transferring the fire into his loins.

'Jonty! Oh Jonty, that's so good!' Angelica said, tenderly stroking the back of his head as he bathed away her pain.

Jonty's tongue worked higher, up the underside of her young, firm breast, onto the small dark nipple that swelled like ripening fruit. And then Angelica lay back across the bed. Jonty stood up, tugged the nightdress under her backside and threw it behind him. Her thighs were so strong, but as she parted them he saw the delicate pink petals behind her damp brown curls. They seemed to suck at him.

'Won't I . . . won't I hurt you?'

'I want you so much I don't care!'

Jonty tore his jeans open and pushed them down. For a moment the air in the room cooled him, but then it too seemed to be burnt up in the sexual fire. He fought for breath as he put his arms straight out on either side of Angelica. Then he stretched his legs behind him.

'Angelica . . . Angelica . . . I love you!' Jonty said, arching his back and stabbing into her.

In a bedroom of the Grande Luxe Concorde Hotel near the centre of Le Mans, Alex Fitch was reporting to his master.

'Talk me through it again,' Stockwell said, his features tight with interest.

Alex Fitch licked his fat lips. 'It could have been the most terrible disaster. The track rod pulled out – that's the arm connecting the steering rack to the front wheel upright. In other words the car was virtually out of control at 200 miles-an-hour, and that's one of the least protected parts of the circuit. If young Church had been at the wheel and not Angelica, it might well have launched itself over the banking and killed several marshals. And during the race hundreds of spectators use that path.'

'Nineteen-fifty-five all over again?'

'Absolutely.'

'This is what I've been waiting for,' Stockwell said almost to himself. Then he looked at Fitch again and said in a sterner voice: 'You're sure that errr . . . personal factors aren't affecting your judgement of this? Because a lot of questions are going to be asked when we get back to Zürich, and you're going to be my expert witness.'

'Not . . . not at all,' Fitch spluttered. 'In my opinion

Jonathan Church shouldn't be anywhere near a racing car, and that goes for Harvey Trip as well. Frankly I think I could do a lot better than either of them, and I've been out of the game for several years. I was always held back by co-drivers like those two.'

'I'd forget that last bit when we explain this decision to the board.'

Fitch reddened. 'I see what you mean. Anyway, when are we going to drop the bombshell?'

'I got the court orders this afternoon with the help of a Paris lawyer, but I'm not going to hit them until raceday. That gives them the least possible time to fight back.'

'Good idea,' Alex Fitch said, smiling maliciously. 'I can't wait to see his face.'

'Forget Jonathan Church!' Stockwell snapped. 'We're aiming at bigger fish!'

Twenty-Four

Rico Glaser looked nervously across the table at his dinner guest. It was Thursday evening, and they were sitting in one of the finest restaurants in Zürich overlooking the Zürichsee. Even though the sun had nearly set, gaudy-sailed windsurfers raced past on the lake just a few metres away from them.

Darrell Rosenberg, Glaser's American distributor, was a big middle-aged Californian in good shape. There was something comical about his mixture of West Coast and Jewish looks – a fine head of sun-bleached hair and a big hooked nose. But when Rosenberg's steely-blue eyes fixed on somebody, they tended not to laugh at him.

'Is the veal all right?' Rico asked. 'Maybe you don't like it cut up the Swiss way.'

'No, it's fine,' Rosenberg said.

'The vegetables?'

'Fine.'

Rico picked at his food. He had spent the afternoon explaining the new distributors' agreement. The Californian hadn't said much, but he hadn't looked happy about it.

'You are an old friend,' Rico started hesitantly, 'so I think I can ask you frankly what is wrong.'

Rosenberg put down his knife and fork. 'All right. Let me ask *you* something frankly then – which horse's ass produced this new agreement shit, 'cos I'm sure as hell it wasn't you?'

'Horse's ass?'

'Yeah, because you know Rico, your business is making prestige cars and mine is selling them. I used to fly over and we'd discuss . . . oh . . . engines, options, shutlines. Now you're spouting half-assed management jargon I don't understand, and I'm not sure you do either. So what I want to know is this – who's responsible?'

Rico sighed deeply. 'As you know, about a year ago I sold out to a Swiss-American holding company. They put in their own man, Curtis Stockwell, as vice-president. He's a Harvard Business School graduate.'

Darrell Rosenberg raised his hands, palms upwards, and shook them like a prophet of doom. '*Oy vay! Oyyy vayyy!* I'd sooner have the receiver in – at least you know where you are!'

'It's not so terrible, surely?'

'What's so terrible is your cars, Rico. Where's the turbocharged model you promised me? Why don't the doors fit properly anymore? I sell expensive toys to rich boys, and let me tell you, if they're not 100 per cent right I lose their custom. And what do I get from you? A half-assed attempt to ram a quota down my throat. That's not the business we're in Rico, either of us, and if we try to play take-it-or-leave-it we're going to be finished pretty damn fast!'

Rico put his hands up to his forehead. 'You're right of course, Darrell. Where do we go from here?'

Rosenberg forked strips of veal into his mouth and looked as though he was enjoying them for the first time. 'My old friend Harvey Trip is racing at Le Mans.'

'You know Harvey?'

'Sure. He's one of my best customers. I was hoping to go over there with you and see the old horse perform.'

'Perhaps we could still go,' Rico said, brightening considerably. 'I was only staying in Zürich for your sake.'

'Well, that's settled. But first I want to talk to someone. Who d'you say owned this Swiss-American holding outfit?'

'Salomon Loewenstein; but he's a difficult man to talk to.'

Rosenberg laughed. 'I think you'll find we've got something in common.'

'We'll go back to my house and try to phone him,' Rico suggested. 'Then I'll book some air tickets to Paris.'

'Air tickets?' Rosenberg frowned. 'Don't you think that turbocharged prototype of yours could use a little exercise?'

Jonty woke up slowly on Friday morning, and sat up with a start in the unfamiliar bed. Then he saw Angelica beside him. He sank slowly down again so as not to wake her, and lay on his side admiring her.

She looked so young and vulnerable asleep, the planes and angles of her face somehow softened and rounded. Jonty felt an urgent desire to pull back the bedclothes and feast his eyes on her fabulous body. She was so fit and lithe. He tried to remember the things they had done together the previous night, and felt aroused and amazed at the same time. This was the girl who had been ordered to rest!

As though reading his thoughts Angelica suddenly stretched like a cat, and the sheet fell over her breasts baring them. Jonty rolled towards her and took a nipple in his mouth. Gently, lovingly he licked her into consciousness. Low moans of pleasure rippled up her throat. There was a movement under the bedclothes, and then Jonty felt himself gripped and tugged towards her.

'At least I've found a way to keep you in bed in the morning,' Angelica teased him afterwards.

'No you haven't,' Jonty said, swinging his legs out of it.

'Where are you going? I haven't finished with you yet!'

Jonty leant back and kissed her lightly on the lips. 'The feeling's mutual, but I want to talk to Ian as soon as possible. Keep the bed warm until I get back!'

Friday was meant to be a day of rest, the calm before the 24-hour storm. But the paddock seemed busier than ever as the teams made their final preparations. For the unlucky ones that meant a virtual rebuild of their damaged cars. Even the 'fortunate' mechanics faced engine changes as team managers made nail-biting choices.

Jonty arrived there at 10.30am to find the Church mechanics hard at work on the stripped down aluminium tub. After exchanging small talk with Steve Driscoll, he found Ian Mottram working on a gearbox in the transporter. Nobody else was with him, so Jonty climbed inside the box-like interior to talk to him.

Ian had been with Church Racing since Michael had started it, and Jonty trusted him implicitly. Apart from anything else he had been a close friend of Michael.

'Any ideas since yesterday?' Jonty asked in a low voice.

The lanky mechanic looked grim. 'I can't be certain, but I think it was a genuine accident. I measured up the steering geometry last night and the rack's very slightly off-centre. The arms are the same length, but when we set the bump steer it left enough thread in one upright but not in the other. Of course we *should* have taken both arms off, checked the threads, and then set the whole thing up again but . . .'

'Time?'

Ian nodded unhappily. 'You've got to remember the car's virtually a prototype. We're finding out about it as we go along.'

'So what the hell's going to go next?'

'I'm really sorry, Jonty. I promised you I'd check everything. I feel I've let you down.'

Jonty put his hand on his shoulder. 'No way. I know you're doing all you can. Been keeping your eye on Dennis?'

'I can guarantee you he didn't tamper with any of the suspension components. I made sure of that. But why are you suspicious of him?'

'I'd rather not say,' Jonty told him, 'but I'd appreciate it if you keep him covered.'

'Sure,' Ian said with a puzzled shrug.

Late on Friday afternoon, Darrell Rosenberg drove the Glaser Turbo into the little village of La Chartre-sur-le-Loir, thirty miles south-east of Le Mans. Beside him Rico Glaser looked fondly at the picturesque streets and houses. They crossed the River Loir, much smaller and prettier than its near-namesake, and drove into the main square. One side was completely taken up by the venerable Hotel de France. On the terrace in front of it sat multiple winners and first-timers in the 24-hour race, sipping non-alcoholic drinks and relaxing. Harvey Trip excused himself from one of the tables, and walked over to the Glaser 822.

'Well I'll be damned!' he said delightedly, opening Rosenberg's door. 'Didn't think you two were going to make it.'

'Wouldn't miss it for the world, old buddy,' Rosenberg said. 'How's it been going.'

Trip frowned as he led them back to the terrace fronting the pavement. 'Not so hot. And these guys you've sent to look after us this year, Stocksy and Futch or whatever they call themselves, are a real pain in the whatsit.'

'The horse's ass?' Rico said gravely.

Harvey Trip stared at him in surprise. 'You got it Rico!'

'We kind of figured you might be having problems with them,' Rosenberg said. 'As a matter of fact, Rico and I have got something pretty important to discuss with you that kind of affects them.'

'Shoot,' Trip said. 'I'm all ears.'

Twenty-Five

EARLY ON Saturday morning the first waves of the annual mid-June invasion reached Le Mans. All through the day the spectators would keep coming until by the four o'clock start over 200,000 of them would fill the stands and terraces in front of the pits and every viewpoint around the circuit.

Just what was it that made the Le Mans race one of the worlds's greatest spectator events? Why would the attendance be four or five times greater than that year's French Grand Prix?

Perhaps the answer was that at a Formula One meeting, the spectator remained an outsider, whereas at Le Mans he became part of the event. For one weekend of the year he would have to adjust his mind and body to a 24-hour race, staying awake when he would normally be asleep, and half-sleeping to a background howl of racing engines when he couldn't keep his eyes open any longer. For 24 hours he would literally *feel* the race.

For the 20,000 British fans who had crossed the channel there were legends of winning Bentleys, Jaguars and Aston Martins, a chance to wave flags and remember greatness. And once more Britain was resurgent, some of those great names coming back with low-budget amateur-assisted teams to challenge the mighty Germans. One year soon . . .

Or perhaps the lure was the atmosphere, a symphony of sounds made by nearly quarter-of-a-million people gathered together, an emanation of cooking smells from hundreds of stalls and camping stoves, all overlayed by the ear-splitting shrieks and burnt-oil scent of some of the world's fastest racing cars.

Conrad Church had caught the first Dover-to-Calais hover-craft early that Saturday morning, and had reached the Le Mans paddock in his black Glaser 822 by ten o'clock. Now he stood next to Jonty, watching the final touches being put to the rebuilt C5.

'It looks all right to me,' Conrad said.

Jonty sighed. 'Hope you're right.'

'Here's something that'll cheer you up – that £100,000 was transferred into Church Racing's bank account on Wednesday. Well, ninety-eight thousand-something-hundred after deductions.'

Jonty looked at his brother in surprise.

'What's the matter?' Conrad asked. 'I promised I'd get it through didn't I?'

'Yes. It's just there were, you know, delays and I began to wonder . . .'

'Well it's there now anyway. Sorry it took so long.'

Jonty shook his head. 'No, it's me who owes you an apology. I've been pretty rude to you about it.'

'Forget it.'

Just then, Alex Fitch marched under the transporter awning looking self-important. 'Morning, Conrad,' he said, ignoring Jonty completely. 'My vice-president wants to see a senior representative from your team in quarter of an hour. We'll be in one of the ACO's pit lane offices. I'd advise you to be prompt.'

'What's all this about?' Jonty asked.

'You'll find out soon enough,' Fitch said with a self-satisfied smirk.

The Automobile Club de L'Ouest, the race organisers, had a row of offices halfway down the pits. Fifteen minutes later, Conrad and Jonty were directed to one of them by a secretary. The plain, white-walled room was just big enough for a square wooden table and a dozen stacking chairs arranged around it. Fitch and Stockwell were already seated in two of these, with their backs to the window overlooking the pit lane. Derek Lomax sat at right angles to them, looking as mystified as the Church brothers.

'Right,' Stockwell said as soon as they had sat down. 'Now that representatives of both teams are here, I'd like to inform you of the decision which Alex Fitch and I have taken. As you know a Glaser-powered car crashed in the Silverstone 1,000-kilometres race, killing its driver. In second practice for this race, a car using our engine suffered total steering failure. We believe that only good fortune saved us from another potential disaster. In view of both incidents, we've decided to withdraw our engines from this race before further and possibly irreparable damage is done to the company's image.'

There was a stunned silence.

'You . . . you what?' Derek Lomax asked disbelievingly.

'We're withdrawing our engines.'

'Are you out of your mind?' Conrad said. 'You can't do that!'

'Can't I?' Stockwell brandished a sheaf of official looking papers with obvious relish. 'These court orders empower us to seize *our* engines any time we feel like it. All we have to do is hand them over to a gendarme. Of course, you're free to obtain engines elsewhere.'

'On race day morning!' Lomax shouted. 'It's deliberate bloody sabotage! If you go through with this, I'll make sure every team manager knows about it. They'll never use your engines again.'

Stockwell smiled. 'I think I can live with that.'

Suddenly, the wooden door screeched as it scraped open across the concrete floor. All eyes turned towards it as Rico Glaser, Harvey Trip and Darrell Rosenberg walked through it – a somewhat comical procession of stocky Swiss mountain guide, middle-aged racer, and tall Jewish beach-boy. Now it was Stockwell's turn to look flabbergasted.

'Rico! Wh . . . what are you doing here?'

'I don't believe you've met our American distributor, Darrell Rosenberg,' Rico said, waving a hand at him in introduction. 'He particularly wanted too see his old friend Harvey race at Le Mans, so here we are, just in time for your important announcement.'

'Just in time for the end of Glaser's racing programme more like!' Lomax said. 'Your vice-president's just told us he's seizing our engines, with your racing manager's full approval, apparently!'

Rico turned to Stockwell. 'Is this correct?'

'It most certainly is,' Stockwell said, recovering fast. 'There was a near disaster in practice involving one of our cars, yet again.'

'Nonsense!' Jonty interrupted. 'A steering arm pulled out, and Angelica Hofer had to broadside our car along the Armco, that's all. No-one was hurt.'

'If spectators had been walking along the path . . .'

'There was absolutely no reason why our car should have been launched into them.'

'And anyway,' Derek Lomax said, 'whether it would have been or not, what's this got to do with me? Neither of these incidents involved my team.'

'Didn't they?' Jonty said. 'Did you know your team manager bribed one of my mechanics to cause the Silverstone accident?'

All eyes locked on Jonty. Derek Lomax's went ice cold with anger.

'I hope you've got proof of that, because I've a good mind to sue you for slander.'

'Would you like me to bring the mechanic here now, or d'you think you'd better check where Cambell got five hundred pounds in used tenners from first?'

Lomax was just about to say something when a terrible realisation seemed to freeze his jaw. In that instant Darrell Rosenberg crashed his fist down on the table.

'Well, the shit really is hitting the fan! I suggest we clean up one bladefull at a time.' Rosenberg nodded from Lomax to Jonty. 'Why don't you two talk this thing out in private.' The Californian turned towards Stockwell and Fitch: 'As to withdrawing Glaser's engines, I'd like to know who in hell gave you two authority to do that.'

Alex Fitch shrank down in his seat, looking as though he wished he was anywhere but in the claustrophobic little office, but Curtis Stockwell met Rosenberg's glare with a look of superior contempt.

'I don't know what business this is of yours. We took the decision on our own initiative, but there happens to be a gentleman in Zürich called Salomon Loewenstein, who shares my opinion of our motor racing involvement 100 per cent.'

'He certainly does,' Rosenberg nodded.

'He does?'

'Sure. And Since Solly is also bored stiff with his purchase he was only too glad to sell out to us.'

'S . . . sell out! Us?'

Darrell Rosenberg nodded slowly. 'That's right, mister business school smartass. You're talking to the new owners – Rico, Harvey and me. And our first decision concerns you and your friend Fitch. Your employment is terminated as of right now. Get the hell out of my sight, both of you, and stay out of it!'

Ralph Cambell was telling Wolfgang Schnering a joke as they strolled towards the Lomax Team's motorhome. He reached the punchline as Wolfgang opened its door, and both of them were laughing as they climbed into it. Their smiles vanished as they saw the grim expressions on Harvey Trip and Derek Lomax's faces.

'Sit down you two,' Derek Lomax said coldly. 'I've got a question that needs answering right now.'

'What's all this about?' Ralph Cambell said. 'There's only half-an-hour left before the warmup and I'm needed . . .'

'Sit down!' Derek Lomax said. 'Now, I'd like to know exactly what went on at Silverstone.'

The team manager tried to look bewildered. 'What d'you mean, what went on at Silverstone? We came fifth.'

'I meant *before* the race. Is it true you bribed one of the Church team's mechanics to sabotage their car?'

Cambell's head went back as though he'd been punched in the mouth. 'Christ! Who told you that? He must be out of his mind!'

'Maybe, but he's quite prepared to come here and repeat it to your face. D'you want me to arrange that?'

'Nah,' Cambell said disgustedly. 'You'd probably take that Cockney prat's word rather than mine anyway.'

Lomax stared at him. 'I didn't say who it was, Ralph, but *you* just did. And what about the £2,000 that went missing in February? You told me it was stolen from your motel in Daytona. Maybe if I called in the police . . .'

'All right, all right!' Cambell shouted. 'So I did pay the little bastard a sweetener. How the hell else were we meant to beat them this year, with a car that's a joke and a co-driver who's way off the pace? It's all right for you, Derek. You own the team, but me and the lads are just employees. There's three million unemployed back home, and we're not too keen to join them. So I decided to win that Glaser support any way I could.'

'That's not winning!'

Cambell gave a contemptuous snort. 'You know what they say Derek – show me a good loser, and I'll show you a *loser*. I think I'm looking at one right now.'

The two men stared at each other with hate-filled eyes, until Lomax spoke.

'We'll do this race, and then we'll split. I used to admire your ambition Ralph, thought about making you a partner, but now I don't want anything more to do with you. Ever!'

'Count me out too,' Harvey Trip drawled. 'What Derek hasn't told you is that Darrell Rosenberg and I have bought out the Glaser Company. He's the American distributor, in case you didn't know, and he's as keen on racing as Rico and I are. We're looking for a team to support next season, so in all fairness I'm going to back out – I wouldn't want to prejudice your chances. Frankly I wouldn't rate them too highly right now!'

As Ralph Cambell stepped dejectedly out of the motor-home, Wolfgang caught his arm and steered him to one side.

'Everyone's kicking you, but I think you had the right idea. I'm not a good loser either, Ralph.'

'Thanks,' Cambell said, 'but it looks as though we've both had it.'

The German's thin lips parted in a cruel smile. 'Do *I* look like a loser Ralph? The race hasn't even started yet.'

'They were bloody well going to seize the engines half an hour before the warm-up!' Jonty told Angelica for about the tenth time. 'Then Rico and the US cavalry came charging to the rescue . . . you should have seen their faces.'

Angelica smiled: 'I wish I had done, but right now we've got a race to do, so let's get changed and talk it through one more time.'

Jonty grinned mischievously. 'That means I get to see you strip again.'

'Any nonsense and I'll lock you out of the motor-home.'

She led the way towards it, and they walked into the back half and closed the partition. Jonty sat down on one of the lower bunks whilst Angelica went into the end section and disappeared from view.

'Now, we've got an hour-and-a-half warm-up session,' Angelica said. 'I'm going to take the car out and make sure everything's working. When it is, I'm going to run a fuel consumption test because that got messed up by the shunt, so don't feel hurt if I don't hand over to you.'

'I've got over the spoilt brat bit,' Jonty said.

'Good. Then you won't be offended by what I'm going to say next. From now on, whenever you get in the car tell yourself this is a 24-hour race, *not* a sprint. Make every gearchange nice and smooth, otherwise halfway through the night it's going to start jumping out of gear, and that's it!'

'Right.'

'Same with the brakes. They feel . . . I don't know . . . not quite right to me, so kiss the pedal with your left foot before you brake hard at the end of the straight.'

'Got it.'

'Remember to give two quick lifts to cool the turbo every time you go down the straight. And Jonty, one more thing,' Angelica said quietly, stepping into the gap and zipping up her red race-suit. 'I love you.'

Jonty looked up at her and smiled. 'I love you too Angelica, very much. When this is over . . .'

'Shhh!' she said, kneeling down in front of him and holding his face tenderly between her hands. 'Take care,' she whispered, and bent forward to kiss him.

Twenty-Six

JUST AFTER 12.30pm, Angelica brought the C5 back into the pits and climbed out of it. There was a surprised grin on her face as she pulled off her balaclava and fished out her yellow foam earplugs.

'What happened?' she asked. 'It ran perfectly!'

'Bad dress rehearsal, good first night,' Conrad intoned.

'Or the gods have decided to look after us!'

As the mechanics refuelled and checked the car, the pre-race razzmatazz was already starting. A procession of famous Le Mans cars of the past toured the circuit, their proud owners reliving former glory for two heady laps.

When the track was clear, a team of stunt drivers two wheeled their cars up the pit straight, handbrake-turning at the end of it to appreciative whoops and applause from the packed stands and terraces. They repeated the balancing act with a succession of larger and larger vehicles, using a monstrous tractor for their finale.

In the bright blue sky overhead, an aerobatic display seemed to be a version of 'chicken' – who could do multiple loops at the lowest level, and how nearly could they miss when flying straight at each other.

The military band started the long hot march from Tertre Rouge to the pits, led by majorettes in gold jackets and ultra-mini skirts. When they finally got there, they were completely upstaged by a group of near-naked Florida beach girls in the pit lane, their bronzed bodies and briefest of brief bikinis advertising a brand of suntan lotion.

At 2.30, the fifty-five cars in the race lined up diagonal to the pit wall in starting order. Drivers, wives and girlfriends, sponsors, mechanics, officials and photographers swarmed around them until the track was almost as crowded as the terraces. Finally a human chain of marshals managed to clear it.

At 3.15 a midnight-blue Mercedes saloon car topped by revolving lights led the field away on the reconnaissance lap. After completing it, the sports cars were held at the beginning of the pit straight, then sent up to their positions on the start grid one by one. As they switched off their engines, the carnival atmosphere changed to an expectant tension.

Inside the C5, Angelica poked a fingertip through the eyeslot in her red-and-white helmet, and dabbed sweat away from her eyes. The hot afternoon sun had turned the cockpit into a sauna, but it didn't particularly bother her as she sweated out the final minutes before the start. Angelica's mind and body had slipped into an altered state, the world she always entered when she was about to race. It had been just the same in a downhill ski-race start hut high on a mountainside. Then she had hardly noticed the freezing cold either.

Angelica was on the right of the track, with a private Porsche 956 alongside her. Works Porsches and Ferrari-engined Lancias shared the two rows ahead of her. At 3.53 an official held up the one-minute board in front of them. She reached for the ignition switch and the Glaser engine rumbled into life. Even now Angelica was thinking about the 2,210 litres maximum fuel allowance, and revving the engine as little as possible.

Six rows further back, Wolfgang blasted his turbocharged V6 into life and gave the accelerator a series of savage stabs. The noise and the vibrations sent adrenalin racing round his body, and flipped a mental switch to the *charge* position. Wolfgang loved starts. They were his trademark, and he had often stolen wins in sprint races with an aggressive attack right at the beginning. He liked to think they had their place in endurance racing too. It let everyone know you meant business, and they tended to stay out of your way for the rest of the race. So what if you burnt up a little extra fuel – the reality of a 24-hour race was about two thirds of the cars retiring anyway, and the rest limping home like a flight of shot-up fighter planes.

Three fifty-four. The midnight-blue Mercedes moved off at the head of the field, starting a chain reaction through the twenty-eight rows of the grid. Two long lines of racing cars followed the saloon like multi-coloured kite tails, weaving from side to side to heat up their tyres. It took them much longer than normal to complete the final warm-up lap, but as the Mercedes came out of the final chicane and fled for the pit lane, the Le Mans clock halfway along it read five seconds to four. Suddenly the race was on, and the pack was in full cry, howling up the pit straight in a haze of dust and smoke, and already losing cohesion.

Wolfgang had started his charge even before reaching the double chicane at the end of the warm-up lap. Deliberately leaving his braking too late before the first left-hander, he slithered between the Rondeau and the March on the row ahead of him. In a sprint race that would have started a wheel banging session to hammer him back into his place, but nobody wanted to be knocked out of a 24-hour event before it had even begun! A huge gap opened up for him, and Wolfgang used it to straight-line the exit from the second chicane. He was going so fast when he hit the pit straight that he carved through the next two rows before he'd even reached the clock. Six places in sixteen seconds! Now Wolfgang was as fired up as a boxer who had landed a stunning punch, and realized his opponent was going. He swung the Glaser-Lomax violently right without even checking his wing-mirror, and forced his way inside an orange Lola turning into the first corner. As they crested the rise under the Dunlop Bridge, Wolfgang saw what he was looking for – the maroon C5 was in fifth place and braking at the bottom of the hill. Seconds later he reached the same spot, braked late and shot across the bows of the Lola to grab the line into the Esses. He had made enough space to get a clean run through Tertre Rouge and out onto the Mulsanne Straight. As Wolfgang started down it his left hand reached for the boost control knob under the dash.

Angelica kept to the left of the straight, closely following the fourth-placed Porsche. She had held her starting position and was satisfied with that – let everyone else do whatever they wanted as long as they stayed out of her way. Now she alternated glances between her right-side wing-mirror and the instruments. She wanted to settle into the pace they had decided on as quickly as possible. Suddenly she spotted a brown shape among the vibrating blobs in her mirror. It was growing larger at an amazing rate, and with sudden certainty Angelica realised who it was – Wolfgang must have turned up the wick.

Half a minute later he was right on her tail and jinking out to the right to overtake her. But Wolfgang was playing paint shaving. As he drew alongside he kept as close as he possibly could without touching her. Angelica tried to hold her line but the bumpy road-surface moved the cars about so that they needed constant correction. Now Wolfgang was right beside her, both cars travelling at 220 miles-an-hour. He must have lifted slightly, because he was staying level. She tried not to look at him, but suddenly the cars made contact and she glanced sideways. As she saw Wolfgang's black-and-gold helmet, a wave of anger overwhelmed her. The vicious bastard had played a similar game with Michael. The cars slapped together as they shot up the final rise before the kink neck and neck. Then they were on the crest and the bend was a frightening reality ahead of them, Wolfgang on the inside might make it, but she wasn't going to unless he gave her space. Knowing that he wouldn't, Angelica whipped her foot off the accelerator and touched the brakes.

Let the *Arschloch* have his moment of triumph, she thought, as she fell into line behind him. She knew she had done the right thing, but it left a bitter taste in her mouth. Only revenge would wash it away, and Angelica swore to herself that she would get it.

As they raced towards the double chicane to complete their fourteenth lap, Wolfgang was about 200 metres ahead of Angelica. Either he had turned the boost back to normal, or he still had it high but didn't have the handling to get away from her. Whichever it was, Angelica laughed delightedly as she saw him peel off into the pit-lane and head for his first refuelling stop.

'Great tactics, Wolfgang!' she shouted as she flashed past his slowing car.

She glanced down at the big red fuel light between the boost gauge and the rev counter. This lap was the moment of truth. She tried to concentrate on the other instruments and the track, but her eyes kept wandering back to the perspex hemisphere. She ticked off the corners one by one – Mulsanne, Indianapolis, Arnage, the Porsche Curve, where the new track section started. Halfway through it the red light flickered and then died again. Angelica looked at it nervously, but it stayed out. Then as she took the double chicane it flashed repeatedly on and off. She took a deep breath and kept going. As she charged up the pit straight, she glanced right at the crowded pits and spotted both works Porsches refuelling. So the Glaser engine did have a fuel advantage, *if* it kept going!

Her sixteenth lap seemed to last forever. By the time she reached Mulsanne corner, the red light was glowing continuously. The IN signal she received just after it was entirely superfluous. On the way to Indianapolis Angelica felt giddy, and realised she wasn't breathing properly. She gulped in air, but couldn't keep her eyes off the hypnotic light. Finally the chicanes came into view again, and with a great sigh of relief she steered into the pit lane.

Three-quarters of the way up it, Steve Driscoll stood on the yellow centreline with one hand over his head and the other pointing to their pit. Marshals waved flags and blew whistles to slow her down as she hurried towards him. As soon as she had stopped, a mechanic forced a polythene overflow churn over the valve behind the left-side door. Opposite him, the refueller bayonetted an identical valve with the fuel hose. This led back to a miniature petrol pump on their pit's side-wall, which a third man flicked on, and fuel began to flow into the C5's tank. The pit marshal assigned to their car rushed up to log their stop and the reading on the pump.

Angelica clambered out of the car and went up to Jonty, who was standing in front of the pit ready to go. She put her helmeted head right up to his, and yelled to make herself heard above the background noise.

'Looks like we can do sixteen laps between fuel stops even running hard, but watch the fuel light – if it goes on *after* the Porsche Curve you can do another lap. The car is fine.'

'Who hit you?' Jonty asked, pointing at the side of the car.

Angelica turned towards it. For the first time she saw the ugly black abrasions caused by the wheel banging session on the straight. Suddenly she was overwhelmed by her love for Jonty, and the realisation that in a few minutes he would be sharing the track with Wolfgang.

'Schnering,' she said. 'For God's sake be careful of him. He's crazy.'

Jonty's eyes flicked up at the name. There was a chilling anger in them that frightened her, because it matched her own.

'I can handle it,' Jonty said, stepping past her and climbing into the car.

He slid down into the cockpit and adjusted the seat and safety harness quickly and surely. Now that the moment had come he *wanted* to race again. He was glad he was back in Michael's car, carrying his name and colours out onto his favourite circuit. There were scores to be settled, and if Schnering wanted to sort his out on the track, that suited Jonty fine. When Steve Driscoll slammed down the driver's door and gave him the go signal he hustled the C5 away from the pit with impressive purpose.

It took him just half a lap to tune into the car again. Then it was part of him, and he began to drive it with the smooth precision he had discovered in practice. Angelica was right, the car felt fine. Only one thing worried him – how long would it last?

Dennis Morrell staggered along the tunnel and into the pit carrying a huge rear wheel and tyre. He dumped it against the back wall, and then went out to the tyre trolley in the paddock to fetch its twin.

Jonty had come into the pits half an hour earlier for fuel and new tyres. Now Angelica was circulating in a trouble-free fifth position, and the delighted team had a little time to relax – *most* of the team anyway.

'Would you go for fresh tyres Dennis,' Steve Driscoll had ordered him, as Angelica raced away from the pit.

That meant lugging the set of wheels that had just come off the car out to the tyre trolley one by one, wheeling it to the tyre company's compound outside the paddock, waiting for the old tyres to be stripped off and new ones fitted and balanced, and then carting the whole lot back again.

As Dennis dumped the second rear wheel on top of the first, Steve Driscoll walked into the stall and came up to him.

'Thanks. Would you go and see if Sharon can rustle up some sandwiches. The lads are a bit peckish.'

Gofor this, gofor that! Dennis had been hearing it all week. Okay, he was the youngest, but bloody Driscoll might give him a break every now and then, Dennis thought as he wandered towards their motorhome. Through its open door he could see Sharon working at the stove and smell stew. He tiptoed up the steps and gave her a playful slap on her backside.

'Hiya doll! Howya doing?'

'All right if you'd stop molesting me!' Sharon laughed, turning to give him a quick kiss.

'Any chance of some sandwiches. I know you're trying to get supper ready, but we're starving.'

'Sure,' Sharon said, stirring a huge pot and then reaching for a pack of sliced bread. 'You know, I could do so much better if I had the right equipment. What we need next year is a microwave so that I can pre-prepare . . .'

'Next year?'

'Yeah. Mum and Dad have got one in the pub now. I could do proper meals within a minute of anyone wanting one.'

Dennis stared at her. 'You mean you *want* to come back and do this again next year?'

'Course I do. Wouldn't have missed this for anything, and I don't think microwaves are that expensive anymore.'

'What about the baby?'

'Mum'll have her for a bit. I know she hasn't exactly been all over us, but you watch her turn into the doting granny when the baby comes. She'll be only too . . .'

Sharon stopped because Dennis had turned away from her, but not before she'd seen him give his eyes a quick wipe with the back of his hand.

'All right love?' she asked quietly.

'Course,' Dennis said, finding it hard to keep the emotion out of his voice. 'Just something in my eye, that's all.'

Just before seven o'clock, Wolfgang brought the Glaser-Lomax into the pits for its third refuelling stop. As he scrambled out of the car, Ralph Cambell grabbed him by the elbow and pulled him into a huddle with Helmut Hahn, the second driver who was just about to take over.

'We're using far too much fuel,' Cambell said urgently. 'Any idea why?'

'Goddammit!' Wolfgang snapped. 'For once I have an engine that could win this race, but the goddam car isn't up to it. I'm having to drive like a maniac just to stay on the pace.'

Cambell's eyes narrowed. 'You haven't turned up the boost have you?'

'What do you think? How else am I meant to get this wonderful aerodynamic device of Derek's down the straight in a reasonable time?'

Cambell shrugged. 'Well, you two are going to have to slow down, or we'll use up the juice before the end of the race.'

'How are the others doing?' Wolfgang asked.

'The works Porsches are in first and third . . .'

'Not them! The Church.'

'Sixth place, just behind us,' Cambell said. 'But our lot at the signalling pits say they seem to be managing sixteen laps between pit stops. That's going to give them an advantage of . . .'

'I can figure it out for myself!' Wolfgang said bitterly. He should have finished it when he had his chance, he told himself. He was *sure* he had suckered the bitch into an impossible situation on the first lap, but at the last second Angelica had dropped back. If only she had tried to race him through the kink, he would have had her.

The refuelling was nearly completed, and Hahn was already in the car ready to go. Suddenly, Wolfgang recognised a familiar engine note howling up the pit straight towards them, slightly higher than a Porsche 956's. Seconds later the maroon C5 blared past, stealing back fifth place from them. He turned to Cambell and put his mouth close to his ear.

'Helmut and I are doing all we can. It's up to you now.'

'Early days yet,' Cambell said, almost to himself. 'A little birdy tells me they might just hit a problem.'

Twenty-Seven

As DUSK began to settle on the circuit, the purple light halfway down the pit straight flashed on. It was the signal for all cars to turn on their lights, but it also marked an important psychological moment – five-and-a-half hours of racing completed. In a 1,000-kilometre event, the chequered flag would be out to signal the end of the race by now, but this one was not even a quarter run yet! Everybody who saw that purple glow wondered just what they had let themselves in for.

Those lucky spectators with accomodation in Le Mans began to think of slipping back for a good French meal and then some sleep in a comfortable bed. The majority faced starker choices – for the campers, a meal out of cans and a night in a sleeping bag; for the coach trippers, snacks from one of the innumerable bars and fried food stalls, and then a cramped seat in the bus that had brought them there; and for the really hardy, a blanket round the shoulders and a night on the terraces.

Many of them would visit the funfair, its huge Ferris wheel now lit up and revolving slowly in the darkening sky. Its passengers could look down on the sports cars shooting under the Dunlop Bridge, twin swords of light stabbing out into space, then slapping down onto tarmac again as they charged downhill towards the Esses.

And some drivers too were looking for something else to occupy them. A surprising number of cars had already retired. Some of them had tried to stretch the distance between refuelling stops, gone for an extra lap, and simply run out of petrol. Refuelling was only allowed in the pits, so perfectly serviceable cars sat impotently on the trackside whilst their teams wondered if they would ever get over the frustration.

Some had suffered major failures – blown up engines and turbochargers, seized gearboxes, or suspension collapses. Running a racing car absolutely flat out for several miles along a bumpy road was a good way to discover weak spots. Other cars were stranded out on the circuit with a minor problem that a skilled mechanic could have solved in minutes; but once out of the pits only the driver was allowed to work on the car with the tools and spares he carried in it. For any car to have a trouble free run to the finish was almost unheard of. Far from feeling smug, the teams who hadn't been caught out so far wondered uneasily when it would be their turn.

As night fell, the rapidly cooling air found the C5's weak link. Angelica was braking hard at the end of the straight when the pedal suddenly kicked back at her. She tiptoed through Mulsanne corner – no problem. But as she accelerated away from it the steering wheel began to vibrate violently in her hands – the brake discs had cracked. Angelica cursed out loud. One of the works Lancias had just retired with engine problems, promoting the C5 to fourth position, and she couldn't bear to lose the place so quickly. She kept going for another four laps until it was time to pit for fuel anyway. By that time the wheel was punching and blistering her hands, and she was having difficulty controlling the car.

As the refuellers went into action a mechanic connected a compressed air line to the side of the car. With an angry hiss the four built-in airjacks telescoped out and pushed the C5 clear of the ground. Three more mechanics air-gunned off the wheel nuts, pulled off the front wheels, and then set to work to remove the red-hot discs. A scream and the smell of barbecued meat meant that fingers had touched red-hot steel.

Jonty was watching from behind the pit counter, and Angelica stepped into the stall to join him. She yanked off her helmet and gloves.

'You all right?' Jonty asked.

'Yes, but I could *scream* with frustration! How we've fought to save a few seconds here, and a few seconds there, and now we're throwing them away.'

She shivered in the cool night air, and Jonty took off his anorak and draped it round her shoulders.

'Thanks,' she said, turning towards him and touching his cheek with her fingertips. 'What are you doing here anyway? It's not your turn to drive yet.'

'I know, but I can't sleep. I lie down in the motor-home, but all I think about is what's going on in the race, so I may as well be in the pits.' Jonty turned his head to kiss Angelica's hands, and saw the blisters. 'How did you get those?'

'When the discs went. It was like riding a bucking bronco, but they're all right now it's stopped!'

'That's how they'll look when I get you home anyway,' Jonty said with a teasing smile; 'all the washing and scrubbing you'll be doing for me.'

'Huh! That's what you think,' Angelica laughed. 'I don't mind cooking, but I *hate* washing up. That will be one of your jobs!'

As their eyes met, their smiles were replaced by a sudden seriousness.

'Oh Jonty,' Angelica said quietly. 'What are you saying?'

'That I want you to stay with me after this; that I want you to . . .'

He was interrupted by a noise like slow machine-gun fire. As they looked down the pit lane, they saw the Glaser-Lomax limping towards them at a drunken angle. Something had broken on its rear suspension, and a shredded tyre thrashed the tarmac as it staggered home.

It stopped at its pit and the Lomax mechanics tore off the shattered rear bodywork. Now a race was on between the teams' mechanics, a competition every bit as fierce as the action on the track. An electric hostility seemed to arc between the rival pits as both teams struggled to get their car away first. There wasn't just a position at stake – the mechanics' jobs depended on the result of this race, and they knew it. In case they needed reminding, Rico Glaser, Darrell Rosenberg and Harvey Trip were in the pits, taking an intense interest in everything that happened.

Ten minutes later the C5 made it away first with Angelica back at the wheel.

Trouble would strike almost every driver at some point in the 24-hour race. For those who hadn't met it yet, it seemed to lurk in the darkness like some ghostly wolf pack, watching and waiting for the moment to pounce. It found Jonty shortly before dawn, just when he thought he had escaped it.

He had just powered the C5 neatly through Tertre Rouge and out onto the Mulsanne Straight when his headlights picked out the back end of a car several hundred metres ahead. Automatically Jonty aimed straight at it to try and pick up an aerodynamic tow. He seemed to be gaining on it surprisingly quickly. Did it have a problem? As he came nearer he could tell from its narrow track and distinctive rear wing that it was one of the works Lancias. One of them was in second place Jonty realised excitedly. It was ejecting occasional puffs of dirty yellow smoke, but they quickly disappeared in its slipstream. Jonty closed in for the kill.

He was right behind it when its engine exploded. Something hard flew straight at Jonty's face, and bounced off the windscreen. The next second it was blacked out by oil. Frantically Jonty twitched the steering wheel right, expecting to slam into the Lancia at any moment. He couldn't see a thing through the windscreen, so he looked out of the side window and steered by keeping parallel with the Armco barrier, just a dull grey blur beside him. After what seemed like an eternity the C5 had slowed down without hitting anything. Jonty gave a great sigh of relief, feeling his heart thumping against his ribs. When he turned on the windscreen wiper it smeared the oil into a yellow distorting lens, but he could just see enough to guide the C5 back to the pits. The new Glaser directors were paying a visit to his team when he finally made it.

'Lancia blew up in front of me,' Jonty shouted, staying in the car and keeping the engine running. 'Was it the one in second place?'

In front of him two mechanics were using yards of blue paper roll to clean the tarry layer off the windscreen. It had a crazed star in it exactly at eye-level. As soon as they had done their job Jonty roared back out onto the track again.

Rico Glaser was standing next to Conrad behind the pit

counter. 'Your brother is doing a marvellous job,' he said. 'You must be very proud of him.'

'Yes, I suppose I should be,' Conrad said.

Was it just that they were all tired Rico wondered, looking at him curiously, or was there an edge of bitterness in his voice?

Shortly after the Glaser directors had left the stall, Steve Driscoll walked in from the pit lane. Conrad caught his eye and nodded towards the back door. His chief mechanic followed him through it into the dank passage behind the pits.

Conrad looked up and down it to check that no-one was eavesdropping before speaking in a low voice. 'I thought I just had to get him back in a racing car and he'd do the rest for us, but it looks as though we're going to have to have to give him a helping hand. He's driving as smoothly as Michael did.'

'And look what happened to him,' Driscoll said with a flicker of a smile.

'Shut up Steve! That was an accident. If it'd happened to this little prat we wouldn't be here now.'

'But as we are, you'd like me to do something about it, right?'

Conrad gave a curt nod.

'It's not going to be easy,' Driscoll said.

'You're not chickening out, are you Steve. Just remember what's at stake – a quarter share of the business for you once he's out of the way.'

Driscoll shook his head. 'It's not that. You've already admitted that we underestimated your little brother. I think he knows what's going on at the garages, and I think he suspects something's wrong here. Ian Mottram's double-checking everything anybody does, and I've seen him in a huddle with Jonty several times this week.'

'But there *must* be a way.'

'Oh there is,' Driscoll said, 'but not yet. The lads are all fired up and alert at the moment. Let's wait until they're getting exhausted and complacent. That's when the little mistakes start creeping in. And the fatal ones!'

Twenty-Eight

TWO-FIFTEEN ON Sunday afternoon. Angelica had just driven the C5 out of the pits to start her last stint. Now the Church team's mechanics wandered into their stall and slumped down against its back wall to snatch some rest. *Their* car was in third place in a race they'd thought would be a disaster, so despite the grime and stubble on their faces they looked distinctly pleased – except for Dennis. With a groan, he bent to pick up one of the wheels that had just come off the C5, and started to carry it towards the tyre trolley in the paddock.

He had just finished loading it up when he felt a hand on his shoulder. Dennis turned round to find Steve Driscoll smiling at him.

'You must be knackered,' the Team Manager said. 'I'll take a turn.'

'Thanks,' Dennis said in astonishment, but he wasn't about to complain. After twenty-two hours without proper sleep he was only too glad of the chance of a short nap. Walking back into the pit he sank down on a tyre next to his mates and closed his eyes.

Once when Dennis half-opened them he saw Driscoll struggling through the back door with one of the freshly fitted tyres. Then he noticed that there were already four new slicks stacked against the counter at the front of the pit. Driscoll was bringing in a set of treaded wet-weather tyres. Must be taking precautions in case there was a last minute cloudburst, Dennis thought, grateful that he hadn't been made to do the double journey. Old Stevie Driscoll wasn't so bad after all.

240

Five-past-three. Angelica accelerated out of Mulsanne corner and looked for the Church team's signaller on the low white wall. He was leaning right out with his board to make sure she saw the IN signal.

Nearly there! Angelica thought, mentally relaxing as she drove towards her final pit stop. The C5 had eaten up two more sets of brake discs, and its entire exhaust system had had to be replaced, dropping it back to fifth place during the Sunday morning. But now it was running beautifully, and back in third position.

As she swept through the new section and the main grand-stands came into sight she gave a great sigh of relief. So Jonty's fears of sabotage had been groundless. Thank God for that! For the first half of the race she had been living on her nerves, remembering the steering arm pulling out, wondering what was going to break next and whether Jonty was going to be in the car when something did. She couldn't bear to think of any-thing happening to him, not now, not after Michael. But it was Conrad who had turned out to be right. What was it he had said? His words came back to her as she steered into the pit lane – bad dress rehearsal, good first night.

The instant she brought the car to a halt the refuellers went into action, and Steve Driscoll dived down by the front wheel arch. 'Tyres!' he snapped, and the mechanics rushed to change them.

Funny, Angelica thought as she climbed out of the car – a new set had been put on the previous stop, and she didn't think she'd been rough on them. Driscoll must be playing double safe, because a new set would give just that little bit extra protection against a last minute puncture. Good for him!

Jonty was standing in front of the pit counter, ready to jump in the car. 'Everything okay?' he asked her.

'Fine. How are we doing?'

'Works Porsches in first and second places three laps ahead of us. Then a private 956 four laps behind us, and the Lomax just behind it in fifth place.'

Angelica screwed up her eyes in concentration. 'I think you

can afford to slow down a little – ten, fifteen seconds a lap. There's no way we can catch the leaders unless they hit trouble, and we can't be caught unless we break down. Make sure that doesn't happen!'

'Right,' Jonty said, and dived for the cockpit.

When Steve Driscoll gave him the go signal he took a little more time to select first gear, and let the clutch out with extra care as he accelerated away from the pit.

Dennis watched the C5 until it disappeared round the right-hander after the pits. Then he wandered back into their stall. Driscoll was leaning against two of the tyres he had stacked just behind the pit counter. That seemed a good way to take a rest but still be able to watch the cars as they howled past on the pit straight, so Dennis leant against the other pair of wets. For no particular reason he began to fiddle with the top one's valve cap, twisting it loose and then tightening it up again.

'What're you doing?' Steve Driscoll suddenly asked.

'Nothing,' Dennis said.

'Why don't you go and see how Sharon's getting on then. I'm a bit worried she's been doing too much.'

'All right. Good idea.'

The bloke really wasn't as bad as everybody made out, Dennis thought as he walked towards the Team's motor-home. Through its open door he could see Sharon bent over the sink.

'Howya doing? Need a hand?' Dennis said, climbing up to join her.

Sharon turned round and wiped the back of her hand across her forehead. Her eyes were red-rimmed with fatigue, but she managed a smile for him. 'I'm fine, love. Just clearing up the debris from lunch. What're you doing here?'

'Just done our last pit stop, so Driscoll said I could come and see you.'

'Hmmm!' Sharon went, tossing blonde curls over her shoulder. 'What does he want?'

'Nothing! I told you, he's given me compassionate leave.'

'That man *always* wants something. He's the one member of this team I'm not looking forward to seeing next year, I can tell you.'

'Come on, Sha,' Dennis said, 'Steve's not as bad as I thought. He even took a turn at the tyres this time, and you know what a bastard that job is.'

Suddenly Sharon's blue eyes were wide open. 'He *what?*'

'He took a turn at the tyres; you know, taking the used ones to be stripped off and bringing back new ones. *And* he had to do two sets because it was the last pit stop.'

'He's never lifted a finger to help you before,' Sharon said suspiciously. 'Why should he now, and why two sets?'

'In case it rained, dummy!' Dennis said, as though explaining it to a child. 'We sent Jonty out on a new set of slicks, but if it'd been raining we'd have put him on wet-weather tyres.'

'But it hasn't rained during the race, has it?'

'No.'

'So why did Driscoll fetch a new set of wets? You'd already got some in the pits that haven't been used.'

'How d'you know Sharon? I didn't even realise you knew what wets were!'

'Because you were sitting on them when I brought in breakfast this morning, and I asked you why they'd got chunky bits on, you know, like a road tyre.'

'Blimey, you got a point there!' Dennis said slowly. Then he shook his head. 'Nahhh! You're trying to read something into it because you don't like the bloke. He must have had some reason that we don't know about.'

'So ask him what it was! Jonty wanted to know about *anything* unusual.'

'Leave off, Sha! If I'd told Jonty everything that's gone on he'd have had a nervous breakdown. I mean, that berk Cambell . . .' Dennis let the sentence trail off.

'Yes Dennis? Tell me!'

'Well . . . after first practice Cambell asked me to fix the car again.'

'And why didn't you tell Jonty? Why didn't you tell me?'

243

'I've told you! Because Jonty was in such a state . . . I thought he'd got enough to worry about. I meant to tell him the next day, honest, but then the steering arm went and I thought someone might think I'd done it.'

'Oh *Dennis!*' Sharon shouted. 'Won't you ever learn? Well, you're going to tell someone about this tyre thing! At least what Cambell did was in character, but Driscoll offering to fetch and carry for you – don't give me that!'

Suddenly Angelica appeared in the door of the motor-home. 'What's all the shouting about? I could hear you two in the tunnel!'

'Tell her, Dennis!' Sharon said fiercely.

Jonty loosened his grip on the steering wheel as he drove through the Esses, trying to feel what was different about the C5. There was more roll in the corners – the car sort of wobbled like a jelly, and it tended to wander about on the straights. It was definitely sloppier than when he'd last driven it. Not really surprising though after twenty-three hours of racing, Jonty thought.

'Which sets?' Angelica asked Dennis as they ran back through the tunnel towards their pit.

'The wets nearest . . . the pit counter. The slicks . . . are on the car,' Dennis gasped as he tried to keep up with her.

Angelica burst through the back door first, and made straight for the tyres Dennis had been leaning on a few minutes earlier. Steve Driscoll was still lounging against the pair beside them.

'Anything wrong, Angelica?' he asked with a forced smile.

'I don't know,' she murmured, staring down at the tyres, but just seeing brand new rubber on clean wheels.

Ian Mottram had seen the fear carved on her face as she rushed into the pit. Now he jumped up and went to her side. 'What's the matter?' he asked.

'Driscoll took these wheels for new tyres instead of Dennis. Is there anything wrong with them.'

'Just a minute!' Driscoll said. 'Nobody touches anything without my permission!'

Ignoring him completely Ian ran an expert hand round the tyre wall. Nothing obviously wrong with it, and the wheel rim was in good condition as well. His hand stopped at the tyre valve. Putting his thumb and index finger on the stainless steel valve cap, Ian gave it a twist to the right – it was on nice and tight. Almost as an afterthought, he put his hand down to the large silver nut that held the valve in place, and gave that a twist to the right as well. Ian's hand jerked off it as though he'd been bitten by a snake.

'The value nut's loose!' he croaked in a strangled voice.

Dennis yanked the top tyre away and threw it behind him. His hand went down to the lower wheel's valve nut. 'Christ! This one's loose as well.'

'So what?' Driscoll said, starting to walk past them. 'They'd have been checked before they went on the car.'

Dennis rushed at him and slammed him round against the sidewall. 'The tyre fitters *always* tighten them, and whoever goes for new tyres double-checks that. *Your* orders, Driscoll! Did you loosen the other set as well?'

'The other set?' Ian asked.

'He went for two sets!' Dennis shouted. 'The slicks are on the car now!'

Behind them Angelica's face had lost its colour. 'What will happen?' she asked Ian.

'Running that fast for that long the air'll be forced past the valve. Centrifugal force'll keep the tyres up down the straights, but at some point when he brakes or takes a corner they'll just tear off.'

For a moment Angelica just stared at him with horrified eyes. Then she started screaming: 'The telephone! For God's sake tell them to stop him!'

As Jonty accelerated out onto the Mulsanne Straight the C5 felt distinctly odd. It wandered across the track and back again despite his corrections on the steering wheel. The funny thing was though that as he speeded up it seemed to get better. In fact as he changed into top gear by the Hunaudières Restaurant it seemed to be behaving almost normally.

'Got it!' the team's chief signaller yelled into the old black telephone that connected him to the main pits. Slamming it back on its cradle, he ran out of the concrete stall and up the embankment in front of it.

'Just two words,' he told the man with the signal board. 'IN and SLOW. DEAD SLOW if you've got the letters!'

Jonty raced over the final brow before the kink at 220 miles-an-hour. He thought about lifting off the accelerator, but then a quick smile stretched his lips. The C5 seemed to be handling all right again, and it gave him a buzz to take the kink flat. He moved his wrists to start the turn, and without any warning the back end started to snake. Jonty held his breath. He couldn't stop the weird movement with the steering wheel, so he tried to damp it out with the accelerator, easing gently off the power, and then squeezing it on again. As the bend straightened out he began to get the car under control again. As he crested the final brow of the straight everything seemed fine. Jonty let out his breath.

The instant he lifted his right foot off the accelerator and squeezed the brake pedal, the car went mad. One moment he was slowing down on the left-hand side of the road, the next the tyres were shrieking and he was pirouetting round and round in thick clouds of tyre smoke.

Desperately Jonty stood on the brakes. The spinning motion seemed to be slowing down, and then he was travelling backwards and towards the Armco barriers on his right. He just had time to feed on some left lock before the C5 broad-sided into them. The violent impact slammed the front wheels flush with the bodywork, whiplashing the steering wheel straight and breaking Jonty's right wrist as it did so. The car bounced away from the Armco, kept going backwards for another 200 metres in a storm of tyre smoke, dust and debris, and then ground to a halt on the left of the track.

Silence. The car had finally stopped, but instead of relief Jonty was overwhelmed by the pain in his arm. It surged up it and into his head in nauseating waves, and for a moment he thought he was going to black out. Then he reached for the starter switch. The engine roared into life. He tried to put the gearlever into first, but his right hand dangled uselessly from his arm. Using his good hand to do everything, Jonty found the gear and steered the car round in a great U-turn so that he was facing the right way again. Something was thrashing against the rear bodywork, but he was utterly determined to make it back to the pits. Painfully slowly he began the long journey.

'Is he all right? Is he all right?' Angelica yelled frantically into the telephone at the back of the pit.

'He's just limped past us,' the Mulsanne signalling pit chief yelled back. 'The right rear tyre's in shreds and its smashing up the bodywork. Something's leaking out under the back, but he's keeping going.'

Shakily Angelica replaced the receiver and turned round. Dennis was still pinning Driscoll against the pit's sidewall, with Ian and the other mechanics surrounding him. Conrad was just outside the stall in the pit lane, shouting at them to let Driscoll go.

'Why?' Dennis kept repeating. 'What was in it for you?'

'What the hell's got into you lot?' Conrad bellowed. 'Let him go this instant or I'll have you all up for assault!'

Suddenly Angelica's eyes widened, and she stared at Conrad. 'You two . . . working together! This is something to do with the business isn't it, something to do with the trust. With Jonty dead you'd be able to . . .'

'You don't know what you're talking about Angelica. Now tell this lot to get their hands off Driscoll or I'll make real trouble for you!'

Just before Indianapolis corner, Wolfgang shot past the stricken car. His head jerked back in disbelief – had he seen what he hoped he'd seen? Quickly he checked in his wing-mirror, and saw a maroon blob crawling along the right of the track. As he took the bend Wolfgang let out an animal howl of delight. His last signal had told him he was four laps down on the bastards. Now he'd reduced that to three. His black-and-gold helmet dipped forward as he started to charge.

As the C5 reached the pit lane, the clock halfway up it read quarter-to-four. Jonty was having trouble seeing where he was going because the terrible vibration from the back of the car was shaking his eyeballs. Great belts of rubber were flailing round and round, carving chunks of fibreglass out of the body-work. His right hand felt as though it had been crushed by a sledgehammer. Suddenly he spotted Ian Mottram ahead of him, waving at their pit. He swung the car towards it, but when he pressed the brake pedal it went to the floor. Frantically Jonty pumped it, just managing to stop before running Ian over. Angelica opened the driver's door.

'Are you all right Jonty?'

'My wrist,' he tried to say, but it came out as grunts of pain.

Then she was undoing his safety harness and helping him out of the cockpit. He stepped out onto the pit lane, and she stood in front of him, easing his helmet and balaclava over his head. Jonty looked around. Already the airline had been connected, lifting the C5 off the ground. The rear bodywork was off and Ian Mottram and another mechanic were under the car yelling for tools and parts. All around them marshals fought back waves of onlookers eager to watch the drama.

'Lost it under braking for Mulsanne,' Jonty grunted. 'Don't know why.'

'Oh Jonty,' Angelica said with infinite sadness; 'Driscoll loosened the valve nuts on your wheels. I think Conrad had something to do with it as well.'

Jonty stared at her, his eyes filling with horror. He sensed other eyes boring into him, and when he looked towards the pit stall he met Conrad's. A white-faced Driscoll was standing beside him. Stepping past Angelica, Jonty began to walk towards them. Both of them turned away and made for the back door.

'Just a minute!' Jonty yelled, breaking into a run. Every jolting pace made his wrist feel as though it was going to explode. Conrad had just stepped into the passageway behind the pits when Jonty reached the door.

'Why?' Jonty shouted, stepping into it after him.

Driscoll kept going, but something made Conrad turn and face his youngest brother. His face was shadowy in the gloom of the tunnel. Apart from them it was empty now – nobody wanted to miss the climax of the race – but a stench of stale urine and tobacco smoke hung in the air.

'Why?' Conrad mimicked. 'I'll tell you why, you little bastard. Take, take, take! That's all your life's been hasn't it. Anything you've ever wanted . . . motor racing . . . my wife. Maybe I just decided to take something from you for a change.'

'What the hell are you talking about? You tried to kill me, you fucking maniac! You killed Michael!'

'Michael? Oh no, that really was an accident. He was worth a thousand of you, you little shit. But when I realised who would benefit from his death, who'd be taking all the profits whilst I slaved away at the business . . .'

'Profits from the garages! You've practically bankrupted them, Conrad! That's what this is really all about isn't it – you needed me out of the way to get control of the trust.'

Conrad gave a mad laugh. 'At least it's cost you 100 grand to work that out.'

'You never transferred the money, did you?'

'Got anything in writing that says I agreed to?' Conrad sneered. 'It's rather like the problem with your tyres – a misunderstanding. You can't prove a thing.' He turned round to walk away.

Jonty leapt towards him and swung him round with his left arm. 'I don't have to Conrad,' he said, looking him straight in the face. 'I used to be frightened of you. You could bully me into doing just about anything, but not any more. Now it's you who's scared of me, and you're going to have to live with that for the rest of your life.'

'Steve!' Conrad screamed.

Over his brother's shoulder, Jonty could see Driscoll coming back towards them, bunching his hands into fists.

Angelica stared at the brown-and-beige Glaser-Lomax as it howled past on the pit straight. Inside it she clearly saw Wolfgang's black-and-gold helmet. She turned and looked up at the Church team's time-keeper perched above her on the pit counter.

'How far behind us is he now?' she asked.

'One lap. When he comes past next time he'll have overtaken us.'

Angelica hurried to the back of the car and knelt down behind it. Ian Mottram was on his back under it tightening up a replacement suspension wishbone. A honey-like fluid was dripping down onto his overalls.

'How much longer?' she asked him.

'Nearly done this, but the brake pipe's gone. That'll take at least ten minutes to fix.'

Angelica twisted round and stared at the Le Mans clock – 3.54pm. 'Forget it!' she snapped, already pulling on her balaclava.

Steve Driscoll punched Jonty in the face, sending him crashing back against the tunnel's wall. He bounced back off it into a crouch, teeth bared in fury, and his left hand balled into a fist.

'That's just about it, isn't it Conrad,' Jonty snarled; 'someone to do your dirty work for you. Well I've only got one good arm, but I'll take you both on right now if that's how you want it.'

Conrad stepped towards him, his face a picture of hate. Then he stopped, another emotion flickering in his eyes. Jonty could read it quite clearly – there was fear in them.

'Come on Steve,' Conrad said in a low voice. 'We don't need this.'

'See you in England,' Jonty shouted at his departing back, 'with the trustees!'

Suddenly he heard the distinctive sound of the Glaser engine roaring into life. Jonty turned and ran towards it, through the open pit door and out onto the pit lane. Angelica was strapped into the car, and he joined Ian Mottram by the open driver's door.

'But Angelica, we haven't done anything about the brakes yet,' Ian was yelling.

'No time. Close the door!' Angelica yelled back, grinding the gearlever into first.

'You're crazy!' Jonty shouted. 'Wait until . . .'

'Close the door, or I'll go with it open!'

They stepped back and Ian slammed the door down. Instantly Angelica blasted the C5 away from the pit, scattering onlookers out of the way as she did so.

As Wolfgang charged up the pit straight he kept glancing right. The clock showed two minutes to four, so he was starting his last lap. If the C5 was still in its pit he would have unlapped himself and be leading it – but it wasn't there! A terrible depression hit him like a hammer blow.

Then suddenly Wolfgang was shouting and laughing like a madman. The maroon car was further up the pit lane, building up speed to join the track, but he was going to overtake it before it got there. As he flashed past the C5, Wolfgang spotted a familiar red-and-white helmet in its cockpit.

'Got you, you dirty bitch!' he screamed.

There was no way *she* was going to get past him on the last lap.

'*Scheisse!*' Angelica snapped, as she watched Wolfgang overtake her on her left. She was accelerating as hard as she could out of the pit lane, but already he was disappearing round the right-hander after the pits. There was a tremendous vibration from the front wheels, and the spokes of the steering wheel were out of position. Angelica gripped it tightly with her right hand, whilst her left went down to the boost control knob under the dash. She twisted it to the right and glanced at the boost gauge – one-point-five.

As she shot under the Dunlop Bridge, she could see the Lomax about 200 metres ahead of her, already slowing for the Esses. She tried the brake pedal with her left foot. It went straight to the floor! Angelica whipped her right foot off the accelerator and pumped at it frantically until there was some resistance. The C5 started to slow, but she had to throw it into a hair-raising slide to make the first corner. She had to brake early for Tertre Rouge, and as she accelerated out onto the Mulsanne Straight, Wolfgang had made ground on her.

Angelica's left hand reached for the boost control knob again. All or nothing. When she glanced at the boost gauge this time it read one-point-seven. The Glaser engine seemed to be pressing against her back. She could feel its heat, and its note gradually rose to a hysterical scream. The vibration was so bad now that Angelica was having difficulty seeing where she was going, but she hung onto the steering wheel and followed exactly in Wolfgang's tracks.

He had seen her coming, and was weaving in and out of the other cars on the straight to break up his slipstream. Now there was a horrifying speed differential because most drivers were cruising to the finish. As Angelica steered through these mobile chicanes, she saw that she was gaining on Wolfgang; but even if she caught him how was she going to stop at the end of the straight? The front brakes still worked because they were on a separate circuit from the rears, but for how long? She was asking them to do more work than all four brakes had done before.

As they shot over the last brow before the kink, Angelica was still 100 metres behind Wolfgang. The whole car was shuddering like a plane about to stall, but she kept her right foot hard down as she took the kink. The C5 bucked in protest, as though trying to get rid of its rider, but then it settled and charged on towards Mulsanne corner. This was it. If Wolfgang got away from her now she would never be able to catch him through the twisty sections.

Wolfgang moved to the centre of the road to block any outbraking manoeuvre, but Angelica stayed right behind him.

She flashed past the 500 metre board, the 400 metre board, but still she didn't brake, waiting for Wolfgang to do so first. Suddenly he was slowing, and she pumped madly on her brake pedal. The gap between them was rapidly closing, but Angelica aimed straight for the Lomax's tail. Just as Wolfgang started to turn into the corner she slammed into the back of him.

There was an explosion of fibreglass as the Lomax's rear bodywork disintegrated. Then it was spinning madly round and round down the escape road with the C5 slithering after it in a straight line. The crunching impact had speeded up Wolfgang, but slowed Angelica down so that she was able to stop first. Quickly she booted her car round and charged back up the escape road. Something was making a violent scraping noise under the front of it, but she couldn't see what it was. No time to worry about that. In her wing-mirror she could see Wolfgang coming after her.

'You dirty whore!' Wolfgang screamed into his helmet. 'Nobody does that to me and gets away with it! Especially not you!'

As the Le Mans clock reached four o'clock, the annual pit straight invasion began. Each year, thousands of spectators defied whatever extra precautions the organisers tried to take, and this year was no exception. Even before the winning Porsche came into sight the first of them began to scale the high walls separating the terraces from the track. Then as the works Porsche reached the chicane hundreds more followed suit, charging through from the back of the pits, or storming the fences beyond them. Within seconds wave after wave of excited fans were surging onto the track, and the winner was forced to a standstill under the clock. He scrambled out of his car as if it was on fire, and leapt over the pitwall to escape from the rampaging mob.

Angelica hammered the brake pedal and slammed the gear-lever down through the gears to slow for Indianapolis corner. She clung to the left of the track – the inside line – and glanced in her wing mirror. Wolfgang was gaining on her rapidly, leaving his braking to the last possible moment. Then he was slithering alongside her with his tyres wreathed in dirty white tyre smoke. As Angelica turned into the bend, she floored the accelerator, deliberately provoking a slide. The C5 broadsided into the Lomax, knocking it onto the grassy trackside. Wolfgang crashed and banged along it for a few seconds, and then disappeared behind her again.

Now she stayed on the right of the track, blocking the inside line into Arnage. As she hit the pedal she could feel the front brakes giving up and fading away to nothing. Again she had to violate the engine to slow herself down, and it shrieked in protest. Wolfgang took a better line through the corner, so that as they raced away from it he began to overtake on her right-hand side. Angelica was still half a car's length ahead of him as they reached the braking area for the Porsche curve. This time she didn't even touch the brake pedal, ramming the gearlever into fourth, and flinging the C5 towards the apex. She shot across Wolfgang's bows, forcing him to lift off again for an instant.

Through the new section, Angelica made her car as wide as possible, blocking the inside line into each corner, then sliding wide on the exit. The C5 seemed to be going faster and faster, getting a little more out of shape and out of control all the time. And then as she turned onto the final flat-out run to the chicanes, Angelica felt a slamming impact behind her, and the car began to spin.

For the first minute of the track invasion, the chicane marshals waved their flags angrily at the spectators, as if flapping fabric would drive them back behind the barricades. Then they gave it up as a hopeless task, and waved them in greeting at the incoming cars instead. After all, the race was over, and this had become almost a traditional part of it.

And then they heard the savage roars of two racing engines still locked in combat.

'My God! My God! Clear the track!' the chief marshal began to scream.

Angelica fed on opposite lock and eased back on the accelerator. She just managed to stop the C5 from spinning, but as it fish-tailed back into line Wolfgang started to overtake her again. He drew level, and she felt him staring at her. As she glanced at him he raised his forearm, fist clenched, and jerked it upwards – *fuck you!*

Angelica looked ahead. They were nearly in the braking zone for the chicanes now. Without brakes, there was no way she could stop him unless he lost concentration and made a mistake. Quickly she lifted a hand off the steering wheel and jerked it up and down in an international gesture of sexual contempt.

Wolfgang's eyes bulged with fury, and then his helmet rocked backwards and forwards as he screamed obscenities at her. His front wheels were ahead of hers. He could have taken her cleanly. Instead he flicked his steering wheel left and slammed into her one more time, knocking her onto the grass. Too late Wolfgang looked ahead and realised he'd sailed past his braking point. Desperately he stamped on his brakes and flung the wheel over. As his smoking tyres lost grip, there was nowhere for the Lomax to go but onto the grassy trackside and deep into the waiting catch-fencing.

On the opposite trackside, Angelica was trying to straight-line the chicane in the brakeless C5. It took off over the kerbing at the first apex, crashed down on the track in a shower of sparks and shattering fibreglass, then took off again over the second apex. This time it crash-landed on the short straight to the final chicane. As she hurtled towards it, Angelica saw the solid mass of people on the pit straight beyond it. One last time she battered the lever down through the gears, the engine note rising higher and higher like a desperate soprano, until it reached an ear-splitting crescendo and exploded. Still she hadn't slowed down enough. Angelica aimed at the end poles in the rows of catch-fencing and slammed into them, tearing them out by the roots. They battered and clawed at the underside of the car as though trying to tear its guts out in revenge, and then the C5 was free, rolling silently and slowly onto the pit straight and towards the crowd. A sea of faces turned to stare at her. Somehow the waves parted to admit her, and then as she finally stopped, closed round her again.

For some time, Angelica sat quite still, eyes tightly closed, hearing only the piercing note in her ears. Then she shook her head as though waking up, fumbled the safety harness open, and pushed up the door. The car was marooned, an island in a stream of people. She stood on the doorsill to see over their heads. From a balcony halfway up the pit lane the crew of the winning Porsche were spraying champagne over the crowd below them. Angelica turned away and looked back towards the chicanes. She could just make out a brown-and-beige shape wrapped up in wire netting.

'Fourth place,' Angelica said out loud. She had won her private race, but had it been worth it? It had nearly cost Jonty his life. Suddenly she desperately wanted to see him, and then she heard him calling her name.

'Angelica! Angelica!'

He was fighting through the crowd towards her, holding his broken wrist with his good hand and shouting her name over and over again.

'Jonty!' she yelled back, jumping off the car and struggling towards him.

And then they met and were laughing and crying, hugging and kissing, oblivious to the looks and catcalls from all around them.

'Jonty, Jonty; are you all right?'

'Am *I* all right? What about you, you crazy woman?'

Angelica wiped her eyes and clung to him. 'We're both crazy, but somehow we've made it. Thank God it's all over. I'll never let you do anything like this again!'

To her surprise Jonty pulled away and stared at her. 'What are you talking about?' he said.

He turned to look at the victorious crew on the balcony halfway up the pitlane. They were almost hidden by a golden mist of champagne. Then Jonty turned back to Angelica.

'All over? Next year we're coming back to thrash those bastards!'